PRAISE FOR FARAH NAZ RISHI

"Incredible . . . this story ripped my heart in two, had me grabbing for the tissues, and then put me back together again."

—Mindy Kaling

"With forthright prose and dashes of acerbic humor, Rishi does justice to the complexities of inchoate affection and cross-cultural clashes. It's powerful stuff."

—*Publishers Weekly*

"This memoir is incredibly unputdownable—readers will leave it breathless and in awe of Rishi's clarity and strength . . . All will be endlessly grateful to Rishi for sharing so generously her experiences of the beautiful contradictions of family."

—*Booklist* (starred review)

"Eloquent, intimate, fascinating, and memorable."

—*Midwest Book Review*

THE FLIGHTLESS BIRDS OF NEW HOPE

OTHER TITLES BY FARAH NAZ RISHI

Memoir

Sorry for the Inconvenience

Young Adult

If You're Not the One

I Hope You Get This Message

It All Comes Back to You

THE FLIGHTLESS BIRDS OF NEW HOPE

A Novel

FARAH NAZ RISHI

Published by Lake Union Publishing, Seattle
www.apub.com

EU product safety contact:
Amazon Media EU S. à r.l.
38, avenue John F. Kennedy, L-1855 Luxembourg
amazonpublishing-gpsr@amazon.com

ISBN-13: 9781662532290 (paperback)
ISBN-13: 9781662532306 (digital)

Cover design by Ploy Siripant
Cover image: © white snow, © arfy_harvy, © Anastasiia Guseva / Shutterstock; © Bullet_Chained, © Mykola Syvak / Getty

Printed in the United States of America

For those who've felt the unbearable loneliness of losing a sibling, and would cross any distance to bring them home. And for Kisa, who was (and will always be) family in every way that matters.

"Hope" is the thing with feathers—
That perches in the soul—
And sings the tune without the words—
And never stops—at all.

—Excerpt from "'Hope' is the thing with feathers"

by Emily Dickinson

AUTHOR'S NOTE

I fear that, as a society, we do not give our animal companions enough credit for what they can teach us. For what they *reveal* about us.

But throughout history, our interactions with animals have been profound reminders of our essential capacity for empathy.

In *Life and Fate*, Vasily Grossman writes of the transcendent power of what he calls *senseless kindness*:

"The powerlessness of kindness, of senseless kindness, is the secret of its immortality. It can never be conquered. The more stupid, the more senseless, the more helpless it may seem, the vaster it is."

In a time seemingly dominated by building walls and unanswered pleas, I think about Grossman's words often—the sheer vastness of kindness. A vastness that grows not from raw strength or logic, but from refusal to be practical, earned, or repaid. Because real kindness doesn't need a reason. It just *is*.

But animals already know this. Their acts of generosity arise not from expectation, but from a deeper understanding that everything is connected. We hear stories: Of a humpback whale shielding divers from a circling shark. Of a gorilla cradling a lost child who'd fallen into her zoo enclosure. Of a sea lion who helped an injured man stay afloat after he'd jumped off the Golden Gate Bridge.

I believe we are meant to help others, not because we must, but because we can. Because something deep in our bones remembers, as animals do, that kindness is never wasted. Every action, every gesture, every moment of care ripples outward in ways we never see—in a grand, interconnected butterfly effect.

It reminds us that our place in this world is not one of dominance, but of *belonging*.

This book is, at its heart, about that belonging: between siblings, between species, between ourselves and the fragile world we share. And it is a call to remember the quiet magic of kindness—the invisible thread that, despite everything, still binds us.

Chapter 1

Aden Shah's parents flew before they died, and even he couldn't miss the morbid punch line in that. After all, no one loved birds more than the Shahs.

Sheriff Elwood had described it like this: Aliya and Jay Shah, for the eighth year running, had wrapped up another successful weekend at the California Exotic Bird Expo in San Francisco. They'd gone out for dinner, just the two of them, and were winding their way back to a hotel outside city limits.

But the route had taken them along a cliffside road—the kind that feels like a scenic thrill in broad daylight but a reckless gamble after dark, especially in a speedy little rental Miata. They took a corner too sharply, lost control, and *flew* off the edge before plunging down, down, down to an untimely death.

A terrible tragedy, the sheriff had called it. *A freak accident.* But at least they'd died instantly; the sheriff had offered that detail as consolation, as if that made any of it easier to swallow.

It didn't.

Now their remains were en route to New Hope, Pennsylvania, where two newly dug plots awaited them at Thompson Memorial Cemetery. Aden's aunt, Reema khala, was already taking care of everything: the funeral arrangements, the rental car company, and, most important, the transport home of Coco Chanel—the Shahs' prized Major Mitchell's cockatoo, who'd been left behind at the hotel.

All that was left was for Aden to show up.

He wondered whether Coco had cried when they didn't come back. She used to squawk her head off whenever she was left alone for more than five minutes. He could almost hear it, the shrill ringing in his ears.

On the other line, the sheriff had coughed, once—sharp and dry, like he'd swallowed something wrong.

Your aunt will be in touch soon. She, er, sounded like she wasn't sure you'd pick up if she called first.

Aden's stomach wrung.

I see.

Anyway, my, uh—condolences. For your loss.

Yes. Thank you.

Thank you. What a stupid thing to say to someone who'd just told you your parents were dead.

Aden ended the call and sat there, staring into the silence. It settled in layers: first the quiet hum of his computer. Then the tick of the clock on his wall. Then, finally, the void in his chest.

He'd been barely twenty-one when he decided never to return to New Hope, young enough to believe that distance alone could erase his parents' existence from his life. It had mostly worked; his mom had stopped trying to reach out about five years ago, when he hadn't picked up her call on his birthday, again. He still remembered the voicemail she'd left:

I know you don't want to hear from us, but . . . Aliza's been asking about you. Not that she'd tell you herself.

An obvious lie.

Except now Aden couldn't shake the image of his little sister sitting on the edge of the couch at home. Alone now. Wondering whether *this* was what would finally drag him back.

His own leather couch crinkled beneath him—a jarring squawk that bit into the quiet. The same couch where he and Sẹ̀yí had spent lazy weekends tangled in blankets, her humming along to the soundtrack of whatever movie they weren't really watching. The same couch where they'd had The Talk, and eventually, The Breakup.

Now, especially, the couch felt too big, too empty, without her.

He rubbed his face, fingers dragging down his cheeks. Maybe it was time for a new couch. Something to think about when he got back.

Hours slipped away without Aden realizing. The sun had long sunk behind the hills, and now night pressed in, draping the room in darkness. He blinked, trying to shake off the haze, and rubbed at his dry eyes. Mechanically, he reached for his laptop on the coffee table, nearly knocking his vintage glass ashtray to its own untimely death. The ashtray had been a gift from Sẹ̀yí, a remnant of another life teetering on the edge of a cliff.

Aden did not miss the bitter humor in that, either.

He steadied the ashtray, opened his laptop, and stared at the blank email window. A few keystrokes later, he'd sent a curt note to his boss, who didn't pay him enough for feigned politeness.

Then—chewing his chapped lower lip—he booked a flight to Philadelphia.

As soon as Aden walked into his childhood home—a modest brick Colonial with a black roof—the noise hit him first. Creaking floors. The muffled voices of too many people trying to sound normal.

Then the sharp tang of lemon spray burned in his nose. A pitiful attempt to mask the stubborn scent of Coco. But there was none of her usual shrieking, no *A-den! A-den!!* echoing down the hall.

He glanced instinctively toward the living room, half expecting to see her cage, her crown of feathers ruffling in disapproval.

No sign of her, thank God. Aliza must have moved her somewhere quieter. Somewhere she wouldn't get too stressed.

Still, the quiet made him uneasy, as if Coco were simply lying in wait somewhere.

Then came the glare of those ungodly overhead lights. His parents had always used bulbs that sucked the life out of everything, casting a cold, sterile glow that made Aden feel trapped in a waking dream. The kind where he was naked and about to embarrass himself in front of a faceless crowd.

He smoothed down his hair as he passed a mirror by the front door, quickly adjusting his tie. Muscle memory, mostly; years of client meetings had trained him to tidy himself before walking into uncomfortable situations.

The living room looked virtually the same as he remembered it, minus Coco—though now it was also filled with clusters of people in black, a jarring contrast with the wooden furniture and his mother's embarrassingly tacky red-and-yellow palette.

He'd expected more people at his parents' funeral. Not a lot, but more. Maybe fifty. Instead, he counted twenty, maybe thirty people if he was being generous.

They stood around awkwardly, clutching their drinks and plates of food like anchors and attempting stilted, hushed small talk. Over half was made up of other South Asian Muslims from their small community—people he'd see only around the Eid holiday, people who'd come now to pay their respects.

Not that the Shahs were particularly devout; Aden couldn't remember the last time he'd seen his parents pray. He couldn't remember the last time *he'd* prayed.

His eyes finally landed on Aliza, half swallowed by the herd of aunties, and next to her—

His heart clenched like a fist.

Sammy.

His younger brother, who looked like someone had hit the fast-forward button on his childhood and forgot to press pause.

The last time Aden had seen him, Sammy had been three years old—all soft edges and oversize, snot-covered T-shirts. A toddler who still tripped over his shoelaces.

But now Sammy's limbs were gangly branches too long for his body, and his hair, once a patch of neat black curls, was now a wild bramble that probably hadn't seen a brush in days.

But what hit Aden hardest were his eyes. Wide. Vacant shells. Maybe he just had no idea what was happening. Was still trying to process it all.

Still, Sammy stood at Aliza's side like her shadow, as he always had, even when he was a toddler.

But seeing an awkward teen where that toddler should be—it put Aden's stomach in free fall. He'd missed it all: the voice cracks, the weird hobbies Sammy had probably picked up. Teaching him how to shave. All of it, gone.

And Aliza—she'd changed, too. The past ten years had carved her face into sharp, severe angles, and she'd cut her black hair short, just past her ears, revealing a neck that was an inch or two too long. The new ring in her nose glinted gold under the stark lights, and an unfamiliar sliver of some tattoo peeked from the sleeve of her simple black dress. Not that this was surprising. If anyone in this family was going to get a tattoo, it would be Aliza.

She didn't notice him at first, too distracted with talking to their neighbor Shreya aunty, whom Aden had known since he and his family had moved in from San Francisco. She lived in the yellow house on their right, the one with carnations in the front yard, and had always been nosy, though not unbearable.

She was better than Carol and Peter Lowell, at least, who lived in the house across from theirs and copied everything their parents did. When his dad planted hydrangeas in their front yard, a week later so did the Lowells. When his mom installed solar path lights, so did the Lowells. When his parents introduced them to Coco, two weeks later the Lowells bought Gus, a macaw who was a raging piece of shit.

Aliza nodded politely at something Shreya aunty said and gave her a rickety smile, though her eyes were glassy and rimmed with red.

She'd been crying, Aden realized.

Aliza rarely cried, not even when she'd broken her ankle skateboarding when she was ten. She'd hobbled at the front door on one foot, face stubbornly set, barely wincing as Aden wrapped her ankle in a makeshift splint.

You can cry, you know, he'd told her. *You don't have to hold it in.*

But then I'll feel like I lost, she'd muttered.

That part had always stumped him. Lost what? Who was she competing against?

The one time he did see her cry was when the neighborhood cat, Freddie, didn't greet them while they waited for the morning bus to school.

But he always says hello! she'd whimpered, snot dribbling down her chin like egg yolk. *What if he's hurt? What if he hates me? What if I did something wrong?*

You're an idiot, Aden had replied.

Aliza was always emotional, always ridiculous, when it came to animals.

But now—now he wondered if maybe crying, for her, meant letting something slip past her defenses. Admitting that something really mattered.

He wasn't ready to talk to them. Not now, not yet. What do you say after ten years of silence? *Nice weather we're having? Sorry I ditched you?*

If Aliza punched him in the face in response, he couldn't blame her.

His chest suddenly felt too tight, his skin too small. So he made a beeline for the kitchen. He hadn't eaten on the plane, and his stomach grumbled in protest. It was almost comforting, in a way, how despite the grim circumstances, his body still stubbornly insisted on its usual needs. Life went on. Even when you didn't want it to.

On the counter sat a plate of egg-and-tuna sandwiches, cut in rough, jagged triangles. Definitely Aliza's handiwork: an almost pitiful attempt at being a hospitable host even when no one would expect it. The sandwiches sat beside a plate of mini quiches and a cheese platter, along with the not one but *two* bottles of Martinelli's—items brought by some responsible adult. Next to them, the sandwiches were like sad, wilted afterthoughts. She shouldn't have bothered.

Aden took a paper plate and an egg-and-tuna sandwich. Took a bite. Coughed loudly. Promptly searched for a napkin to spit out the mouthful.

Just as he managed to find one, Aliza's voice cut through the muffled murmurs of the other guests.

"What the hell are you doing here?"

Aden froze, still chewing. He swallowed quickly, wiped his mouth, and turned, finding his sister in front of him, eyes blazing.

Took her long enough.

"Hello to you, too," he replied dryly. He gestured to his plate. "You're still too stingy with the mayo in your tuna salad, by the way. This is dry as hell."

"Mayo's disgusting," Aliza shot back, her eyebrow twitching. "And you've got some fucking nerve showing up like this."

"Wow, hostility," Aden deadpanned. "Can't a guy eat?"

"You know what I mean. You can't just walk in here like nothing's changed."

"How about this, then? My parents *also* died, so I have as much a right to be here as you. And, by the way, I'm an attorney now. You'll need my help."

"*Your* help?" Aliza let out a sharp laugh. "I've been doing just fine without you for the past *ten years*. I don't need your help."

"Yeah?" Aden smiled thinly. "Sorry, remind me again, are you the executor of our parents' estate? Because last I checked, it's me. And correct me if I'm wrong, but do you know how to organize the estate assets, debts? Notify the banks? Deal with the Social Security office? Not to mention taxes and asset disposition—"

"I can figure it out," Aliza hissed, before her face crumpled in a sneer. "Ohh, I get it. You're just here for the money."

"Jesus, that's not—"

"Oh, my *babies*," interrupted Reema khala, sweeping them both in a suffocating hug.

Aden's entire body went rigid. His eyes met Aliza's over Reema's shoulder in a fleeting look of mutual discomfort.

Reema khala was their mom's younger sister. She rarely visited, despite living just an hour away in New Jersey. And when she did, she never stayed the night, wrinkling her nose at the house like it reeked. She wasn't wrong. After all, their house always smelled like Coco: talcum powder and bird poop and tangible irresponsibility.

It had all begun almost thirty-two years ago, before Aden was born. His parents had bought Coco on a whim during their honeymoon—a fifty-dollar impulse from a roadside breeder in Bali. They hadn't been thinking about longevity or legality or anything remotely practical. They'd just wanted a pet. Something bright and lively. Something to love.

And for a while, that was all she was. Coco—loud, needy, ridiculous—held court in her oversize cage in the corner of their San Francisco apartment. Apparently Aden had been a little afraid of her as a baby, and he didn't care for her much as a toddler, either. But after the family moved to New Hope, when he was about seven and Aliza was two, things shifted.

His parents both worked long hours back then—his mom a systems analyst, his dad a programmer—and somehow, the everyday care of Coco fell to him. He was the one refilling her water, sweeping her feathers, picking the millet husks from her food dish with quiet precision.

He hadn't done it out of affection. He'd done it because his parents had once praised him when he did—ruffling his hair, telling him how helpful he was being, how good. And Aden wanted to be good. He wanted to be the kind of person people loved. The kind of person people kept.

His parents' obsession with Coco came later. After they quit their tech jobs and threw themselves into the world of competitive bird shows. It began innocently at first: a local showcase here, a community pet fair there. But once Coco started raking in ribbons, his parents were hooked. The competitions got bigger. The stakes, higher. And Aden got dragged along for the ride.

He'd hated every second of it. The competitions were circuses filled with lonely eccentrics who spent obscene amounts of money on specialized diets, toys, and training for their birds, all to bring out the best in their little feathered prodigies. The whole thing reeked of midlife crises and misplaced ambitions.

Before long, though, his parents became fixtures on the circuit. Aliya and Jay showed up with suitcases full of homemade bird treats, elaborate perches, and even costumes for Coco, moving through the competitions with a kind of effortless charm. And Coco? Coco was a star. With her radiant pink feathers, her uncanny ability to mimic snippets of Bollywood classics, and her perfectly synchronized dance moves, she became something of a celebrity in the bird world.

The story of how they got her—their "bargain bird from Bali"—became part of their performance. They recited it like gospel at every expo and competition, polishing the details every time. It never included the dubious breeder. Never touched the ethics of importing wild cockatoos before the ban in '92.

"Coco was our training wheels for having real kids," his mom had joked more than once, always with a laugh.

But Aden never laughed.

Because Coco wasn't a warm-up act. She was the main event.

Aden still remembered overhearing one of Reema khala's attempts to talk sense into his parents. He'd been only ten at the time, sitting on the stairs, hidden behind the railing as he listened to the three of them talk in the kitchen.

You can't just quit your jobs for bird competitions, for God's sake. How will that bring in stable money? What about your kids?

We have savings. They'll be fine, Mom had argued. *They understand the importance of having passions.*

Do they? What about their future? How will you pay for their college?

They understand.

Aden hadn't understood. Not really. All he'd known was that his parents were suddenly home a lot more—working with Coco in the backyard, building elaborate props and perches, teaching her to bob her head to old Bollywood songs. They'd seemed happy, happier than he could remember. So—at least at first—Aden had tried to be happy for them, too.

That was when Reema's visits became even more infrequent, though Aden couldn't blame her.

And now she was hugging them both tightly, as if she had known this day would come.

"It's good to see you both," she said softly, voice thick. "I just wish it was in better circumstances. I'm so sorry."

"Thank you," both Aden and Aliza replied automatically.

Reema pulled away with a sigh, her eyes meeting Aden's. Her lips curved into a faint, melancholy smile. "It's been so long. When did you fly in?"

"About two hours ago. From Chicago."

"And work?" she asked Aden. "They didn't give you too much trouble for taking time off?"

"My parents' funeral seemed like a good enough reason."

Her expression sparked—too quick to read, but Aden felt its weight. She was gathering more questions, he could tell, so he answered to save her the trouble. "I'm an associate attorney now at Farley Law. It's a midsize corporate firm."

"I see," Reema said, her voice light but edged with something sharper. "Well, looks like things are working out for you."

Aden tensed. Maybe it wasn't intentional, but the words carried a faint sting, an unspoken accusation.

Reema turned to his sister, her demeanor softening. "Coco's already settled in her room. Though she tried to bite me—several times. Is that normal? You'd think she'd realize I'm trying to help."

Her room? So Coco had been bestowed her own designated space in the house now? He supposed he shouldn't be surprised.

Aden's eyebrows furrowed. The important question, though, was *which* room.

"She's probably just really stressed," said Aliza quietly. "We all are."

"How's Sammy handling it?"

Aliza shook her head. "He hasn't said anything. I'm worried about him."

"*Bechara.* He's in a state of shock, I'm sure." Reema gave Aden another pointed look. "What are your plans?"

Aden's throat went dry. He hadn't planned on having this conversation here, certainly not now, beneath hungry, prying stares and that god-awful lighting that washed out everything. "I'll stay here for a couple weeks, at least until the big things get sorted."

"What big things?" asked Aliza, her eyes narrowing. "You don't have to stay here. You can just sort everything from your penthouse in *Chicago*."

"I don't live in a *penthouse*." He couldn't afford that, not with his associate salary, not so soon after law school. Not that Aliza had any reason to know that, since they hadn't spoken in ten years. But still.

"What's going on?" Sammy's voice startled Aden. He hadn't even noticed his little brother standing there, as silent and slight as a ghost.

Aden took a breath. "I also want to look into selling the house," he said.

Aliza's face twisted. *"What?"*

"You can't afford to keep it," Aden said matter-of-factly.

"It's not a big deal. I'm a vet tech now. I'll ask for more hours, I'll"—she glanced at the floor—"I'll make it work."

A vet tech? A *part-time* vet tech? Aliza had always wanted to go to veterinary school. It'd been her dream for as long as she could talk—a stupid one, in Aden's opinion, but hers, nonetheless. She should have been well into her final year by now. What the hell had happened?

Aden shook his head. "It's not that simple. The taxes, the insurance, the HOA fees, the upkeep—it's way too much to deal with. New Hope isn't exactly cheap. And it's just the two of you. It'd be easier to sell and downsize. Move somewhere more manageable."

Aliza's mouth fell. "You can't just sell our family home without even considering what *we* want! And what about Sammy? He still has school. You want to just uproot him and have him start school somewhere else?"

Sammy said nothing; instead, his dark, dazed eyes remained focused on boring holes in the floor.

Aden shrugged. "So we'll put you two in an apartment or something, until he graduates."

"We're not selling the house," Aliza hissed, taking a step closer. "You shouldn't even be the executor. You're just lucky they died before they could change the will. Mom and Dad would have appointed someone who *actually* had our best interests at heart."

"Would they, though?"

Aliza opened her mouth to argue, but Reema stepped in swiftly, her voice cutting through the tension. "Aden, Aliza, please. Not here," she said firmly. "We can talk about this after the funeral."

For a moment Reema's tired eyes wandered across the room. "I still need to greet a few people, before Shreya starts sobbing all over again. Play nice, all right?"

She patted Sammy's head, giving him a sympathetic look. And then she was gone, disappearing into the loose throng of unfamiliar faces, leaving the three siblings in the dim kitchen.

Aliza grabbed Sammy's hand without a word, already pulling him toward the hallway—but not before she spat, "Your hair's thinning at the front."

"No, it's not."

But she was already gone, leaving him standing there with the sad tray of sandwiches and the remnants of their half-finished conversation for company.

The room felt too quiet now, the muffled hum of small talk barely reaching him as he tried to calm himself. He ran a hand through his hair reflectively, only to pause mid-motion as his fingers brushed against the front of his hairline.

Of course it wasn't thinning, he reassured himself. Aliza was just trying to get under his skin.

It was working.

The Past

I open my eyes and there's a big face a giant face big and round like big light and it comes close to mine I hear sounds warm sounds garbled sounds but sweet you're home now it says but I don't understand I am cold and its naked wing is warm there is another next to her another big face it looks at me too shows me teeth but no bite, no bite at all just warm warm warm

There is another hiding with small face so small, but he does not show teeth he does not bite he does not hold me

he only looks and does not garble like the others he just looks because he is small like me like me he does not know like me does not have feathers like me is

he scared like me

Aden come see how pretty she is today!

more warbling I do not understand

small face A-den quiet he coos I like

I am home

this I understand

Chapter 2

The funeral was a blur.

Aden had driven to the memorial grounds by himself, using his parents' Toyota Camry, but he barely remembered the drive. Now he stood apart from the rest of the funeral goers, his expression flat, watching as his parents' shrouded bodies were lowered into the earth. The sky sagged with gray clouds, thick and swollen, threatening to burst at any moment—so the whole ordeal felt quietly rushed, for which Aden was grateful. The sooner it was over, the better.

Earlier, Reema khala had asked whether he wanted to see his parents' bodies after they were cleaned, to have a private moment to say goodbye before they were buried. To this, Aden politely declined. He'd already said his goodbyes years ago. Today was just a formality, which was why he wasn't surprised that he felt nothing.

In any case, this was good enough: There were no coffins, per Islamic custom, which meant he could at least make out the familiar forms of his parents' bodies, the contours of their faces, through the thin layers of fabric. There was no smell, no malformation, either. No other indication they were dead. As if, at any moment, his mother would throw off the covering, sit up, and bellow *Surprise! We're alive!* And his father would follow, grinning as Aden's mother's cackling filled the air.

Then Aden would have to scold them for pulling a sick joke just for attention—although he wouldn't be surprised.

An imam led the modest group of mourners in prayer, his voice a soft, rhythmic hum that barely floated through the heavy air. That led to a mini sermon about how the Shahs were good people; how those left behind must not mourn too long, for all life is borrowed. A gift.

His parents would've wanted something more—something louder, more theatrical. The kind of funeral people talked about for weeks. But their children wouldn't even stand together to mourn them. Aden stood a few paces back, hands in his pockets, while Aliza and Sammy lingered by the graveside.

They made an odd pair: Aliza with her many piercings, and Sammy, awkward like some sickly brown Victorian child.

Like Aden, though, they didn't cry.

Instead, there was a quiet determination in Aliza's stance, like she was holding herself together through sheer force of will. Her hand never left Sammy's shoulder. A tether, keeping him close. And Sammy—dark circles beneath his eyes—clung to her just as tightly, fingers curled in the fabric of her sleeve like he was afraid she'd slip away, too.

The imam then looked to Aden to say a few words, but Aden shook his head, even as the imam's lips pressed together in a thin, disapproving line.

He hadn't even brought flowers for his parents' grave. Flowers felt like an offering for people who deserved it. A symbol of love, gratitude. Maybe even forgiveness. But Aden didn't know what he owed them.

Flowers were expensive, anyway—and what were flowers to the dead?

You never give me flowers, Ṣèyí's voice echoed faintly in his mind, more mournful than anything here, tugging at old wounds. Knowing her, if they were still dating, she would gently encourage him to see a therapist after the funeral. But the last time he'd seen his therapist, when he had begun his 1L year, he'd thrown words around like *abandonment issues* and *Why not try talking to your parents?* and *Have you considered ECT?* He was a quack.

Aden stamped out his thoughts like a cigarette.

"Oh, Aden."

A bony hand clamped on his shoulder. He turned, startled.

The Lowells had shown up after all.

"I can't believe you're here," said Carol, her wispy blond hair swishing around her neck like spiderwebs. "I was telling Peter—right, Peter?—that I didn't think you'd show."

"She did," Peter added unhelpfully, not looking up from his shoes.

Aden offered a tight-lipped smile. "Well, here I am."

"I know this must be so hard on you. I can't even imagine the guilt you must—" Carol shook her head. "But you're right. You're here now. Your parents would be so happy."

Aden blinked, the corner of his eye twitching. His parents hated the Lowells. Hated them. The fact that Carol acted as if they were best friends was almost laughable, especially when Aden knew the Lowells hated them, too.

He nodded instead. Meanwhile, someone was wailing loudly—Shreya aunty, probably. That, at least, he knew would satisfy his parents.

"When we looked out our window," Carol went on, "and saw all these cars piling up to your house, we knew something was wrong, but we didn't think . . ."

"Yeah." Aden's voice was flat.

"Oh, it's such a shame!" She placed her bony hand on her chest. "Such a *shame*! They were good people. We'd even thought about meeting up with them at the bird expo, but my knee was acting up too much for the drive. How's Coco handling it all? I'm sure she's *devastated*."

"The bird's fine." As far as Aden knew.

"Well, you know," said Carol, leaning in as if she were sharing some secret, "if it gets too much for her, she can always stay with us. Gus would love the company. And you know cockatoos can be very delicate—too high-maintenance for someone who doesn't understand them."

"I'm aware." As much as he would love to give Coco away, even he couldn't stomach giving her to the Lowells. He refused to give them the satisfaction.

"Okay, hon. We'll be waiting to hear from you." Carol gave his shoulder one last squeeze.

Aden hadn't attended many funerals, and perhaps he should've counted that as luck. But standing there now, he decided he despised them. Something about facing their own impending death made people stupider, more self-serving, than usual. Funerals weren't for the dead—they were for show. A way for people to pretend they understood something that was, at its core, impossible to understand.

And the longer he watched the mourners, the more absurd it felt. Nothing anyone said mattered; none of it brought people closer—not to each other or the dead. They were here out of obligation, reciting their lines, performing grief because that was what you did. His own presence felt just as hollow. He hadn't come to mourn. He'd come because that was what a son, the eldest son, was supposed to do.

Maybe that was the point. Maybe death was the one thing that stripped away the illusion that anything mattered at all.

Finally, the funeral ended—a clumsy full stop to a sentence no one knew how to finish. Everyone muttered their final half-hearted condolences and dispersed, including his siblings, who jumped into Aliza's car without so much as a glance in his direction.

So Aden drove back to his family's house, alone.

Reema khala was the only one who followed the siblings back, only to inform them that she would be staying at a nearby hotel.

"You have food in the fridge," she said, hovering in their front doorway. "One of your neighbors brought some kind of casserole. Looked less than appetizing, though. If you get hungry, you still have those mini quiches left."

Aliza barely looked up. "We'll be fine."

Reema hesitated. "Right. Okay. Well, you know how to reach me."

Aliza waved her off, shutting the door behind her. Silence spread thick and heavy, like layers of dust settling over the house.

Aden stood in the living room, feeling as out of place as the dead plants by the window. Aliza and Sammy stood, flanking him, unsure of what to say, or maybe unwilling to acknowledge him at all. His very presence had unsettled the house, made the walls themselves hold their breath.

"I'll, uh—" Aden cleared his throat, though it did nothing for the stickiness lodged there. "I'll just sleep in my room."

"Wait—" Aliza started, but he was already moving.

He made his way down the familiar hallway, threw open the door to his old bedroom, and froze. The room was the same in shape, a boring square with a cream carpet even more worn than before, with a single window on the back wall half covered by faded-gold curtains. But that was where the familiarity ended. His bed was gone—so, too, were his shelves. In his bed's place stood a large white aviary, surrounded by old newspaper.

And inside the cage, staring back at him, was Coco Chanel.

The bane of his existence. A living feathered demon. If Satan himself had ever taken physical form, he would no doubt have chosen the body of this particular bird.

Coco fluffed up her red-and-yellow mohawk, her beady eyes gleaming with a wicked sort of curiosity. "Hello! Big kiss!" she squawked, hopping from one foot to the other.

Aden blinked, trying to process. His old room, now a cage. There was morbid poetry in this somewhere, but he didn't have the patience to dwell on metaphors.

"What the hell is this?"

Aliza appeared behind him, arms folded. "It's Coco's room now. You were gone so long, Mom and Dad figured it'd be a better use of the space."

"Of course they did," Aden muttered, a stale laugh threatening to escape. "That's crazy. They're *crazy*."

"Well, you did say you were never coming back," Aliza said flatly, leaning against the doorframe. "Guess we believed you."

Her voice wobbled slightly on the word *believed.*

Aden rubbed his hands down his face. "Maybe I should have just gotten a hotel."

"You said it, not me. Or better yet, go back to Chicago."

"I told you, I'm not leaving," said Aden tiredly. "I'm the executor. I have to meet with the lawyer tomorrow."

Aliza's expression shifted—cool indifference sharpening to something angrier. "Exactly. There's already a lawyer involved. You don't have to be here. Just appoint me as the executor, and I'll handle the rest."

Aden's chest tightened. He hadn't come back just to be dismissed like this. "It's not that easy," he said, frustration bubbling. "You're being stubborn. Just let me help."

"Help?" Aliza scoffed. "You mean sell the house, grab the cash, and then bail again? No fucking way." Her brows yanked together, forming a large, angry crease on her forehead. "No. You need to mind your business and let me handle it. Sammy and I will be *fine.*"

"Hello, Coco! Hello, Coco!" the bird squawked, pacing in her cage.

"You're twenty-five," Aden said, trying to ignore the bird. "Your prefrontal cortex has barely finished developing, if even. You need an adult."

"Don't infantilize me," spat Aliza, her eyes flashing. "Who do you think has been the adult since you left? Who do you think took care of Sammy, who made sure our parents didn't spiral into complete chaos? You have no idea. You have *no idea* what we've been through."

"Whatcha doin'? Whatcha doin'?" Coco piped in again.

"Not *now*, Coco," snapped Aden. "Look, Aliza, that's all the more reason why you should let me take over. Be logical. A part-time vet tech salary isn't going to be enough to take care of you both. Let me sell the house and handle everything."

Aliza's face contorted in anger. "You're so selfish. You really think you know best?" Her voice trembled. "You don't get to show up after *ten* years and act like a big brother."

"I'm trying to help—"

"No. You're trying to swoop in and play hero to make yourself feel better—like that's going to fix anything."

Aden bristled. Was she being stubborn just to get back at him? Aden wasn't blind—he knew his leaving had hurt her and Sammy. But it wasn't like they were suffering, not the way he had been. Their relationship with Mom and Dad had been different. They were the ones who got to stay. They had each other.

He had no one.

But he was the eldest. He had responsibilities. He'd been out there, in the real world, learning what it took to survive. It was obvious he was best suited to clean up after their parents' mess.

"Someone should," Aden said finally. "You don't even have your shit together. Whatever happened to vet school, huh?"

Aliza flinched as if he had struck her. Coco had stopped her incessant squawking and was now quietly preening herself. Even the bird seemed to understand that Aden had crossed a line.

Sammy, who had been standing in the hallway, finally spoke, his voice barely a whisper.

"It's not her fault."

Aden jumped, startled. "Jesus, Sammy—how long have you been standing there?"

"This is exactly what I mean." Aliza's voice cracked, her anger dissolving into something raw. "You don't even *see* us. You don't care. Just go back to Chicago, Aden. No one needs you here."

That stung more than it should have. Aden wanted to say something—to tell her she was wrong, that he thought about them far more than they knew, that he wished things were different—but there was no point. He didn't have the right.

Coco let out a shrill laugh that quickly devolved into an earsplitting scream. The noise hit Aden like a punch in the gut—it was too similar to their mother's raucous cackle.

Aliza groaned, covering her face. "Coco-baby, *please*—"

"This fucking *bird*." Aden took a step toward the aviary, his fists clenched.

Aliza stepped in front of the aviary protectively, grabbing his arm. "What, you're just going to punch poor defenseless *Coco* now?"

Aden stopped, his frustration deflating. "I wasn't actually going to do anything," he muttered. "I'm not a monster."

"You could've fooled me."

Aden ripped his arm from her annoyingly ironclad—God, had she gotten into weight lifting while he'd been gone?—grip. Then he sighed, running a hand through his hair. "This is pointless. I'll sleep on the couch in the living room. We'll talk about this tomorrow, after we've cooled down."

Aliza threw her hands up. "Fine."

"Fine."

He waited for Aliza and Sammy to leave before letting out a groan, feeling more exhausted than he had in years. His eyes drifted back to the aviary—only to find the bird once again staring back.

"Hello, big kiss!"

Chapter 3

Aden sat on the porch with a half-empty carton of Parliament Menthols and a bottle of cheap white wine someone had left on the kitchen counter.

He didn't normally drink. Muslims weren't supposed to. Not that he was the religious sort; it was just something he'd been taught, and the teaching had stuck.

Sẹ̀yí didn't drink, either.

"Growing up, I always heard people talking about how having a glass of red wine was good for you, but now it's been debunked," she'd mentioned once over dinner. "Turns out, it messes with your sleep, inhibits memory." She'd smiled and added, almost in a whisper, "Allah knows best." Like it was a secret she was letting him in on.

She had that effect—making faith feel less like a list of rules and more like something warm and steady, something you could slip into like a beloved sweater.

But Sẹ̀yí had always been a good person, a good, practicing Muslim, the kind who fasted every Ramadan and prayed on time. The kind who went out of her way to help a stranger struggling with their bags or their stroller. The kind who truly believed that God—despite His lack of interference, despite His silence—cared deeply for all His creations.

Aden hadn't planned on dating someone like her. But as soon as their eyes had met at that 1L mixer at Northwestern Law, he'd been a goner.

He'd loved her. God, he'd loved her.

The worst part was how she made him *want* to be better. Sometimes they'd be curled up on his couch, watching a movie, and she'd politely excuse herself to pray in his bedroom. She'd always leave the door slightly ajar, and he'd catch glimpses of her cream-colored scarf fluttering as she moved, like wings. He'd think, *Maybe I'll pray with her.* Maybe he would download some prayer app to keep him on track. It might feel good. It might connect to her in some deeper way.

But then he'd remember the last time he'd tried. How he'd stumbled through the motions, awkward and unsure, his mind drifting the whole time—to emails he needed to send, to his parents' latest half-hearted attempt to reconnect, to the fact that he never really felt anything when he prayed. Not like she did.

And so he'd make some excuse instead. Some things were better left to people who knew how to believe.

That was nearly a year ago. Before the funeral. Before he'd buried his parents.

He'd never claimed to be a perfect person, but tonight of all nights—he lifted the wine bottle in a mock toast to his dead parents, wherever they were—well, at least he had an excuse.

As for the cigarettes, he'd dabbled when he first started law school, more for the image than anything else. He wanted something to hold at parties, an excuse to keep his hands busy instead of awkwardly shoved in his pockets. Smoking had become a rare occurrence after he discovered that too many cigarettes left his skin irritated with a scaly rash around his mouth—and Aden was vain, not that he'd admit it. Vanity, after all, worked best when you pretended it wasn't there, even if you couldn't walk past a mirror without stopping to admire your reflection.

He took a long drag from his cigarette. Choked down a cough.

At least the sky was pretty tonight. The kind of pretty that only showed itself when the world was asleep. The moon hung like an unpolished mirror—too dull for reflection, but enough to make Aden look anyway—casting the porch in pale silver. Ten, twenty, thirty minutes passed in a haze of menthol plumes and cheap, sour wine that left an acrid sting on his tongue, like asparagus piss. And then, as the buzz took hold, the rage settled in.

No one loved birds more than the Shahs.

Or perhaps it was truer to say that the Shahs loved nothing more than birds.

So much so that the Shahs had given up Aden's bedroom for Coco.

You were gone so long, Mom and Dad figured it'd be a better use of the space. That was what Aliza had said, like it was all some kind of joke. Like his existence in their family could just be uprooted and rearranged, as easily as moving furniture.

He crushed his cigarette underfoot, stared out at the moon, and then, somehow, was on his feet. The room that used to be his felt like a taunt, a wound that hadn't scabbed over. He didn't even remember deciding to go back inside the house, didn't quite register climbing the stairs. The door was cracked open, just enough for a low shaft of light to stretch across the hallway floor, an invitation.

He slipped inside his old bedroom.

Aden had realized early on that his family was not like other families. It had begun in fourth grade, when his birthday rolled around and his parents forgot to give him cupcakes to share with the rest of his class, even though his teacher had reminded them. Aden, too, had reminded them every day of the week leading up to it. But his parents had argued that birthdays were never a big deal with them—growing up, they'd never celebrated their own birthdays, so why should he?

That part, Aden could almost accept. Almost.

But he couldn't shake the feeling that this wasn't just about birthdays. It was about how his parents had seemed to forget about him altogether. How he could be standing right there and still be invisible.

He'd spent a long time convincing himself it didn't matter. Maybe if he tried harder—if he kept his room clean, if he got better grades, if he helped with Coco—then maybe they'd notice him. Really notice him. Love him.

He could live without the cupcakes.

But then, a few weeks later, his parents celebrated what they referred to as Coco Chanel's "Gotcha Day"—the day they'd brought her home from the breeder. They bought a custom cockatoo cake. Spent $2,500 on a photo shoot with Coco, when there were already more framed photographs of their bird than there were of him.

That stung. Not the cupcakes. Not the photos. Just . . . this. The fact that Coco was easier to see. Easier to love.

His parents had cried when Coco developed a feather cyst. But when Aden was sick with the flu for a week, they merely dropped off bowls of lukewarm soup and Gatorade at his door with equally lukewarm wishes to "get better soon"—mostly because they needed him to mow the lawn on account of Coco's "allergies."

He'd told himself it wasn't a big deal. He wasn't a baby—he could handle this, accept it, not want more.

He'd told himself this for years.

But some things—some things never stopped hurting.

"A-den!" the bird greeted him, raising a clawed foot—the one with her ID band. "Coco! Say hi, Coco!"

Aden did not say hi. His head was swimming, his vision bleary.

"Pretty bird, pretty bird, A-den," she crooned. Her beak opened wide as she unleashed a piercing, metallic laugh.

Aden flinched.

There was a time when that laugh delighted him. Back when he was practically a toddler, and he'd finally gotten over his initial fear of her, her mimicry had become part of a game they'd played together. She wasn't like parrots—cockatoos didn't mimic human speech as deftly as other bird species—but Coco had a knack for sounds. When he was maybe six or seven, he'd coax her into copying sneezes, funny whistles, ringtones. He'd laughed himself breathless the first time she'd barked like the Shreya aunty's Maltipoo, proudly calling her a genius as she pranced in chuffed circles on her perch.

But now that laugh was like a knife scraping the back of his brain.

The problem was that Coco was always loud. Sometimes too loud. As Aden got older, she'd shrieked whenever the phone rang, mimicked the sound of a doorbell, forcing him to rush to the front door—only to find nothing there. She'd screech loudly enough to rattle the windows, waking Sammy when he was just a baby. Sammy wouldn't even cry, only whimper his complaint, too timid to join her raucous chaos.

Coco let out another skin-crawling laugh. Aden felt his nerves unspool.

"Please *shut up*," he muttered, but Coco only tilted her head left and right, feathers ruffled in triumphant display. Daring him to do something about it.

Aden didn't love animals the way his sister did, but he knew a lot about cockatoos. He knew they craved attention, nay, an audience, desperately—lest they wither and drop dead from neglect. Coco especially treated the world like her stage; anyone who didn't adore her was, by default, an enemy to be punished.

Aliza always swore Coco wasn't like that. "She's just . . . gotten more anxious lately," she'd argued once, back when they were kids. "You just have to talk to her—like you used to, remember? And then she's sweet. I think she just wants company. Maybe all the competitions have stressed her out."

Maybe Coco was sweet to Aliza, but ever since Coco had begun raking in the ribbons, she'd seemingly decided that Aden's general indifference was punishable by beak and claw. Too often, his hands were left a bloody mess after he'd finished cleaning her cage.

Worse, the world seemed full of people like Coco—spotlight chasers who trampled everyone else. In law school, there'd been James Alderman, who strutted around campus like he owned the place, fishing for admiration. He'd corner Aden after exams and ask, *loudly*, about Aden's scores, taking Aden's nonanswer as an invitation to boast about his own. When Aden had started dating Sẹ̀yí, James proclaimed—*so fucking loudly*—that Sẹ̀yí could do better. And when they'd both interviewed for an associate position at Sterling, Landry, and Abbott, it was James, of all people, who snagged it. *Better luck next time, huh, champ?* he'd said, slapping Aden on the back and then letting out a laugh that made Aden want to rip off his own ears.

Like Coco, James viewed the world as his stage, and Aden was left standing in the wings.

Still. That was better than the role his parents had given him: the family cleaning crew, summoned only to scrub up their messes.

Now he was back for another round. Like some sick glutton for punishment.

Coco squawked once more—"A-den! A-den!"—and Aden's jaw tightened.

He leaned close, his voice razor thin. "You haven't struggled a day in your life, huh?"

Coco cocked her head, dark eyes glittering as she peered back at him.

"Stupid fucking bird," he muttered. "You don't even know. You have no *idea* what it's like out there. Sure, yeah, maybe you spent your whole life in a cage—big freaking deal. *I'm* the one who's been trapped."

For once, Coco was quiet. She ruffled her feathers, the faintest rustle as she shifted from claw to claw. Still, she held his gaze.

"Yeah, all *you* gotta do is stand there and people love you," he went on. "You're treated better than ninety-nine percent of the human population. Do you even know that? You don't know that. People are starving—*star-ving*—and here you are, eating *organic fruit* like . . . like inflation doesn't exist!" He pointed a wavering finger at her. "Look at you! You don't even know what the economy *is*! You"—he swallowed—"you don't know *anything*."

Coco merely fluffed herself up in that peculiar, self-important way she had.

"And yet, you have the nerve to bite people." Aden barked out a short, hollow laugh, reaching for the cage door. "But hey. You're a bird. You're supposed to be free, right? Right?" His hand fumbled with the latch. "Maybe it's time someone showed you what the real world is like."

Coco hopped onto the perch closest to him, her gaze steady as the cage door opened.

"Yeah," he said, softer now. "You could just fly away. No one would . . . no one would even blame you for it. Must be nice."

She stepped onto his arm without hesitation. Her claws light yet certain—an act of trust, despite it all.

Her wings fluttered gently against his sleeve.

Aden felt it then: that cold twist in his chest. A familiar knot of guilt, aching, the same one he'd been choking down for the past ten years.

He took a long breath. With Coco settled on his arm, his steps grew deliberate, heavy as he carried her out of his childhood room, down the stairs, and toward the waiting dark.

The world spun, and his thoughts roiled, a tangled, drunken mess—but he lifted his arm toward the night sky.

"Because that's what birds do," he whispered.

"They *fly*."

The Past

Small A-den good boy good boy he coos at Coco sing at Coco Coco dances

I clipped her wings yesterday so you can take her outside—but stay right outside, okay?

Big face warbles

A-den take Coco on shoulder sunlight so warm so bright A-den so warm flowers so sweet

Pink like Coco! *A-den sings*

Coco no understand but Coco show big feathers and dance and A-den laugh

He speak so small now

We're going to be a big brother and sister soon *he garble to Coco*

So Coco dance more for A-den and A-den dances too

Chapter 4

Aden awoke to the sound of his sister screaming. "Coco! Has anyone seen Coco?"

The noise splintered through his skull like shrapnel. He winced, cracking his eyes open and blinking against the harsh morning light. His joints protested as he attempted—but failed—to sit up in his bed.

Wait. No. This wasn't his bed. He was outside, sprawled on the front porch. His entire body ached like some sick freak had replaced every bone with rusted rebar as he slept. Almost thirty-one years old, and already his body was throwing in the towel. Fantastic.

His gaze drifted down to the empty bottle of wine a few inches from his outstretched hand, and a dull trickle of memories from last night began to seep in: the stars overhead, spinning, his thoughts a numb haze. The anger.

Right. He was hungover. Not the smartest move, considering he was supposed to meet with Abigail, his parents' lawyer, later today. And based on her emails—blunt, straight to the point—it would be about as pleasant as a root canal.

The front door burst open, and Aliza stormed out, her eyes sharp and wild, darting around until they found him lying on the porch like roadkill.

"Where is Coco?" she demanded.

Aden stared back groggily. "What?"

"Coco is missing! Her cage is open, and now—now she's *gone*."

Aden finally sat up. His brain whirred painfully, sifting through the fog, and slowly, the memories replayed in high definition: him sitting on the porch, looking out over the empty yard, the wine loosening his every thought. Buckling beneath the sheer weight of it all—Reema's questions, Aliza's accusations, the house and its thousand small burdens.

And then the faint echo of a feeling he barely recognized, something like defiance, paired with an absurd urge to just . . . let something go.

Coco.

He remembered unhooking the latch on her cage, his hands moving with a strange, drunken resolve. Remembered whispering, "Go on, then! Fly! *Fly!*" like he was in some melodramatic scene from a movie. Like *Free Willy*, but far less inspirational.

Shit.

"Okay, don't panic—" he began, but Aliza's face reddened.

"What did you do?"

"Look, I'm sorry, I don't want to fight. I just—I made a mistake."

"Oh my God." Aliza put her hand on her chest, trying—and failing—to steady her breathing. "I knew it. I *knew* it! You always hated Coco, but I didn't think you'd be evil enough to kick her out, you idiot. She's just a bird. And now she's out in the real world, hungry and cold and *defenseless*. What the hell is wrong with you?"

"I told you, it was a mistake. An accident."

"And what good does that do me?" Her glare had him pinned, but her breathing was ragged, too fast. She mussed her hair violently, like she could scrub the panic away if she just tried hard enough. "God, Aden, you're—" Her voice cracked. "I swear, you're worse than the *Lowells*."

"Hey, I know you're pissed, but that's unfair."

When he was twelve, the Lowells had tried to steal Coco during the Eastern Regionals. They were discovered sneaking her into their hotel room, the cowards. *She looked so under the weather, so overworked; we just wanted to take her somewhere she'd feel more comfortable,* they'd argued with Aden's parents.

"Then you need to fix this. *Now.*"

"Aliza," said Aden, rubbing the back of his sore neck, "I know you're upset. I get it—but do you have any idea how hard it would be to drive around looking for a cockatoo? She could be anywhere. And I've got a meeting with the family lawyer in, like, two hours."

"That's not my problem."

"What's wrong?" Sammy poked his head from inside, his swollen eyes giving him the appearance of a sickly owl.

"Aden *released* Coco," she spat through gritted teeth. She gave Aden a look like she might punch him. More than that, he was worried it would hurt. "And now he's going to spend however long it takes to bring her back home."

"Coco has a tracking chip in the ID band on her ankle," Sammy offered quietly. "I think there's an app—it should make it easier to find her."

"Show me," Aliza commanded.

Sammy nodded and disappeared back into the house. Aden raked his fingers through his hair. "Aliza . . ." he said. But Aliza didn't let him finish.

"Aden, Coco could *die*. Because of you." His sister took a long, shaky breath and rubbed her eyes. Was she crying? "God, I should have trimmed her wings. But I was caught up in everything for the funeral and . . ."

Aden ran his tongue across his teeth.

Coco dying—well, it wasn't like he *wanted* that. Again, contrary to popular belief, he wasn't a monster.

But if he was being honest, a small, selfish part of him wondered whether her absence would make things . . . easier.

She was a needy thing—not just in her constant desire for company, but also in making sure she finished all her food and supplements, cleaning her cage, bathing and hygiene, mental stimulation (which, frankly, she needed a lot of). And still she was a brat—one who could easily live for at least another thirty years.

With Mom and Dad gone, who was going to take care of her?

Aden seized the thought like a lifeline:

He couldn't undo what he'd done, but maybe in a way . . . maybe this was for the best.

"There are worse things than Coco disappearing," he said simply.

Aliza's hand lingered on the edge of the doorframe. Her eyes found his again, but they didn't hold the sharp edge of anger anymore. Instead, there was an unfamiliar distance, as though she were staring at a stranger. A cold, quiet severing.

Aliza's anger—even her disappointment—he could handle. But this . . . this, he didn't know what to do with.

"I'll find her," she said finally, before turning and walking back into the house.

Aden opened his mouth to stop her but thought better of it. Instead, he laid his tired body back down on the hard, uneven floorboards of his family's porch. Alone, with his empty wine bottle and the obnoxiously early sunlight.

Aliza cared too much, he thought absentmindedly. But she was still young. Still clinging to the idea that things could be fixed if you just tried hard enough.

Aden knew better.

He almost laughed. At least his siblings already hated him. No skin off his back.

He closed his eyes a moment longer. Then, slowly, gingerly, he pushed himself upright, only to catch a whiff of something stale. Rotten.

He'd need to shower before meeting with Abigail.

Aden eased his parents' car onto the narrow residential street, Harper & Linwood LLP's address punched into his phone's navigation app, its dead monotone instructing him to turn right in four hundred feet.

He drummed his fingers on the steering wheel, eyes skimming the web of cracked asphalt ahead. His skull still throbbed—a dull, persistent reminder of last night's wine, which churned unpleasantly with every bump in the road. It didn't help that the seat felt wrong. No matter how much he fiddled with the settings, it wasn't quite comfortable, and one of the tires was definitely losing air.

He glanced at the clock on the dashboard. He'd remembered to bring a briefcase, which was currently sitting in the back seat, filled with the documents he'd pulled from his parents' filing cabinet. A copy of their will. Insurance policy. Social Security. And he still had fifteen minutes to spare. More than enough time to sit in the parking lot and prep himself to wrestle with the bureaucratic circus that would be Abigail Harper.

He imagined her sharp suit, clipped voice, and sterile conference room that smelled like paper and disappointment. He'd had a professor like her at Northwestern, the kind who refused, on principle, to let herself be impressed by any student, even if they gave her the perfect answer on a cold call. That professor had made her dislike of him clear, but at least she'd also equally hated James Alderman.

She'd liked Ṣẹ̀yí, though. *Everyone* liked Ṣẹ̀yí Ariyo in law school, *everywhere* she went. She was the one who'd raise her hand in class when everyone was too afraid to answer. Aden loved her unabashed laughter when someone said something funny, like bright, warm sunlight spilling through an open window. The single dimple on the left side of her mouth. The way she'd sigh and let out a *"Mtcheww,"* especially if Aden had said something ridiculous, sounding *just* like her Nigerian mother (not that Aden would ever tell her this). But she was soft, too. Gentle. The kind of person who'd come home from her immigration law internship after talking to a victim of female genital mutilation from the Ivory Coast and cry silently on the couch before staying up the whole night researching. Determined to *do* something about it.

But apparently Aden's association with her during law school had not been enough to place him in anyone else's good graces. Not that it mattered to him; he was used to that anyway. Maybe even deserved it.

His thought was interrupted by movement on the sidewalk—a flash of bright fabric, someone wearing a ridiculous neon windbreaker, their short black bob bouncing with every step. Aliza, he realized. And beside her, Sammy's unmistakable slouch, as if trying to fold himself in half.

Aden slowed the car, watching them through the windshield. Aliza's expression was grim as she scrolled through her phone while Sammy adjusted the laptop tucked beneath his arm. They looked like two Dickensian orphans—lost and pitiful—the kind that would make some do-gooder roll down their window and offer directions, or a shilling.

Though he supposed they were orphans now.

For a second, Aden almost kept driving. What good would stopping do, anyway? He'd tried to help, but they didn't want him here.

But then, uninvited—as they so often are—a memory surfaced. One from before things had unraveled.

He remembered a rare summer evening when their parents had been gone—off at some breeder's house for "networking," whatever the hell that meant. Not that he cared. Because for one night, the house belonged to Aden and his siblings.

Aliza had dragged the box fan into the living room, while Sammy, who'd just learned how to use the microwave, brought in a plate of pizza rolls. Aden, still sweaty from mowing the lawn, had stood beside Coco's cage, flicking his fingers through the bars until she finally tapped his hand with her claw.

"High five!" he'd declared, triumphant.

Aliza squealed, her gap-toothed smile wide. "Do it again!"

When Coco tapped his fingers again—enthusiastic this time, like she knew she was being clever—Sammy had almost dropped the pizza rolls in awe.

Their parents never saw, of course. But that was part of what made it—the moment, the laughter, the triumph—*theirs*. And maybe that was why Aliza and Sammy still held on so tightly now. Not just to Coco, but to whatever scraps of that feeling were still left.

Aden's grip tightened on the wheel.

Yeah. He should keep driving. He'd already apologized for losing Coco. He didn't owe them anything. Hell, he was already doing them a favor by handling the legal end of things, even if they didn't appreciate it.

But that memory clung to him: Aliza's laughter. Sammy's wide, bright eyes.

A knot coiled tightly in his chest.

Before he could second-guess himself, he made a sharp U-turn, pulling up beside them. He rolled down the window.

His siblings stopped—and immediately met his stare with twin expressions of disinterest. Like they'd already decided he was about to waste their time.

"You look ridiculous," Aden informed them flatly. "It's embarrassing."

"We're literally just walking," said Aliza.

"Have you made a post on craigslist or something?" he asked. "There's also bird-watching sites. If you share a photo of Coco, bird-watchers will keep an eye out for her. They live for this shit."

"I . . . haven't. Yet. But you can go now."

Aden did not. "Don't you have work?"

"I told the vet office I wasn't coming in today."

"You told the vet office you weren't coming in?" Aden repeated, arching an eyebrow. "Is gainful employment a joke to you, or . . . ?"

Aliza shot him a glare. "Did you stop just to lecture me, or are you here for a reason?"

"Lecture, mostly," he said, tapping his fingers against the wheel. "But also . . . you're clearly bad at this. What's your strategy here? Wandering around looking homeless, hoping Coco just conveniently flitters over in your general direction?"

"The proper term is 'unhoused,' you ass. And we're *trying*."

Sammy squinted at him silently, shifting the laptop under his arm again. Clearly, it was heavy for the kid.

"I can see that," Aden replied. He tapped the wheel again. "Do you need help or not?"

Aliza blinked, startled. "What?"

"Do you? Need? Help?"

"You were on the way to the lawyer," she pointed out.

"And I'll get there eventually," Aden said, popping the door lock. "Get in before I change my mind."

Sammy, always so quiet, glanced at Aliza for a cue.

"What's the catch?" Aliza asked, narrowing her eyes.

Aden shrugged. "No catch. Except maybe I don't want to hear you whining about this bird for the next twenty years. Consider it self-preservation."

Aliza gave him a long, searching look—one that felt too much like the one she'd given him earlier that morning. But instead of snapping at him, she just climbed into the car, dragging Sammy in after her.

"Fine," she muttered. "But don't think this makes up for anything."

"Wasn't trying to," Aden replied. His voice was breezy, but his hands gripped the wheel just a little too tightly. He shifted the car into drive. "I'm just here to show you that wandering the streets isn't a viable strategy. Call it a learning experience. You're welcome."

Aliza rolled her eyes but didn't argue, sinking into the passenger seat with her arms crossed; Sammy stared out the window in the back seat, wordlessly fiddling with the tracking app on his laptop.

With the two of them settled, Aden guided the car down another cracked, sun-faded street, the suspension creaking beneath every bump.

Disappointment was a quiet thing, he'd learned. It wasn't the slam of a door or the shatter of glass; it was softer, like sand slipping through fingers, leaving an ache you couldn't name. He didn't want that for them.

But maybe that was inevitable. Maybe this was all he could offer as their older brother: the chance to learn for themselves. To keep looking for Coco until, inevitably, they gave up.

Until they learned, as he had, that some things drifted too far to come back.

The road stretched ahead, dappled with sunlight and shadows, seemingly endless. Aden flexed his fingers on the wheel, loosening his grip, and tried not to think about how long it would take before they gave up searching. Or how long he was willing to let them try.

Aden glanced one more time in his sister's direction, but she was leaning away, her back turned to him. Lately it felt like her back was always turned to him.

"Point me in a direction, Sammy. And put your seat belts on," he said, biting back a sigh. "Let's get this over with."

Unfortunately, his siblings were persistent. Two hours had crawled by like a slow, painful bleed before Aden finally had to say something.

"Look, maybe the tracking app isn't working. There's no way Coco has been flying around for *hours* without a single break."

"She's never had complete freedom," Aliza snapped. "Of course she'd be flying nonstop."

"But she's not built for flying all day," said Aden. "She's spoiled. Lazy. Barely used her wings because she was carried half the time."

"She's not *spoiled*."

"Fine, then she's *dependent*," Aden corrected. "That's what happens when someone spends their whole life being babied."

"Wow, okay, Aden. You want to make this about us now? Because let me remind you how all of this is *your* faul—"

From the back seat, Sammy leaned forward. "So if Coco's been constantly flying, doesn't that mean she could burn herself out really soon?"

"Possibly . . ." Aden answered, hesitating. "It could be that she's just looking for someplace safe first. Again, assuming the tracking app is actually working."

"Good. Because, um. I have to pee."

A sigh pressed out of Aliza.

"Can't you hold it?" She didn't even glance back, her voice fraying. "If we go home now, what if Coco does stop to take a rest? Then we'll have missed our chance to grab her."

Sammy squirmed. "I really have to go."

"*Fine*. We can go home, take a quick bathroom break. But then we need to keep looking."

Aden glanced at Sammy through the rearview mirror, searching for some shared solidarity. But Sammy's eyes stayed glued to the floor.

"Aliza," Aden said carefully, testing the waters, "I think you need to accept that this might not go the way you want."

She didn't answer. She stayed turned toward the passenger-side window, seemingly fascinated by someone's entirely ordinary mailbox.

"Even if we're lucky enough to find her when she stops to take a break, then what?" he continued. "How are you going to grab her? What if she's up in some tree? You really think she's going to come down willingly?"

"She might. She's family."

"You put too much faith in her. Her being, may I remind you, a *bird*."

"I wouldn't *have* to sit here and hope for the best if you hadn't let her out in the first place."

"And I get that. But, again, I just think that maybe you need to consider—"

"I don't want to lose anyone else, Aden!" Aliza's voice cracked like a whip.

Anyone else.

It hit sharper than Aden cared to admit. She'd just lost both her parents, same as him. Only her relationship with them had been different, leaving her grief loud and exposed, desperate to cling to any shred of normalcy. Not like Aden, who wasn't sure if his grief even existed.

She'd hardly even had a moment to mourn.

In the rearview mirror, Sammy's head was down, but his fingers stayed curled tightly around his laptop, knuckles pale. Holding on to something.

Aden stared straight ahead, the road in front of them blurring slightly.

But there was a quiet, angry heat inside his stomach, a feeling he didn't want but couldn't shake. Had that fear of losing anyone else ever included him? Or had he been missing from the picture for so long that his absence didn't even register anymore?

Aliza sat back abruptly, as if realizing how much she'd let slip. She swallowed audibly.

"Coco has watched us grow up," she continued finally, her voice a little softer, but no less jagged. "Coco has Mom's laugh, for God's sake; she even *talks* like her. She's the only reminder of them we have left, and you're fine with letting her starve to death? Getting eaten by a cat?" Her eyes reddened. "I don't care if you hate her. She was Mom and Dad's pride and joy. She deserves better."

A-den! A-den! Coco's familiar voice echoed in the back of his mind.

But that flicker of concern soured quickly—twisting into old bitterness, stirring the memory of being the afterthought in a family that had always seemed to save its love and faith for Coco. And beneath that, the sharp, shameful sting of jealousy. Over, he reminded himself, a stupid *bird*.

A sharp, humorless laugh escaped him.

"Yeah. Yeah, that's exactly my fucking point," Aden said. "She *was* our parents' pride and joy. The same lunatics who valued a stupid bird more than their own kids. I'm sorry, but I, for one, am not wasting my time driving around looking for Coco. Especially when we both know she's not coming home anytime soon."

Aliza flinched like she'd just been slapped.

But she didn't fire back immediately. Instead, she sank farther into her seat, fingers knotting together in her lap, her breaths coming shallow and quick.

"This is exactly why you shouldn't be the executor," she muttered, her voice tight.

"Oh my God. Aliza, it's *done*. Drop it."

"Bullshit." Her voice rose. "You don't even care! About the house, about Coco, about us—about *anything* except your own convenience.

If Mom and Dad were here, they'd be *horrified* at how you're handling this. Sammy and I could—"

"You really think it's that simple?" he cut in. "You think you can just march into court and, what? Convince a judge to give *you* control?"

"I don't know!" Aliza shot back. "But I'll do whatever it takes to get you removed. If you're not going to act like this family matters, then you don't deserve to have a say. *Ever*."

Sammy cleared his throat. "Coco's heading west," he said quietly. "Toward Reading."

Aden blinked, his grip tightening against the wheel. "The hell is she doing?"

"Sammy," said Aliza, "can you look up how long a bird can fly without resting?"

Sammy typed some more then: "Swifts can fly for ten months without stopping. There's also this one bird—the 'bar-tailed godwit'?—that flew from Alaska to New Zealand in eight days straight."

"A bar-tailed *godwit*?" Aden said. "Were the scientists high when they named it?"

"What about a cockatoo?" Aliza asked, ignoring him.

Sammy frowned at the screen. "Cockatoos aren't long-distance fliers. They can do a few hours, but that's about it."

"See?" Aden said. "I was right."

"It's only because she's a cockatoo, not because she's lazy," Aliza shot back. "Let's just drive toward Reading, then. Coco'll hopefully stop to rest soon, and then—"

"No." Aden's knuckles were pale against the dark leather of the wheel. "I'm done driving. We're going back. You can figure out what to do on your own."

The car filled with a heavy stillness, leaving an unsettling, choking hum. Aden stared ahead, his grip unwavering, while Aliza turned toward the window, her reflection sharp in the glass.

It was pointless, after all. Chasing Coco. Trying to fix things. Maybe it always had been. Because no matter what he did, whether he tried to help, tried to make life easier, it would never matter. Aliza would still find a reason to hate him. Not when she was breaking like this—and not when he couldn't seem to show her how he was hurting, too.

He was too tired to fight a battle that felt impossible to win.

"Fine," Aliza muttered at last, her voice barely audible. "We've never needed you anyway."

Chapter 5

Aden wondered whether the wooden "Live, Laugh, Love" sign in his parents' kitchen was meant to be ironic or if they really had reached the age where they thought such signage was cute.

Either way, it mocked him now, hanging smugly by the oven like the house itself was in on a joke he wasn't part of.

It was just past 6:00 p.m., and he'd scavenged through the fridge for leftovers, eventually settling on a bowl of lasagna a neighbor had dropped off earlier. As he ate, he scrolled through his emails, hoping for something—anything—work related. The only one in his inbox was from Abigail Harper: We can reschedule for Friday this week. Otherwise, my next opening is not until two weeks from now.

Aden swallowed a sigh and looked up from his bowl.

LIVE, LAUGH, LOVE

Insufferable.

He finished the lasagna, dumped his bowl and fork into the dishwasher, and jabbed at the controls until it hummed to life. Then he trudged down the hallway, toward the bathroom, to brush his teeth.

He needed to get back to Chicago. The longer he stayed, the heavier this house seemed to grow, its weight creeping into his chest.

But first, the home office. He'd already made a dent—his mom had been organized enough to put their most important documents in a bright-orange folder, which now sat safely in his briefcase. Still, there was more to do: cancel his parents' credit cards, file the life insurance claims, and call a real estate agent.

He'd already looked through his parents' bank accounts, and the damage was worse than he'd thought: just a measly $20,000 left in savings, which was practically chump change if split three ways. From the looks of it, they'd blown their money on Coco's vet bills and insurance, and the fancy hotels they'd stayed in during the competition circuit.

Maybe they'd flown off the cliff on purpose, Aden thought darkly. *Their irresponsibility knew no bounds after all.*

The thought made his temples throb, a familiar heat blooming across his forehead.

He'd have to pass on his share of the inheritance. Aliza and Sammy needed the money more—not that he'd tell them. Aliza would probably fight him on it, thinking it meant she'd owe him somehow. Stubborn shithead.

He pulled out his phone and connected it to his dad's old Bluetooth speakers, scrolling through his music. Ella Fitzgerald's voice, smooth as warm molasses, poured into the room while a trumpet bubbled and popped like champagne. He liked these old recordings—the way the vinyl crackled, bright and a little rough around the edges. He had Sẹ̀yí to thank for that. She loved jazz.

They'd slow-danced together to "Dream a Little Dream of Me" once while taking a break from studying for their Contracts exam. He could still see her face, more familiar than his own: dark, luminous skin catching the warm glow of the kitchen light, high cheekbones framing eyes tapered like black brushstrokes, full lips that curved into a knowing smile. The subtle rose of her perfume. She'd laughed when he twirled her, her voice lilting: *You're ridiculous.*

He'd wanted to tell her then, to say what he couldn't quite admit to himself—that he loved her. Loved her with a kind of clumsy, bewildered certainty that twined in his chest whenever she smiled at him like she knew him better than he knew himself.

But that love felt dangerous. Like a test he was bound to fail.

So instead, he'd buried it. Let it simmer beneath half-formed daydreams. Looked away from it every time it rose up and caught in his throat—because it reminded him of the truth: that Sẹ̀yí deserved more than he could ever give.

His toe slammed into the corner of the desk.

"Shit!"

He stumbled back, muttering curses under his breath as he rubbed his foot. Served him right for getting distracted.

Right. The desk. He hadn't gone through the drawers yet. Maybe there was something useful in them—an old checkbook, a copy of the will, or, hell, even a password list for their other accounts. All things he needed to sort before the government threatened to reap his parents' still-warm corpses for some extra dimes. It was strange that there was so much to get done and a limited time frame to get it done in—time clearly stopped for no one, apparently not even for death.

The first drawer was a mess of paper clips, rubber bands, and a screwdriver sticky with something unidentifiable. The second held receipts, two unpaid tickets, an old road map of the United States—Jesus, how old was this thing?—and a stack of Post-its with half-jotted recipes.

Beneath them, a photo.

Aliza, two or three years old, laughing so hard she was mid-snort. A bright-pink Coco perched on her shoulder, leaning toward her. They were standing by a pink rosebush Aden didn't recognize—his parents didn't exactly have green thumbs—but he recognized Aliza's matching pink T-shirt, stained with juice, her hair stuck up in the signature crooked pigtails she'd worn as a child.

There was a caption on the back, and Aden recognized his mother's handwriting:

Aliza and Coco. April 2002.

He stared at the picture longer than he meant to.

He remembered bits and pieces of that day: His mom had insisted they take the picture, and Aliza—who'd only just learned to walk—had gently held Coco like she was something precious. She had refused to let their mom or dad help, cradling the bird with both hands while whispering, *It's okay, pretty baby.* Coco had been quiet that day, no shrieking—just still, her pink feathers sleek and bright as she pressed close to Aliza. Like she understood that this, too, was home.

Aden didn't think Coco had ever been that calm with him.

His lips twitched upward. He could almost smell the roses, hear the shrill, delighted squeal Aliza used to make whenever he got Coco to bark like a Maltipoo for her. She was a sweet kid back then.

What were the odds, finding this now? It wasn't like his parents to hold on to photos like this, but maybe it was because Coco was in it. Maybe it was part of some photo album tucked away somewhere. Maybe they'd meant to get it framed.

Maybe they'd forgotten about it.

Aden slipped the photo into his pocket before he could second-guess it, a strange tangle of guilt and warmth settling low in his chest. He'd never fully gotten along with Aliza. Not in the way other siblings did, anyway, with their inside jokes and secret alliances.

When he was fifteen, they'd gotten into a cold war over his clothes, specifically, his hoodies. She'd developed a nasty habit of pilfering his favorites, the perfectly oversize ones made soft from years of lacrosse practices and late-night cramming sessions. An unforgivable crime. Worse, a senseless one. No one was holding his sister at gunpoint, forcing her to wear boys' clothes, least of all his. So *why*?

When he'd finally had enough, he'd complained to his parents, practically *begged* for their intervention, but his mom had just sighed and waved him off: "Oh, no," she'd said. "I'm not getting involved. You two figure it out."

As always, so helpful.

That day, he'd stormed back to his room, seething, ready to plot his revenge—only to find her already there, elbow deep in his closet.

"What the hell are you doing?" he demanded.

She turned, a hoodie dangling from her bony fingers like a trophy. His favorite one. Of course.

"I'm just borrowing it," Aliza said calmly. Defiantly.

"Like hell you are." He snatched it back, holding it high above her head, just out of reach. She was only ten then, tall for her age but all limbs and angles, while he had two years of lacrosse training and a vendetta. "You'd look stupid in it anyway," he snapped. "I'm doing you a favor."

The swipe came out of nowhere—a flash of fingernails across his cheek, sharp and stinging, like a feral cat's. For a moment they just stared at each other, stunned. Her chest heaved with anger, her small hands clenched into fists. He touched his cheek, half expecting to see blood.

And then the rage hit. He thought about tackling her right there, pinning her to the carpet until she apologized. But he didn't. The optics of wrestling a ten-year-old girl as a fifteen-year-old teenager weren't exactly in his favor, and that was the curse of being the eldest sibling: shackled by the invisible rope of having to know better, *be* better. Even when your parents couldn't care less.

"GET OUT!" he yelled instead, slamming the door behind her as she fled.

They didn't speak for weeks after that.

But the silence never lasted with Aliza. She was always the first to break it. She was also the only one in their family who remembered his birthday. The only one who nudged their mom to buy red toothbrushes because she knew he preferred them. The only one who'd clean Coco's cage when he was too swamped.

"You owe me," she'd say. But she'd never collect.

Then, when he turned eighteen, he left for college, never expecting to miss much about his life back home. But sometimes, when he saw a red toothbrush in the aisle at Walgreens or smelled laundry softener that reminded him of his hoodies, he thought of her. And in those moments, the way he missed her was a painful prickle—like a scratch across the cheek that hadn't healed.

Aden pulled the photo out of his pocket and smoothed out the edges. She'd probably want to keep it. Unlike their parents, Aliza had always been the type to lecture him for throwing away things like scuffed shoes or tacky ties from high school dances. To her, the older something was, the more memories it had soaked up, like a sponge he didn't care to wring out.

The photo wasn't doing him any good anyway. If anything, it made his chest ache—a stupid reminder of a time when things had been easier. Before everything had gone to hell.

Aden dragged his legs down the hallway to her room, the wooden floor groaning under his weight, which, frankly, felt insulting. He paused at her door and knocked softly, a gesture so out of character it made him feel vaguely ridiculous.

"It's me," he said. "Can I come in?"

Silence.

He waited a moment longer before cracking the door open just enough to peer inside. Aliza lay curled on her bed, facing the wall, her shoulders drawn up tight.

"Hey," he tried again, holding up the photo like a peace offering. "Found this in the office. Thought you'd want it."

She turned sharply, her face blotchy and her eyes rimmed red. For a second she said nothing, just stared—first at him, then at the photo. Finally, she got up, snatched it out of his hand like she was afraid he'd change his mind, and gave it a quick glance. Her lip quivered before she locked her jaw, her expression closing up like a book slammed shut.

"You okay?" he asked.

Her laugh was dry. "Our parents are dead, you've been back for all of five minutes, and now Coco's MIA. What do you think?"

"That sarcasm's doing wonders for your emotional growth."

"Go fuck yourself."

"You've been crying."

"Like you give a shit."

Before he could even form a retort, she slammed the door in his face.

Aden stood there for a moment, staring at the chipped paint on the doorframe, half wondering if he should knock again, half grateful to retreat. He let out a slow breath and headed back down the hall toward the living room. It was late. May as well call it a night.

After changing into his silk pajamas—a self-indulgent purchase for his thirtieth birthday that now felt absurdly out of place—Aden did his best to settle into the lumpy, sagging couch. He arranged and rearranged the patchwork of blankets and throw pillows, but the couch remained no better than a slab of concrete. Comfort, it seemed, wasn't on tonight's agenda.

As he adjusted one last time, he heard the sound of footsteps. Someone was in the kitchen. He frowned, sitting up slightly.

Sure enough, light spilled into the hallway, and a familiar shape moved around near the fridge.

Sammy.

His dark circles looked somehow worse. The kid probably hadn't slept a full night since their parents died. Too restless to sleep, too tired to stay still. For some people, grief turned them into sobbing, inconsolable messes. But for Sammy, it sent him digging into the fridge at odd hours, as if the right snack might fill the emptiness inside him.

Aden cleared his throat.

"Hey, uh—" Aden hesitated, groping for a decent nickname. *Sport? Kiddo? Bro?* "Sam. Sammy."

Sammy didn't respond at first, his focus on the fridge. He pulled out a jug of milk and poured some into a bright-green mug emblazoned with a red *S*. Personalized, probably—a gift, or maybe one of those ugly Christmas mugs you found at the back of a discount shelf. The kind their mother would buy in a weak attempt at motherly affection. He popped the mug into the microwave without a glance at Aden, who was now propped against the back of the sofa.

"We haven't really gotten a chance to talk," Aden tried, forcing his tone to stay light.

Sammy shrugged, his round eyes flicking to him for a fraction of a second before focusing on the glowing microwave display. "Mm."

The microwave beeped, and Sammy carefully pulled the mug out, cradling it like it held something more precious than lukewarm milk. He blew on the surface, the steam rising in lazy spirals, before he squeezed in some honey from a bear-shaped bottle.

Aden cleared his throat again, determined not to let the silence stretch. Talking to his little brother felt like pulling teeth, but if he couldn't get through to Aliza, maybe Sammy was the answer. He could explain the necessity of selling the house, convince him it wasn't betrayal—it was a fresh start. Sammy was still young; the possibilities were endless. New school, new friends, a chance to leave all the painful baggage of this place behind.

"You've gotten taller since the last time I saw you." Aden cringed at the pitiful attempt, but Sammy didn't seem to notice; he busied himself stirring honey into his mug.

"Okay," Sammy answered. The single word landed with a soft thud. Not hostile, just . . . neutral.

"And, uh, you're doing okay?"

Sammy hesitated, his gaze drifting toward the mug. "I don't think so," he said finally. "But I guess that's normal."

"Yeah," Aden said softly, not sure what else to offer.

Sammy looked at him then, his expression unreadable but not unkind. "Why are you sleeping here? Don't you have . . . I don't know, somewhere else to go?"

It wasn't accusatory, just a quiet observation. But somehow that made it sting more.

Aden shifted uncomfortably. "I figured . . . you know, it'd be easier if I stayed."

"For who?" asked Sammy.

Aden opened his mouth, then closed it. He didn't have a good answer.

Sammy didn't press. He just nodded, as if Aden's silence had told him everything he needed to know.

Then, without another word, he padded out of the kitchen, leaving Aden alone with the faint, lingering scent of milk he hadn't been offered.

Chapter 6

Aden woke to the pale light of dawn creeping through the curtains, its unwelcome intrusion highlighting every new ache in his body. His neck and back popped and cracked enough to put Rice Krispies cereal to shame, all thanks to the couch—unforgiving as ever.

He stretched with a groan, his silk pajamas somehow making him feel even more absurd. As if he were pretending he was lounging in luxury instead of tossing and turning on a sagging couch in a house that barely felt like home.

There was no chance he'd fall back asleep now. He sat up, raking a hand through his hair as last night's conversation with Sammy floated back to him.

For who?

Sammy hadn't said it with malice, but the words still clung to Aden's skin like a polyester coat in summer. He glanced at the hallway, half expecting to see his little brother lingering there, his soft eyes sharpened by quiet questions.

The house was quiet, save for the occasional creak of the floorboards settling.

Aden had always prided himself on being practical. The voice of reason. Yet here he was, camped out on a couch that hated him, surrounded by people who didn't want him there, trying to convince them that selling the house was the right call.

But Coco.

Aden exhaled sharply, scrubbing his hands over his face. It was ridiculous, really, the way his siblings had latched on to the bird like she was some kind of lifeline. Yes, there'd been a time he might've loved Coco, too, but age had brought perspective. Now Aden understood just what Coco had cost their family: Time. Money. Sanity. The way their parents had treated her like royalty while the rest of them had to make do with scraps.

What baffled him most was how Aliza and Sammy didn't see it, too.

Still, Coco had mattered to them. Had *always* mattered. He remembered how when they were just kids, Aliza would spend her own allowance on mangoes and pomegranates because "even Coco deserves a sweet treat now and then." And while Aden had called it a waste of money, he'd still peeled the mangoes for her, slicing them into neat cubes so Aliza wouldn't cut her fingers.

And Sammy? Aden didn't know exactly what Coco had ever meant to him. Sammy had been too young when the bird became the centerpiece of their parents' lives, too quiet to ever voice an opinion. But something about the way he'd looked last night—that inscrutable flicker of disappointment—had told Aden that Coco wasn't just a bird to him. She was a fixture of the house. One that belonged there, no matter what.

Aden pulled himself to his feet, stretching out the worst of the kinks in his back. Maybe it was stupid, but he couldn't shake the feeling that if they found Coco, it would be . . . something. Not a fix, not a solution. But *something.*

The kitchen smelled faintly of the warm milk and honey from last night, a sweetness oddly comforting.

Aden poured himself a glass of water, staring out the window above the sink. The sun crept higher in the sky, casting a golden light that spilled over the overgrown grass in the backyard. Across the way, in the Lowells' window, he made eye contact with Gus, their demonic macaw—perched like a feathered gargoyle, motionless and staring straight at him.

Unblinking.

Judging.

Fine, he thought. *One more day.* He'd offer to keep looking for Coco for one more day. It didn't have to mean anything. Wasn't some grand gesture or admission of guilt.

It was just one day.

But as he rinsed his glass and set it gently on the counter, Aden couldn't help but feel like he was lying to himself.

Then again, that was pretty much business as usual.

It was around 8:30 a.m. when Aliza and Sammy landed in the kitchen, their expressions guarded as they took in the breakfast spread Aden had set on the table. He was pouring orange juice into three mismatched glasses, his movements overly careful, like he wasn't sure how to do something so normal anymore.

The spread itself was modest, though ambitious for someone clearly out of their depth: a plate of toast, the slices fat and perfectly browned, despite the faint, accusatory scent of burned crumbs lingering in the air. Beside the toast sat a small bowl of what might have been whipped butter—or perhaps just softened butter hastily mashed with a fork. In the center of the table was a pile of scrambled eggs, slightly overdone and pale, arranged on a serving plate their mom had reserved for holidays and "company."

Aden set the glasses down and gestured toward the table without ceremony. "Bon appétit."

His siblings stared at him, then at the food, then back at him.

The silence dragged just long enough to feel absurd before Aliza finally broke it.

"Your pajamas look stupid."

Aden glanced down at his dark-green pajamas. "They're silk," he said, a little too defensively. "And I usually wear a robe with them."

"Of course you do." Aliza pointed to the table as Sammy wasted no time, already sliding into a chair. "What the hell is all this?"

"A peace offering."

Aliza's skeptical gaze swept over the table again, lingering on the sad pile of eggs. "A peace offering," she echoed flatly.

Aden ignored her and cleared his throat. "Sammy, where is Coco? Has there been any movement since last night?"

"We checked earlier. She's been on the run again since four a.m.," he answered, grabbing a piece of toast and spreading butter with some difficulty. "She's already in Harrisburg."

"God. She's heading to *Pennsyltucky*?" Aden shook his head. "Miracle she hasn't been shot down yet."

"Don't even joke." Aliza sat down at the table; she still looked unconvinced by the supposed peace offering, but clearly her hunger had won her over. She took a plate and helped herself to some toast.

"I'm not," said Aden. "My point is, if you're going to look for Coco, the sooner, the better."

Aliza paused mid-bite, her brow raised. "What are you suggesting?"

"That I help," Aden said. "You'll be the lookout, Sammy can track her on his laptop, and I'll drive. It'll be easier with the three of us. We can get it over with quicker."

Sammy looked up, intrigued, while Aliza narrowed her eyes. "What about your appointment with the lawyer? All the estate crap you keep saying you have to do?"

"I rescheduled for Friday. Which means I'm free today and tomorrow. Between the three of us, maybe we'll have some luck." Aden hesitated, then added, "Did you ever post on Bird-Watching Reddit?"

Aliza swallowed a bite. "I got a response from one bird-watcher who said they'll keep an eye out and reach out to other bird-watching groups in Appalachia. Other than that, nothing."

"Well," Aden said, "we know she'll stick to wooded areas, maybe near water. Sammy's tracking can fill in the rest." He glanced at his younger brother, who was busying himself with covering his scrambled eggs in a troubling amount of ketchup. "If we head to Harrisburg soon, we might actually get ahead of her. So, after breakfast, grab any essentials and then we'll head out?"

Aliza took another large bite of toast. Sammy looked up from his eggs, waiting, while she chewed in thoughtful, deliberate silence. Tension hung in the room like something tangible, and Aden felt himself shrinking from it.

He didn't know why this mattered so much—whether they agreed to his plan or not shouldn't be a big deal. And yet, he hated how clearly he could feel the line dividing them, leaving an unspoken loneliness prickling beneath his ribs.

It had always been like this—even before he'd left for Chicago. Like when he was seventeen, sitting on the porch while their parents fussed over Coco's latest trophy. Aliza had been perched on the arm of the couch beside Sammy, watching some children's cartoon, while Aden sat outside alone because he'd been locked out of the house and no one was picking up the phone.

That was the thing about being the oldest: No one bothered to check if you were okay. They just assumed you were.

So Aden had gotten used to being alone. To keeping his distance. To convincing himself he didn't need them, either. And for a while, it had worked.

But if they let him help find Coco—if they gave him a way to finally, properly, set things right—maybe he could leave again with a clean break this time. He *wanted* a clean break, that much he was sure of. Between Sẹ̀yí and abandoning Aliza and Sammy the first time, he already carried enough guilt to sink him.

He wouldn't let Coco, of all things, be one more weight.

"Fine," said Aliza finally. "It's the least you could do anyway. You'll right your wrong, be on your merry way back to Chicago, and leave us the hell alone." She set down her toast, her sharp gaze pinning him in place. "We can revisit our conversation about your executorship once we figure all this out first."

"I told you, there's nothing to talk—"

"And as I said before, that's bullshit," Aliza retorted. "*That's* the deal. Or else I'm not above choking you out right here and now if that's what it takes for you to stop being a selfish ass."

Aden ran a hand through his hair and bit back a sigh. Was his sister always this stubborn and . . . scary?

"Fine," he said eventually. The word felt like a concession but also, somehow, a relief. Like cracking open a window in a room that had gone stale. Still, even as he gave in, Aden couldn't shake the sense that Aliza held all the cards. Her sharp gaze a reminder that no matter how much time had passed, she could still see right through him.

"Couldn't you have made something besides eggs?" Aliza muttered. "It feels . . . ominous to be eating eggs when Coco's missing."

Aden sat at the head of the table, the one their mom used to claim. "I don't know how to make anything else."

"No wonder you're still single."

They had barely been on the road twenty minutes when Sammy announced, "She's still moving westward."

Aden groaned, tightening his grip on the steering wheel. The car rattled slightly as they hit a pothole. Damn Pennsylvania roads. "Is she heading to Ohio? Who the hell willingly goes to Ohio?"

"She must be terrified by now," Aliza said softly, her gaze fixed on the passing trees.

Sammy didn't look up from his laptop, his brow furrowed in thought. "Maybe that's why she keeps moving. Like what Aden said. Maybe Coco's still looking for somewhere she feels safe."

"In *Ohio*?"

"She's not in Ohio just yet," Sammy replied. "But . . . she's already out of Harrisburg."

"Well, wherever Coco's headed, maybe it's something instinctual," Aliza said, glancing back at Sammy. "Something pulling her forward—something else we can't understand."

Aden's brow furrowed. Cockatoos were smart: He remembered his dad boasting to their neighbors about how Coco could solve puzzles meant for human toddlers, right before slipping a treat into one of Coco's foraging toys. Aden had watched as Coco twisted and pried at the toy's latches and levers, methodical and relentless, until the snack was hers.

Maybe that was what Coco was doing now: trying to outsmart her own panic, pushing forward not out of instinct, but out of some stubborn will to survive.

Aden shook his head, dismissing the thought.

"Being stubborn is a family trait, so I guess that checks out."

His fingers tapped a restless rhythm on the steering wheel. He'd been the one to suggest this plan—hell, it had been his *brilliant* idea—but the reality of chasing a bird across Pennsylvania was beginning to hit, and he was not enjoying it. His parents' car smelled faintly of stale coffee and Sammy's cheddar popcorn, the crumpled bag discarded at his feet. Every jolt of the uneven road sent a twinge through his lower back, a physical reminder of just how long the day was going to be.

Aden groaned.

By the time they reached Michaux State Forest two hours later, the sky's color was drained to a lifeless gray and the rain had started as a drizzle, dampening the windshield and Aden's already dwindling patience.

"Of course," he muttered, parking the car with more force than necessary. "Because what's a fun family outing without rain and mud? Let's throw in a thunderstorm, shall we?"

Memories of childhood summers flitted in his mind. Like how he'd begged his parents for a family camping trip like the ones his classmates boasted about after vacation. His mom's excuse had been laughable: *There are no bathrooms out there,* she had said, making a face. *And Coco will get lonely if we leave her for too long.* They must have felt guilty about it, though, or maybe Reema khala had *made* them feel guilty about it, because a few days later they'd bought him a secondhand bike. Only, with the Northeast Regional Parrot Exhibition coming up, they didn't have time to teach him how to use it. Aden would have to learn on his own.

He took the bike outside. Hopped into the seat, determined.

Gravity did the rest.

He must have fallen a dozen times before the Lowells took notice, stepping out of their house to offer to teach him, patting him on the head like he was a pitiful little village child they'd stumbled upon in the jungle. But Aden wasn't that desperate. In the end, he watched several YouTube tutorials, rode a few laps around the neighborhood, and promptly grew bored.

Now, standing in the rain with mud soaking into his shoes, he wished he could go back and tell that kid that outdoor adventures weren't all they were cracked up to be.

"Coco's been here for at least twenty minutes," Sammy said, squinting at the glow of his laptop screen. "She's not moving."

Aliza tugged her jacket tighter around her as she stepped out of the car. The air smelled of wet earth and leaves, the fog rolling in low and heavy. "That's a good sign, right? Maybe she's resting."

Aden slammed his door shut. "Or plotting how to piss me off more. Let's get this over with."

The forest was thicker than it looked from the road, the ground soft and slippery underfoot. Sammy walked with his laptop half open to shield it from the drizzle, his eyes glued to the screen as he tracked Coco's signal. Aliza stayed close to him, one hand on his elbow to steady him when he tripped over roots or slid on the mud.

"Careful, Sammy," she said for the third time.

"I am careful," he murmured, not looking up.

"You're walking like a zombie," Aden called from ahead, stepping gingerly over a puddle. "Worse, an iPad kid who's never been outside."

"I go outside," replied Sammy, brow furrowed.

"Taking out the trash or walking to the school bus doesn't count. Just don't fall, okay? One wrong move and we're all going to end up in one of those true-crime podcasts about stupid families who get themselves lost in the woods."

"Thanks for the encouragement," said Aliza. "And stop stomping around, Aden—you're scaring every animal within a mile radius."

"I'm walking *normally*."

They trudged farther into the forest, the fog wrapping around them, clinging to their skin with the faint smell of pine needles.

Sammy suddenly stopped, his gaze snapping to the left. "Wait," he said, his voice barely above a whisper.

"What?" Aliza asked, her grip tightening on his arm.

"There." He pointed toward a low branch about twenty feet away. They followed his gaze.

Coco was perched there, casually preening her feathers. She looked okay, almost infuriatingly so—ruffled, a little dirty, but still unmistakably herself.

For a beat, none of them moved.

Aden finally exhaled. "Well, there she is. Let's grab her and go home."

"Obviously," Aliza muttered, pulling a small bag of almonds from her pocket. "Coco!" she called softly, crouching down a little. She shook the bag, the sound faint but hopeful. "C'mere, pretty baby. Look what I've got for you."

Coco paused mid-preen, her head cocking to the side. For a moment it looked like she might actually hop down.

"Yes, that's it. It's okay, we've got almonds, your favorite! I bet you're hungry, huh?"

Coco opened her beak. Aden held his breath.

A soft click of claws on bark. The tiniest shuffle.

Then a dog barked in the distance, followed by a yell of "MAVERICK, NO!"

Coco startled, letting out a sharp squawk before launching herself into the air.

"Coco, no!" Aliza yelled, scrambling to her feet as they all watched, helplessly. The cockatoo disappeared into the fog, her pink feathers fading into the gray sky.

"Shit!" Aden yelled. "Coco, you dumbass! We're trying to *save* you!"

Aliza shoved him. "Don't insult her! It's no wonder she wouldn't come down. She can sense your negative energy."

"Negative energy?" Aden laughed. "Sorry I can't exactly be a walking affirmation board while my new loafers are getting eaten alive by *mud*."

"No one told you to wear fancy shoes, you douche," Aliza snapped. "If you *actually* cared to help, you'd be wearing something practical, like sneakers."

"I didn't bring *sneakers*," Aden said, "because I thought I'd be attending a *funeral*, not chasing after a bird who clearly doesn't want to be found. And now my genuine Italian leather, hand-stitched loafers are ruined!"

He threw his hands up in the air, the frustration boiling over before he could stop it. He could practically hear James Alderman scoffing—at Aden, mud splattered and shouting at trees like a lunatic. The thought made his blood pressure spike.

Damn that bird. She'd vanished into the fog like she'd been waiting for an excuse to leave. Like she knew exactly where she was going, and it sure as hell wasn't back to them.

And the way she'd cut through the air—powerful and sure—reminded him too much of that night on the porch. How she'd flapped hard, wings hammering the air as she shot higher and higher, until she was nothing but a dark blur against the stars. Even then, he'd half expected her to turn around. Circle back home.

But she hadn't.

And now she was gone again.

Aden clenched his teeth, swallowing the sharp, ugly feeling rising in his chest. He wasn't sure what was worse—watching her leave, or realizing how it felt to be the one left behind.

"How about instead of blaming me," he said, his voice rising, "we give a round of applause to whatever genius brought their dog to the middle of nowhere! Hoo-*ray*!" He clapped angrily. "Is that enough *positive energy* for you?"

Aliza's face crumpled, the bag of almonds slipping from her hand into the mud. Her voice broke when she said, "She's—she's really gone."

Sammy, who had been staring at the patch of sky where Coco had vanished, shook his head. "Coco's not gone," he said quietly, though his voice lacked its usual conviction. His laptop battery icon blinked in warning, a cruel reminder of their growing limitations.

Aliza wiped at her face, whether from rain or tears, Aden couldn't tell. "It's getting dark," she said. "We'll have to come back in the morning."

Aden stared at her, incredulous. "Are you kidding? You want to come back here and play bird whisperer again? I hate to break it to you, but guess what? It didn't work. Who's to say it'll work next time? Or ever?" He shook his head. "Unless you come up with a better plan, it's not happening."

"Then we come up with a better plan," Aliza snapped, her voice sharp enough to cut through the rain. "We're not giving up on Coco yet. Not now."

Aden barked out a laugh, short and humorless. "Of course you're not." They wouldn't give up—not on Coco.

Sammy finally lifted his eyes from the screen, his eyes meeting Aden's. "You said you wanted to help. Do *you* have any ideas?"

The question cut through Aden's frustration, giving way to something heavier. He sighed. His hair was damp; he needed a shower. No, a hot bath—far, far away from here.

He looked down at his mud-caked shoes, then back at his siblings, who were both staring at him like he held the answers. Sammy was right. Aden had been the one to offer to help. And they were desperate enough to rely on him now, and it left him off-balance. He knew they didn't trust him. But right now they had no one else.

Which meant he'd need to suck it up.

"No," Aden muttered finally. "But for now let's find a hotel to stay the night. I'm too tired to drive anymore. We can start searching again in the morning."

Aliza blinked. "Really?"

"It is what it is," he replied with a shrug, already turning away. "Also, someone look up where we can grab some food first. And coffee. Preferably through an IV."

Chapter 7

One summer night, when Aden had been ten and Aliza five, their parents had left them home to attend a dinner party. It was one of the last times they'd done something like that—before Coco became the center of their world, before bird shows and ribbons dictated their every weekend. Back then, their parents still had friends outside the competition circuit; they still cared, somewhat, about fundraisers and dinner parties.

Still acted like a family that belonged somewhere.

Aden had made peanut butter and jelly sandwiches for himself and Aliza, then put on *Finding Nemo*—her favorite movie at the time. He let her curl up on the couch, eyelids fluttering, the crust of her sandwich still clutched in one hand. Within fifteen minutes, she was asleep, breath soft and even. The house, too, seemed to exhale: walls settling, silence blooming in the corners. Aden let himself breathe with it, just for a moment. His shoulders loosened by degrees, like knots soaking in a warm bath. A rare indulgence.

Then he peeled himself from the couch and checked on Coco.

She was eleven years old—her feathers a pale pink, her eyes an onyx black. Her cage, all wood and metal bars, sat in its usual corner of the living room, tucked away like a piece of furniture someone had forgotten to move.

On this night, though, it felt less like a cage and more like a small, quiet world Coco had chosen for herself—a space she ruled in her own way.

Aden moved closer, slow and hesitant, as if the bird might read the shift in his breath. Her cage door was open, as it almost always was back then, but Coco's wings had been clipped, and she'd never been one to wander too far anyway. She liked her corner. Her wooden perch. Her order of things.

She turned her head as he approached, black eyes catching his. Watching. Expectant.

The hush of the evening pressed against the windows; pale light pooled across the floor, casting long shadows. Aden reached for the tin of almonds from a nearby shelf crammed with her food, her toys. One by one, he dropped a few into the dish clipped to the side of her cage, the soft clink of the almonds punctuating the silence.

Coco's eyes followed the motion. Then she clambered over, claws scraping wood, and began cracking the almond shells with mechanical precision. Her movements were sharp, efficient—at odds with the stillness of the room.

Aden watched her, transfixed. Coco cracked another almond, then paused, her black eyes lifting to his. She did it again and again: repositioning the almond with her claw, taking slow, deliberate bites, then glancing back at him.

He realized, with a faint pang of surprise, that it wasn't only the food she was interested in. There was something in her gaze—something that seemed to skim past the surface and land somewhere deeper. Like she already knew what was on his mind. Like she always had.

Or maybe it was a quiet request for something more: attention, or something closer to love. Not the kind you earned by being helpful, or the kind you had to chase.

The kind that simply asked: *Stay.*

At the time, Aden didn't see this small, strange creature as an obligation yet. Not the brash, noisy remnant of their parents' world she would eventually become. She seemed delicate, fragile as glass. Out of place, like she'd been dropped into their lives by accident.

And in that moment, Coco felt like a reflection of him: something trying to survive in a too-often senseless world. Something that just wanted affection—wanted to be *seen*. By anyone.

Aden watched her crack another almond. From the couch, Aliza snored softly, the low glow of the TV flickering against the walls. The stillness of the house felt like the world was holding its breath, waiting for something Aden didn't understand.

He leaned against the cage, the metal cool beneath his arm. Coco didn't look at him this time. She just kept eating, calm and certain, as if whatever had passed between them transcended words.

The diner smelled like burned coffee, maple syrup, and cigarette smoke—a mix so familiar it felt nostalgic. He and Sẹ̀yí used to haunt places like this after long nights of cramming for finals. Always the cheapest option, always open. He wondered what she would think if she saw him now: unshaven, slumped in a booth, with the two siblings he'd barely mentioned during their years together.

Sẹ̀yí would have hated this: the squabbling, the lack of direction. No, she was the kind of person who could stare the impossible in the face and reduce it to mere steps, neatly laid out like the diagrams she used to draw on graph paper.

That had never been Aden's strong suit.

Aliza sat across from him, her phone beside her plate of barely touched French toast. Sammy was hunched over his laptop, newly charged, his pancakes cooling as he scrolled. Aden stirred his coffee absently, the clink of the spoon against the ceramic mug creating a faint rhythm in the muffled diner noise.

He was already out almost two hundred bucks for this stupid bird—two motel rooms, gas, and now breakfast he wasn't even hungry for. Technically, he could afford it—his salary was relatively decent, six figures, and only just—but that didn't mean he had money to burn. And the more he spent, the more this whole thing felt like a bleeding wound he couldn't stitch up fast enough.

"We could try heading toward Chambersburg," Aliza said, holding out her phone, the Google Maps screen aglow. "If Coco's heading west, we'd at least be in the right direction."

Aden sighed, leaning back in the booth. His feet hurt—he'd need to replace his loafers once he got back to Chicago. A tragic casualty.

"This isn't the Oregon Trail," he said. "She's not following any discernable path. She's just . . . flying."

Aliza's lips thinned, but she didn't reply. A waitress bustled past them, balancing a tray of greasy plates, and Aden caught the sour tang of ketchup. Was it stress that was making him nauseated? Or the smell of cheap condiments? He rubbed his temple, the air inside the diner thick and oppressive. Pressing him in place, even as he itched to leave.

From the corner of the table, Sammy cleared his throat softly. "Um . . ."

Neither of them looked up.

"Um . . ." Sammy said again, more insistent this time. He shifted his laptop so they could see the screen, now filled with the familiar Reddit post. The one Aliza had put up about Coco. "There's . . . a *lot* of comments on this now."

Aliza leaned over, her frown softening as she squinted at the screen. Sammy spun the laptop toward her, and she scrolled through the thread.

"Look at this—someone said they saw a cockatoo near Carlisle yesterday," Aliza said. "And this person—oh my God—this person says they saw her in a parking lot eating popcorn!"

Aden made a face. "Eating popcorn?"

"She likes popcorn," Sammy said quietly, almost defensive.

Aliza adjusted the laptop around to show him. "Yeah, *look*."

Aden leaned in, studying the grainy photo attached to the comment. It revealed a pale blur of a creature next to an open, crumpled bag of what appeared to be, in fact, soggy popcorn.

He shook his head, sitting back. "We don't even know if that's her. None of this is reliable. People could be trolling us. Making things harder on purpose."

"Most people aren't evil," said Aliza, pulling the laptop back toward her.

"Uh-huh. Next thing you know, someone says they saw Coco do 9/11. Or saw her hitching a ride on some biker gang's Harley."

Sammy tapped on another comment. "Not a bike, but someone did mention a bird on a truck near Mechanicsburg."

For a moment the table went still. The diner noise seemed to fade, leaving only the faint hum of absurd possibility between them.

"Well," Aliza said, her voice firm, "looks like we're continuing west."

"Okay," Aden muttered, the word like gravel in his mouth. "But I need to head back to New Hope tonight for my meeting with Abigail tomorrow. And Sammy—you start school again next week, right?"

Sammy blanched at the word, his shoulders curling inward. Aden had never been the biggest fan of school, either, but Sammy's fear felt . . . different. Deeper.

But before he could ask, Aliza spoke up, her voice hardening. "*Sammy* can go back to school when he's ready. School can wait. *This* can't."

Aden's jaw tightened. "You can't have him chasing after Coco forever. At some point we need to set a line, for his sake. So if we don't find her by tonight, that's it. We go back."

Aliza's gaze wavered, her lip caught between her teeth. Her eyes were sharp with thought, as if weighing each possibility, dissecting it.

"Hey, and maybe you're right," Aden continued, softening just enough to be convincing. "Maybe not everyone is evil. There's always a chance some Good Samaritan catches her and lets us know they have her. We can go pick her up then."

"But you won't be here," said Sammy.

Aden froze for just a second, the words slipping past his defenses like a needle he couldn't quite reach. He forced himself to shrug, even as the silence stretched taut between them.

"Yeah," he admitted after a while. "I won't. But you guys will figure it out on your own, I'm sure."

"Aden—" Aliza began, but he held up a hand.

"Hurry up and eat. We're wasting time," he said firmly. "We'll head west. But if we end up chasing some random seagull, I'm kicking you both out of the car and heading home without you."

Aliza nodded slowly.

"Deal."

"Turn left," Sammy instructed from the back seat, calm as always, and Aden complied with a groan.

"What now?" asked Aliza.

"The car's been acting weird since we went over a pothole," Aden muttered, glancing warily at the dashboard. "Any clue when Mom and Dad last had a car inspection?"

"No idea. Maybe two or three years ago?"

"You're supposed to get an inspection every *year*."

Aliza shrugged. "Well, I don't know what to tell you."

That explained the unpaid tickets he'd found in their home office. If their parents weren't already gone, Aden might strangle them himself. How had they functioned this long, made it this far in life? Every new discovery about their irresponsibility felt like a personal attack. Though he of all people shouldn't be surprised.

"This is why we need public transportation," he said. "People can't be trusted with their own cars."

"Stay in the right lane," Sammy said.

Aden veered the car as it rattled beneath them. "The tracking is up to date, right?" he asked. "We're getting real-time data?"

"It's as up to date as it can be," Sammy replied.

"Jesus."

Coco was showing no signs of slowing down, and it was already the afternoon. They were running out of time.

Aden glanced at the GPS again, then at the blur of trees rushing past the window.

"Maybe we should have a reward," he said slowly. "Incentivize other people to help."

Aliza blinked. "Wait, that's a good idea. I'll post it on Reddit." She pulled out her phone and began furiously typing. "How much? Two hundred dollars?"

Aden scoffed. "Five hundred dollars, at least. Two hundred dollars in this economy is practically pennies."

"Maybe for you."

"We're talking about Coco Chanel. She alone is worth at least twenty-five hundred dollars."

"I didn't realize you cared so much," Aliza muttered.

"I don't. I care about accuracy of value. It's the principle of it."

"Uh-huh." Some more typing from Aliza. "Okay, I put down one thousand dollars. I hope you know you're the one shelling out the reward money, in case someone finds her."

His jaw twitched. "*Fine*. But you better have put your number for any leads or tips, because I don't want to deal with people." Aden glanced behind him. "Sammy, how we lookin'?"

"We're almost at the Bird Enthusiasts of Appalachia. It should be on the left."

"All right." Aden continued forward. "God help us."

They pulled up to a weathered wooden building with a hand-painted sign that read "The Bird Enthusiasts of Appalachia." It looked more like a repurposed bait shop than a hub of, well, *avian expertise*. A few cars were parked haphazardly on the gravel lot, and a rusted lawn chair sat near the door, occupied by a man in camouflage pants and a shirt that read "Bird Life Is the Best Life."

"This can't be it," Aden muttered, killing the engine as the car gave one last sputter, as if relieved for the break.

"Yep, it's it," Sammy said, though he didn't sound fully confident.

Before Aden could object, the door to the building swung open, and a woman with binoculars slung around her neck stepped out. She was wiry, with a wild halo of gray hair that seemed to defy gravity. The T-shirt beneath her knitted vest bore a detailed diagram of a bird skeleton labeled *Columba livia domestica*, and her cargo pants had enough pockets to prepare for any conceivable situation—and then some. Aden wouldn't have been surprised if she started pulling out bird specimens; in law school, Sẹ̀yí, whose best friend, Olive, was an environmental lawyer, had told him about smugglers who sneaked rare birds onto airplanes that way.

He eyed her pockets warily.

"You must be the Coco people," she called, waving them over.

Aliza climbed out first, her phone still in hand. "That's us!" she said, returning the wave.

"'The Coco People.' Perfect," Aden muttered under his breath, stepping out reluctantly.

The woman, whose name tag read "Marcy," led them inside, where a handful of other bird enthusiasts milled about. The walls were plastered with maps, photos of rare birds, and handwritten notes in varying degrees of legibility. A coffee mug reading "Birders Do It with Binoculars" sat on a cluttered table scattered with notebooks and a flyer advertising a Blind Birders Walk. A projector hummed quietly in the corner, displaying a PowerPoint slide titled "The Migration Mysteries of the Ivory-Billed Woodpecker. "

It was overwhelming, like stepping into a living diorama crafted by someone in the throes of a breakdown, complete with its own scent of old paper and unbridled enthusiasm. His parents would've loved it here—not because they were passionate birders or anything. They weren't the type of people to traipse through the woods, marveling at migration patterns before the sun rose. But they loved attention and, thus, anyone who could appreciate the glory that was Coco Chanel.

"Welcome to Bird HQ!" Marcy announced, her voice commanding despite her small stature. "All right, team! This is—sorry, what's your names?"

"This is Aden and Sammy. I'm Aliza."

"Right," Marcy said, grinning. "This is Aden, Aliza, and Sammy. They're searching for a lost cockatoo, and we're here to help!"

"A *Major Mitchell's* cockatoo, actually," Aliza added.

"Ooh, even better. Bill! Where's Bill? Get the maps!"

While Aliza and Sammy chatted with Marcy, Aden hung back, taking in the scene. The group was a mix of retirees, grad students, and outdoorsy types, all with varying degrees of intensity. One man, Bill, wore a fishing vest so overloaded with supplies it looked like it could double as a flotation device. Another sported a headlamp, despite it being broad daylight. A young woman with oversize glasses gave a friendly wave before hauling boxes out to a truck.

"Sorry about the mess," said Marcy. "We're prepping for our monthly meeting tomorrow. You should all join! It's a good time. Bill makes these canapés that are simply to die for."

"Oh, no," Aden said. "We're heading home tonight."

"Really?" Marcy frowned. "Where did you kids drive in from?"

"New Hope," said Aliza.

"That's a long haul. No, no, you should stay! You can sleep here. We have a shed in the back—I promise it's cozier than it sounds, and there's a big bed. I've used it when I need to stay up prepping for our meetings."

"No, thank yo—" Aden began, but Aliza cut him off with a smile. "We'll think about it."

Aden glanced at his sister, but she avoided his eyes.

"All right," Marcy said, clapping her hands together. "So tell me about Coco."

For the next fifteen minutes, they recounted the story—her escape (with extra emphasis on Aden's carelessness, thanks to Aliza), her route so far, and the faint hope of tracking her with the GPS.

Marcy nodded gravely, occasionally interrupting to pepper them with oddly specific questions.

"What's her wingspan?"

"Uh, I don't know," Aden said. "Bird-size?"

Marcy frowned again. "We'll estimate. And how old is she?"

"Almost thirty-two," Aliza answered.

"Oh, so that explains it!" Marcy let out a bellowing laugh. "Our girl's just about reached her midlife crisis! No wonder."

Aden gave her a sidelong glance. *This woman is completely nuts.*

Marcy's electric-blue eyes seemed to crackle as she took them all in; then she nodded like she'd just made a decision. "So here's what I'm going to do for you. Send me a picture of Miss Coco, and I'll post it on our newsletter. You'd be surprised at how fired up us bird-watchers can get with a challenge like this. We even took a field trip to New York City when Flaco escaped the Central Park Zoo."

"Flaco?" asked Aden.

"The Eurasian owl? In Central Park? You didn't hear anything about it?" Marcy's face fell. "Shame what happened to him, though. Bill was one of the first to spot him."

Aliza looked worried. "Wait, what happened to Flaco?"

"He survived out there for a year before crashing into a window on the Upper West Side. But he was pretty sickly before that—ate too much rat poison. You'd be surprised how often that happens."

"Oh, God." Aliza held her face in her hands. "What about Coco? I didn't even consider—what if she crashes into a window?"

"And that's why we're going to do whatever we can to catch her before that happens," Marcy said gently. "I tell you all this so you know that we'll have your back. You're not alone. It's clear Coco's important to you."

Bill interrupted to offer them "lucky birdseed," which he assured them had been blessed by "the energies of the universe." Sammy accepted it with a polite smile, even as Aden struggled to fight the temptation to back slowly into the car and drive far away from these people.

But for all their eccentricity, even he had to admit there was also an almost overzealous sincerity to the group. Marcy and Bill debated routes, compared notes, and pored over maps like generals planning a campaign. Another member, Carl—a retired engineer—rigged a makeshift tracker to help refine Coco's GPS signal, while Marcy offered to send updates to their Reddit post if Aliza didn't have time.

"So how'd you get into bird-watching?" Aliza asked Marcy after a while, as they hovered near one of the tables.

Marcy's face softened. "Oh, I taught ecology at Cornell for thirty years, but honestly, it wasn't until my partner passed that I really started paying attention. She loved birds—couldn't pass a tree without pointing out which species was singing. After she was gone, I started listening the way she did. Felt like a way to be close to her again." She paused, blue eyes bright. "Birds remind me that the best things never last. Their lives are short. Ours too. Loss is a part it. But that's what makes everything so . . . worth noticing."

Her casual talk of loss settled over them like a hush. Aliza blinked hard before staring down at her phone. Sammy shifted his weight, his expression as unreadable as always.

Aden said nothing. Her words sat in his chest—awkward and unwelcome, like someone had handed him a glass he didn't know what to do with.

Marcy was one of those people who could transform something unbearable into something lovely. Meaningful.

But to Aden, loss was just . . . loss. A void you couldn't fill. Something that didn't transform you or teach you anything. It just sat there, quiet and permanent, swallowing whatever you tried to build around it.

So he simply ignored it. Hoped it would go away on its own, even though deep down, he knew better.

He looked at his siblings. Aliza's obvious emotion—she always had so much of it—and Sammy's softness . . . it all made him feel like an outsider again. Like he was broken. The one who never cried at funerals, even his own parents'. The one who didn't cry even when Ṣèyí left.

He cleared his throat and looked away, pretending to study a bird map tacked to the wall.

"All right, back to work!" Marcy suddenly broke the silence, snapping them out of the moment. "Bill, what've you got?"

Bill spread a map across the table, his hands moving with the precision of someone who had done this a thousand times. "Based on the sightings Sammy here has logged, she's likely moving along this tree line. It's dense enough for cover but still has open pockets for foraging."

"That's all well and good," said Aden impatiently, "but the longer we think about where she *might* be going, the more time she has to move."

"But this is how we get ahead of her," Bill explained. "It's clear she's not moving haphazardly. It almost looks like she has a destination in mind. If we can figure out where she's headed next, you could ambush her."

"It is *curious*, though," said Marcy thoughtfully, tapping her chin. "Why she's moving west. Any idea what might be driving her there?"

Aliza shook her head. "No idea."

The group grew quiet, the kind of quiet that people took to turn a question over in their minds that no one knew the answer to. Coco had never had this level of freedom before—who could tell what she was thinking half the time? Hell, who could say she was thinking at all?

Marcy, as if sensing the tension, broke the moment with a pat to Aliza's shoulder. "Well, if Coco's a Major Mitchell's cockatoo, then that means she's not just rare, she's resilient. She'll find her way. But the moment you give up the search, it's over—so the important thing is, no matter what, you keep going, too."

Her smile was firm, reassuring, but Aden caught the flicker of uncertainty in her eyes. It was clear that even someone as unwavering as Marcy wasn't immune to the weight of *what if?* But she buried the uncertainty beneath a veneer of confidence—seemingly for their sake.

In that way, at least, she was better than Aden.

The meeting wrapped up with Marcy assigning her fellow bird enthusiasts tasks and promising to check back in with Aliza after they got any news of sightings.

The siblings stepped outside to a sky streaked with the first hints of sunset. Aliza glanced back at the group of bird-watchers gathered on the porch of the Bird Enthusiasts of Appalachia building, her gaze lingering on Marcy's steady stance.

"They didn't have to help us, but they did," she said, her voice warm.

"Yeah," Sammy added softly, his eyes fixed on the fading horizon. "They care."

Aden glanced at his siblings—Aliza with her chin high, like she'd already decided things were going to turn around for the better, and Sammy clutching his laptop, the faintest hint of a smile on his face. As if good luck could be coaxed by sheer will. But in Aden's experience, that was never the case. The world was never that simple.

He turned away, jamming his hands into his pockets. "Let's hope their lucky birdseed actually works," he muttered, striding toward the car.

The Past

A-den no sing for Coco anymore

He does not come to me so I call and call and call I am lonely I say but he does not understand so I say in garbled tongue he knows I say PRETTY BIRD PRETTY BIRD COCO and finally he comes and gives me mango but I do not want mango I want him to stay he does not hold me anymore like the others why

Other little one too small little sister *A-den call her* A-liza

and other big ones make too much—loud noise, loud hands, always wanting Coco to dance but A-den A-den easy garble tongue easy for Coco to call

but he does not like it when I call but he is good, he is soft soft like soft feathers, A-den does not make Coco dance for him, Coco feels good, feels good good boy, Coco is good

PRETTY BIRD? I call

he does not call back

he no sing anymore

Coco like A-den sing, miss sing

Chapter 8

"Sit properly," said Aden, his jaw clenched. "You're stressing me out."

The sun was already calling it quits for the day, sinking behind the horizon and leaving streaks of orange and purple that made everything harder to see. Aden wished he could call it quits, too. He'd never been a fan of driving; after almost two days straight of it, he was even less of a fan. His back ached, his hands were seemingly permanently clamped at ten and two on the wheel, and his skull felt like it had shrunk a size too small. He was certain that with one more provocation, one more thing going wrong, homicide would no longer be off the table.

"How am I supposed to see Coco?" Aliza retorted, twisting in her seat again. "I need a full 360-degree range."

"Then if we get into an accident and you go flying out the windshield, don't get mad at me."

She didn't bother responding to that, just twisted farther, half slipping out of her seat belt.

Aden raked his hand through his hair and groaned when several strands came away in his fingers. He was shedding more than usual—another reason to shove Coco into an oven once they found her. If they found her.

"Sammy," Aliza said, now craning her neck toward the back seat, "I thought you said we were close."

The dim glow from the laptop cast Sammy's face in a ghostly blue. His glasses reflected the map on the screen, dots and lines like constellations. "We are," he answered softly, hesitating. "But . . . I'm confused. It says she's right off the freeway."

"That doesn't make *sense*," Aden said, shaking his head. "She should be in the trees. Sticking to quiet areas."

"Maybe she *is* hitching a ride on a truck," Aliza mumbled.

"Well, whatever the hell she's doing," said Aden, "she's making it a hundred times harder to get her. I can't exactly slam the freaking brakes in the middle of the freeway."

"We might not have a choice," Aliza snapped. She twisted to Sammy again. "Where to next?"

"Turn right," Sammy instructed. "Onto the freeway."

"This is so stupid," Aden said, making the turn.

Worse, it was dangerous. It was bad enough it was almost dark and they were in an unfamiliar area; they were close to the Ohio border now, about five minutes from a town called Masontown. He'd lived most of his life in Pennsylvania, and even he had never been this far west in his home state. But considering he'd already seen four different pickup trucks waving Confederate flags in the past hour, he wasn't planning to visit again.

Sammy fished around in a small bag that Bill from the bird-watchers' group had handed him earlier. He pulled out a pair of binoculars, adjusting the knobs with stiff, unsure movements, then peered through them.

"She should be on the left somewhere . . ." he muttered, focusing ahead.

"On the left?" Aliza leaned over to the driver's seat, her shoulder bumping into Aden's. "Where?"

"Stay seated, woman!" Aden barked, swerving slightly before correcting.

Sammy squinted into the binoculars and adjusted the focus. "Oh! There!"

He pointed ahead, toward a utility pole on the median. A flash of pink caught the last rays of sunlight—a small, unmistakable silhouette perched precariously on the edge of the pole.

Aliza let out a sound that was somewhere between a laugh and a sob. "It's her! Aden! Stop the car!"

"I can't stop here!" Aden barked.

"Then do a U-turn!" Aliza shouted back.

"Are you out of your goddamn mind? Traffic's coming in way too fast!"

"It's an emergency!"

"U-turns here are illegal for a *reason*, idiot!"

"If we lose Coco again, it's on you!"

Aden gritted his teeth, but against his better judgment, he shifted into the left lane and slowed enough to swerve onto the shoulder, ignoring the furious honks of passing cars. The car's tires kicked up gravel. Between his exhaustion and Aliza's yelling, he couldn't think straight. His heartbeat thudded against his ribs as he scanned for an opening in the concrete barrier. But finally he spotted a gap, one probably meant for cop cars and emergency vehicles.

"If this kills us," he muttered, his voice low, "it'll be your fucking fault."

The car shuddered as he made the turn, tires squealing in protest. Sammy clutched his laptop to his chest, and Aliza braced herself against the dash, her knuckles pale. Aden's pulse pounded in his ears as they emerged on the opposite side, heading back toward the pole.

When the car straightened again, Sammy opened a window and stuck his head out. "Coco!"

"Slow down!" Aliza hissed.

"I can't!"

"Coco!"

The bird shifted at the sound of her name, tilting her head like she recognized it. For a brief, fragile moment, she seemed poised to stay.

Her eyes met Aden's, and time stopped.

Then a passing eighteen-wheeler roared by, slathered with the logo held by a happy pig that read "Parker's Pork Rolls," its engine loud enough to shake the ground. Coco startled and flapped her wings wildly, failing to get her bearings. Eventually, she launched into the air, clumsy and panicked, leaving the pole behind.

"Dammit!" Aden swerved onto the shoulder again and slammed the brakes. "She's heading into traffic! What the hell are we supposed to do?"

Aliza took off her seat belt. "If you don't save her, I will."

"Aliz—"

But she was already out of the car, vaulting over the guardrail like it was nothing. "Coco!" she screamed.

"Aliza, stop!" Aden yelled, unbuckling his seat belt in a panic and scrambling after her. Sammy was right behind him, his strides quick but hesitant.

The three of them reached the edge together, just in time to see Coco dip low over the highway. Her pink feathers shimmered in the glow of oncoming headlights, a fragile burst of color against gray asphalt.

The headlights bore down, and for a terrible second, Aden saw it all: feathers scattered like pink confetti, her broken body reduced to an unrecognizable mess of blood and bone and terrifying stillness.

Aden felt his chest split open. He opened his mouth to shout—

But Coco banked sharply, her wings catching the air just in time. She soared upward, her silhouette swallowed by the dark.

Aliza sank to her knees, clutching the guardrail like it might collapse beneath her. Sammy stood frozen, his hands trembling at his sides. Aden stared into the night sky, his chest heaving, the adrenaline still coursing through him.

It was too close.

They'd almost lost her. Coco—frustrating, impossible Coco, so stubbornly full of life—had almost been flattened like mere roadkill.

"She's gone," Aliza finally whispered, her voice cracking.

Aden didn't respond. He couldn't trust himself to speak.

After they caught their breath, they got back into the car, the reality of their failure clinging like an oil slick.

"That was reckless," Aden said, dazed. His voice sounded strange, distant, even to himself. "We shouldn't have done that." More to the point, he shouldn't have listened to Aliza—he was the adult here. He should have put his foot down, not let himself get swept up in her mindless impulsiveness.

"We had to," said Aliza, staring ahead, hands fidgeting with her seat belt. "It's like what Marcy said. We have to keep going, and sometimes that means being reckless in order to get shit done. We only did what was necessary."

Aden shoved his key back into the ignition and turned it. The engine made a hollow, guttural noise but refused to catch.

He exhaled sharply, gripping the wheel tighter. Maybe the car was as exhausted as he was.

"No, it wasn't necessary." He tried again, but the car let out an ugly sputter. "None of this is necessary."

"Don't start," Aliza snapped. Her mouth was taut, but he could see it on her face: the remnants of fear, of a barbed defensiveness, that was slowly overtaking her.

Aden turned the ignition again. The engine groaned but stubbornly refused to move.

"We *saw* her, Aden," Aliza went on, her voice rising. "We were *this* close."

"That doesn't mean we just throw ourselves in harm's way to get her!" Aden slammed his palm against the wheel. The hollow thud startled Sammy in the back seat. "Now we're stranded on the side of a goddamn freeway in the middle of nowhere!"

"What do you want me to do? It's not my fault!"

"It's your fault we're even out here," Aden spat, the words bitter on his tongue. "God, I shouldn't have listened to you."

"May I remind you that *you're* the one who let her go in the first place," Aliza shot back.

"Fine, sure," Aden scoffed bitterly. "But if you're going to act so reckless, maybe it's better we give up on this whole thing."

Aliza's face flushed red.

"If you hate it so much, why didn't you just stay home, Aden? Why bother coming at all?"

"Because someone has to make sure you don't get yourself killed in the process!" Aden took a breath. His jaw clenched so tight it ached. "And what about Sammy, huh? What if *he* got hurt?"

Aliza made a noise like she'd been punched; her eyes widened before she shook it off.

"Oh, yeah, that's rich," she said softly, "coming from the guy who disappeared for ten years without a word."

The air in the car seemed to thicken, like they were all trapped in a jar with the lid screwed on too tight. Sammy shifted wordlessly in the back seat, his fingers twitching against the edge of his notebook.

"I didn't just disappear," Aden growled, his voice low and venomous. "I was forced to leave because I couldn't—" He stopped himself, glancing at Sammy. "Forget it."

"Couldn't what?" Aliza pressed, leaning forward, her eyes narrowing. "No, go on, *say it*. Couldn't handle us? Couldn't handle Coco? Couldn't handle being under the same roof as your family anymore? Come on, you coward!"

Aden slammed the heel of his hand against the steering wheel again, the frustration bubbling over. "Yeah, sure, Aliza! That's it! You've figured me out, congrats! Our family drove me nuts and I couldn't stand any of you people, so I left. There! Happy?"

Behind them, Sammy's laptop nearly slipped from his lap to the floor. Aden's fury hung in the air like a slap, reverberating through the silence that followed.

For a moment no one spoke. The car was utterly still, save for the soft hum of traffic rushing by. Other lives, moving forward. Other people on their way to somewhere, anywhere but here.

Aden stared at the dashboard, his pulse drumming in his ears. He could feel Aliza's eyes on him, burning with an intensity that made his skin prickle. He wasn't sure whether it was anger, disappointment, or something worse.

Finally, her voice broke the quiet.

"You're such an *ass*, you know that?" Each word a deliberate cut. "You talk like you were the victim, like you didn't have a choice. But you did. You *chose* to leave. And now you're here acting like you're doing us some huge favor by sticking around."

Aden exhaled sharply, his grip tightening on the wheel. He wanted to argue, to throw something back at her, but his throat felt thick, and the words wouldn't come.

From the back seat, Sammy shifted, picking up his fallen laptop with careful hands. He didn't look at either of them, his eyes fixed on the screen as if it held answers to questions he couldn't bring himself to ask.

Aden was a decent lawyer, but he'd always been terrible at detangling his thoughts in personal moments like this, moments that really mattered, and saying what needed to be said. His throat would fill with the silt of it all, drowning him in silence until the moment was over. Then he'd spend the rest of the night going over all the right things he could have, *should have*, said.

This, he realized, would be another one of those nights.

Briefly, he thought about Coco's feathers—how they'd almost been stained red; how he could picture her death in his head, clear as day. He'd felt powerless to stop it. It was a miracle she was still alive.

But even if they'd saved her, if they brought her safely back into the car and returned to New Hope—what would have changed, really? His siblings would still hate him; he would still be sitting on the outside, looking in.

His breath still hadn't fully returned to normal. His chest felt cinched too tight—like metal wires had wrapped around his ribs, pulling tighter with each breath.

You chose to leave.

Aliza's voice rang in his ears. But he didn't know how to tell her that leaving hadn't felt like a choice at all.

It had felt like running out of air.

Kind of like right now, he thought.

He reached for the door handle and pushed it open, the rush of cool air hitting his face like a slap.

"I'm going to check under the hood," he said, stepping out before anyone could respond.

Chapter 9

Aden remembered the moment he decided he would never come back home.

In fact, he even remembered the exact thought he'd had: *I'm never going back.* As soon as the words formed in his brain—synapses sparking, neurons firing—it was like some great invisible thread inside him had snapped.

That wasn't right. Not a thread.

A tether.

A *leash.*

It wasn't a dramatic moment, his decision to stay away. No slammed doors. No swelling of dramatic music. No shouting, "I'm done!" in the pouring rain while his parents wept on the porch.

No, he'd simply called his mom to tell her that he wasn't coming home after graduation.

And instead of worrying, instead of asking her son if he was all right, his mother had yelled.

What do you mean you're not coming back home? You're about to graduate—where else do you have to go?

Aden knew she wouldn't be happy. But he hadn't expected that.

As she yapped at him over the phone, his eyes darted around the sterile white dorm room he'd barely lived in. Looking for some kind of escape.

Instead, his gaze caught a bright-orange pill bottle sitting on his desk. The antidepressants his new psychiatrist had prescribed, just before gently reminding him he wasn't allowed to lock his door anymore.

All because he *had* tried to escape from it all.

And he hadn't even succeeded at that.

His mom was still going. *We need you here, Aden. God, how could you do this to us?*

Ungrateful had been the word of the day, with a side of *dramatic*, her go-to insult. And, of course, the kicker:

What do you even have to complain about? Your life hasn't been that bad. Lots of kids have it worse than you.

Ah, yes. The classic "starving kids in Africa" argument. Aden had wanted to clap. It had only reaffirmed his decision.

But what stuck with him today was the *way* she'd said *ungrateful*—like it was a curse, a mark on his character that could never be scrubbed away. Like he'd never given anything back, no matter how hard he'd tried.

Because he *had* tried, even when his parents had long stopped praising him for it. Still tried to help look after Coco without complaint—sitting quietly through her endless competitions—even when it meant being pulled out of school. Never made a fuss when their parents screamed at each other about money; he just led Aliza and Sammy by the hand outside, leaving behind the yelling and Coco's stressed squawking. Figured out how to make dinner for himself and his little siblings when their parents were too tired to cook.

So yeah, maybe Aden hadn't gone hungry. He was lucky there. But that didn't mean he'd been *full*.

Looking back, it wasn't really about that one phone call. It was years of tiny moments stacking up like junk mail—ignorable until the pile toppled over.

"Aden! Come downstairs!" his parents would squawk from the kitchen, and he'd come running—even when he was studying for his exams or elbow deep in homework—only to be asked some inane question they could answer themselves if they just bothered to look.

Where do we keep the misting spray bottle, Aden?

Do we have any more cuttlebones?

Coco's vet appointment—was that scheduled for Wednesday or Thursday?

By the time he was fifteen, his dad had decided he needed "real-world skills," which apparently meant learning to file taxes. Not in a bonding experience kind of way—not to fill the life-skills hole left by the American public school system. No, by seventeen, Aden was filing the family's taxes on his own, praying to the cruel suits at the IRS that he wouldn't screw it up—on top of the usual chores of mowing the lawn, taking out the trash, getting (and sorting) the mail.

As soon as he got his driver's license, he graduated to being the family chauffeur, the one responsible for scooping up Aliza and Sammy from day care and preschool, making sure to tell their caretakers that their parents were simply waiting in the car.

Aden had gotten very good at wording things so that fewer questions would be asked.

The kicker was when his parents tried to send him to one of Aliza's parent-teacher conferences, but her teacher had called to say that it was "inappropriate" for Aliza's brother to show up instead of her own parents—especially when Aden was still a kid himself. Aliza's face had turned red as she scrambled for excuses. But Aden hadn't been the slightest bit embarrassed. He knew it was strange. And he was used to it. His parents hadn't shown up to *his* conferences, either.

His parents never bothered with excuses. *You're responsible for a kid, Aden. Of course we can leave things in your hands, Aden.*

They might as well have added *You're free labor, Aden.*

And then there was that call, days before his college graduation. His mom, telling him how ungrateful he was for refusing to come back.

"After everything we've done for you, Aden."

After everything we've done.

Sure.

Sitting on the edge of his lumpy twin XL mattress in his college dorm, Aden almost laughed. And after he set down his cell phone, he held his head in his hands and let that final thread—the one called familial piety, the instinctual sense of duty—give way.

He didn't even feel angry. Or sad. Just tired. Bone-deep, soul-crushingly tired. If walking away made him a coward, well—so be it.

He'd called himself far worse things anyway.

The clerk at the Masontown Motel—a scrawny man with an airy plume of white hair and a bullfrog voice—eyed Aden and his siblings like they were a pack of stray dogs that had wandered in. The kind that had fleas and dragged in mud.

"You said two rooms?"

"Yes, sir," Aden said tightly, tapping his fingers on the counter to keep himself from looking back at Aliza and Sammy. "Ideally one would have two beds. If that's possible."

He tried not to inhale too deeply.

Masontown wasn't much—just a forgettable dot on the map, about seventy miles from the Ohio border. Not exactly brimming with nice accommodations, which meant this miserable little motel was the best they could do.

Aden was not raking in the dough, by any means, but as a young attorney, he had grown used to a certain standard of lodging. This was not it.

The lobby reeked of mildew and ancient coffee, as if the pot behind the counter had been simmering since the eighties. A lone ceiling fan wobbled overhead, its blades slicing through the oppressive silence. In the corner, a vending machine sat sentinel, its expired snacks faded and curling at the edges like they'd endured multiple heat waves.

Behind him, Aliza's arms were crossed tightly over her chest. Sammy hovered close, clutching his laptop like a lifeline, his eyes darting nervously around the room.

"Mm-hmm." The clerk put on a pair of reading glasses and clicked at an old beast of a computer. A neon "Vacancy" sign buzzed faintly on the wall behind him, the noise occasionally punctuated by a bug insistent on body-slamming into it. "Where're you comin' from?"

"Just the Philadelphia area," Aden answered vaguely. He didn't like it when people asked too many questions. People who asked too many questions were either bored, nosy, or looking for a way to make your life harder.

The clerk squinted at his computer screen. "Well, you're in luck. Got exactly two left. Both doubles. One's upstairs, though. Ain't got no elevator, just so you know."

"That's fine." Aden sighed.

The clerk grunted. "Long way from home, huh." His gaze flicked to Aliza, then Sammy. "Vacation?"

Aden ignored the question. "How much for the rooms?"

The clerk shrugged, clicked a few more keys, and slid a battered clipboard across the counter. "A hundred for the night. Each room."

"Shit, *seriously*? For a *motel*?" Seeing the clerk's expression, which did not budge, Aden cleared his throat. "Fine, fine."

Reluctantly, he yanked out his wallet from his back pocket. The clerk handed over two grimy keys attached to oversize plastic fobs, numbers etched into them in faded gold paint. "Room 104 and 205. Enjoy your stay."

Aden led his siblings to their room, past another vending machine—this one, broken—and an ice machine with a sign that, concerningly, read "ICE AVAILABLE—EAT/DRINK AT YOUR OWN RISK."

When they reached room 104, Aden handed Aliza the key. "Let's just freshen up, walk someplace nearby for dinner, then call it a night. All right?"

Aliza didn't respond; for the past few minutes, she'd been busy staring at something in the palm of her hand. He recognized it as the photo he'd given to her earlier: the one of her and Coco.

Guess she was holding on to it after all.

Once inside his own room, Aden closed the moth-eaten drapes, kicked off his shoes, and dropped onto the bed. The floor was dark-red carpet—probably to disguise bloodstains—and the walls were lined with wood paneling, the kind that had only been stylish in the seventies but persisted in places untouched by time or taste. If he squinted in the dim orange glow of the bedside lamp, he could convince himself the walls were bars, and he was locked in.

He closed his eyes. His body ached, and his wallet was significantly lighter than when they'd started searching for Coco just two days ago. The car refused to start after their near run-in with Coco on the freeway, and they'd had to wait for a tow truck to rescue them. The mechanic at the body shop had warned them that it would take at least another two days for repairs to finish and that, frankly, it was a miracle the car had lasted as long as it had.

"Should've sold it years ago," the mechanic had said.

Yet another thing neglected by his parents. And now they were stuck out here for far longer than he'd planned; they could go nowhere until the car was fixed.

Aliza and Sammy were probably shit-talking him right now, as if the car breaking down was somehow his fault.

If Sẹ̀yí were here . . .

He swallowed hard. What would she say? Something far too generous, perhaps. *You're doing the best you can*. That was Sẹ̀yí—always seeing more in him than he could see in himself. Even though Aden had never told her much about his family, their situation. But somehow she always knew, could always sense more than what was shared.

Once, during the holidays, she'd dragged him to her family's house after learning he'd planned to spend the break alone. She'd barely given him a choice—just showed up at his door with that warm but determined smile that dared him to say no.

Her family had been loud, their house cozy and full of life in a way that made Aden feel out of place. He'd spent most of the evening sitting quietly in the corner, unsure of where to put his hands, unsure of how to speak to people who genuinely seemed to want to know him. Later that night, on the drive home, Sẹ̀yí'd reached across the gearshift and taken his hand—not because he'd said something, but because, once again, she just knew. Like she could feel the sharp little stone of loneliness lodged inside him.

He'd squeezed her hand back so tightly it almost hurt.

Sometimes he wondered if he'd spent too long gripping her hand like that—too afraid to let go but too afraid to tell her everything. Maybe he'd been waiting for her to grow sick of him. Maybe that was why he'd pushed her away.

Forced her hand, just so she'd finally get tired of waiting for him to come around.

There's no point, he'd said the night they'd fought. *It's not something I can explain. You wouldn't get it.*

She'd just laughed—soft but laced with exhaustion. *Yeah, Aden, because no one in the world's ever had a screwed-up family before.*

He hadn't known how to respond to that, so he hadn't.

Just like he hadn't responded to her texts after she finally broke it off.

He opened his eyes again and stared at the ceiling, a sprawling tapestry of old water stains, each one telling its own story of failure. One stain in the far corner looked vaguely like a bird in flight, its wings spread wide, soaring.

Coco. Always Coco. He couldn't even escape her in a seedy motel in Nowhere, Pennsylvania.

Maybe Aliza and Sammy were right to hate him. He couldn't seem to stop disappointing people, himself most of all.

The thought made him shift uncomfortably. The truth was, he didn't know what Sẹ̀yí would say now. It had been months since they'd last spoken, and he was almost forgetting the sound of her voice.

But he remembered her hand—warm in his, always so warm. Grounding him when everything else felt like it was spinning too fast.

She'd tried, he thought. God, she'd tried. And he wished with every fiber of his being that he could have let himself try, too.

Maybe Sẹ̀yí would call him a fool. He'd almost prefer that.

At least it was honest.

Sometimes he wondered whether Sẹ̀yí had taken what was left of his heart with her.

A sharp knock on the door rattled him out of his thoughts. His first instinct was that it was Aliza, ready for round two of their fight in the car, but when he opened the door, it was Sammy.

"Hey," Sammy said quietly, holding his laptop like a shield. His wide eyes darted, as if afraid of being caught. "Can I come in?"

Aden stepped aside, nodding toward the desk chair. "What's up?"

Sammy sat down, fidgeting with the edge of his hoodie. "I was looking at the Reddit post again. The one about Coco." He paused, as if unsure whether to continue. "People are still commenting. Someone said they saw a cockatoo near a gas station west of here, maybe thirty miles away. But it was an hour ago, so . . . I don't know if it's real or not."

Aden rubbed his hair, his frustration simmering. He didn't trust Reddit, didn't trust strangers on the internet to have any clue what they were talking about. But Sammy's earnest expression made it hard to voice his doubts.

"Nothing we can do about it now," he answered finally. "The car's in the shop for the next two days. We'll just have to hang out here until we decide what to do next."

In other words, whether they would go home or continue the search.

Sammy nodded slowly, his body sagging like a deflating balloon animal. He didn't say anything but didn't move to leave, either. Such a tiny kid—was he eating enough?

"What?" Aden asked, sharper than he intended. He exhaled, trying again. "Seriously, what's on your mind?"

"I just . . ." Sammy hesitated. "I don't think we should stop looking. Not yet."

"Don't you want to get back to school? See your friends?"

Sammy's gaze fell to the floor. "I don't really like school."

His tone made something in Aden's chest unfurl. "For what it's worth, I think that's normal. But, Sammy, the car is dead. We're stuck until it's fixed. There's nothing we can do right now, so why don't you just—" He stopped himself, pressing his lips together. Ṣèyí would say he was being too dismissive.

"I know," Sammy said quickly. "But people want to help. I just feel like if we give up now, we'll never find her. And Aliza—she'd be really upset. Maybe forever."

"I get it," Aden said. He reached out a hand to rest on Sammy's shoulder, then thought better of it. "But we can't save her if we don't have a way to get there. So let it go, Sammy. At least for tonight. All right?"

Sammy swallowed hard and nodded again, retreating into his hoodie like a turtle into its shell. Aden felt the smallest pang of guilt as Sammy stood and shuffled toward the door.

Before stepping out, Sammy turned back, his voice quiet, but clear. "You don't have to pretend like you don't care."

The door clicked shut, leaving Aden alone with his thoughts again.

He sat on the edge of the bed, elbows on his knees, staring at the faded red carpet. It wasn't that he didn't care. It was that he cared too much. Caring had cost him before—his sanity, his relationships, his sense of self. Caring meant failing, and failing meant he'd have to admit he wasn't enough. Not for Coco. Not for his siblings.

Not for anyone.

At some point Aden must have drifted off to sleep, because he jumped at the sound of someone banging on his door again.

For a brief, disorienting moment, he thought he was in his childhood bedroom again, Coco screeching in the background. But the smell of damp carpet and stale cigarettes pulled him, regrettably, back to the motel, to the sound of knuckles rapping on wood.

"Aden!" Sammy's voice was muffled but urgent.

Aden groaned, rolling onto his side and glaring at the clock: 6:12 a.m. He stumbled out of bed, his body protesting every step, and yanked the door open.

Sammy stood there, wide-eyed, his hoodie hanging unevenly off one shoulder. He looked like he hadn't slept.

"What?" Aden snapped, rubbing his eyes.

"It's Aliza," Sammy's hands were shaking. "She left."

For a second, Aden's mind stalled, his brain buffering. Left? As in . . . walked to the lobby? Went to grab some of that lukewarm motel coffee? That was a recipe for listeria or E. coli or something. Unless—

"What do you mean 'she *left*'?" he asked, voice sharper now.

Sammy thrust his phone toward him. On the screen was a text from Aliza:

Going to find Coco. Go home with Aden.

Aden's stomach took a nosedive, and the fog of exhaustion cleared.

Damn it, Aliza.

"I think her phone's off now." Sammy's words tumbled out in a rush. "I already tried calling her, like, ten times. But she won't pick up, won't answer my texts." His eyes bore into Aden's, pleading. Scared. "What do we do?"

Aden's pulse thudded in his ears.

She didn't have a car. Or money, as far as he knew. Did she even know where the hell she was going?

His fingers gripped Sammy's phone so tightly his knuckles hurt.

What if she was stranded somewhere? What if someone picked her up? What if—

His mind lurched back to that day at the public pool, years ago. Aliza, maybe five or six, had wandered into the deep end of the pool—the same pool where Mom and Dad would drop them off whenever Coco had a vet appointment, like it somehow counted as day care just because an underpaid teen lifeguard was on duty.

Aden had been floating on his back in the shallow end when he'd heard the splashing. Erratic. Frantic. He jerked upright. His sister's head was barely bobbing above the water, mouth open, choking, too panicked to scream. Aden, still a kid himself, had scanned desperately for a lifeguard—anyone—but no one came.

He remembered that horrible, helpless feeling. The split second where he'd thought, *I'm too late*. And yet, his body had moved before his brain could catch up, cutting through the water on instinct and adrenaline.

He reached her just in time, pulling her out of the water as she sputtered and coughed. He'd spent the next ten minutes yelling at her, shaking—because that was easier than saying, *I was scared out of my mind.*

And Aliza hadn't said a word. Just sat there, dripping, nodding. Like she knew.

Think. Focus.

He was going to have to email Abigail—tell her they'd need to reschedule, again. At this rate, he might even have to take more time off at work. Summers were usually quieter at the firm, but still. His boss at Farley, a man named Richard Albert—a tight-ass who wore his silk ties even tighter—was not going to be happy.

Of course Aliza would pull something like this now.

Anger threatened to surface like hot barbed wire up his throat, but he swallowed it down. Yelling now wouldn't help Sammy, wouldn't help anyone.

"She didn't even take the car!" Sammy went on, his arms flailing. "She's out there, who knows where, and we're just stuck—"

"Hey," Aden interrupted, his voice a steady raft in Sammy's vortex of panic. "She can't be that far. She doesn't have the car, so either she's on foot—and she'll tire out eventually, just like Coco—or, if she's managed to hitch a ride, she'll have to make a stop sooner or later."

"You mean hitchhiking?" Sammy didn't look reassured. "But what if something happens to her? What if we don't find her and she ends up lost in Canada?"

Aden ran a hand through his hair. He could feel the weight of Sammy's fear pressing on him, pulling him down like quicksand. But one of them had to keep it together.

In any case, Canada would be better than here.

"First things first," Aden said firmly. "We're going after her. But to do that, we need wheels."

Chapter 10

The garage smelled like grease and burned rubber, and the hum of fluorescent lights buzzed overhead like a metal hive of bees. The air was heavy, cold, sluggish—still waking up. Aden could relate.

He and Sammy stepped through the open service bay door, the crunch of gravel under their shoes announcing them before they even spoke.

Inside, the mechanic—a stout man with bad posture and a permanent scowl etched into his face—was hunched over a logbook at the counter. He didn't look up, just kept flipping pages with painstaking slowness.

Aden cleared his throat. "Morning."

The mechanic didn't react.

Aden glanced at Sammy, who shrugged, then: "Good morning," he repeated louder, voice tight with impatience.

Finally, the mechanic grunted, the noise like a single scrape against concrete.

"You're early," he drawled.

"Yeah, well," Aden said tightly, "we have a bit of an emergency on our hands. Is there any chance the car's ready?"

The mechanic took a long sip from his coffee thermos.

"Ready?" He chuckled. "Buddy, you think I work miracles at dawn? Parts aren't in yet. Two, three days—if the shipping gods are kind. You'll have to be patient."

Two or three days.

They didn't *have* two or three days.

Aden inhaled slowly through his nose, biting back the immediate urge to say something sharp. Losing his temper would get him nowhere.

"Is there a rental-car place in town?" he asked.

The mechanic barked out a laugh. "Here? Good luck. Closest place is Uniontown, and they won't be open for a couple'a hours." He took another long sip of coffee, damn him. "Guess you'll just have to sit tight."

Aden felt his eyebrow twitch. Uniontown was back east, back the way they had come. That wouldn't work. *Think:* What were his options?

"Look, I *get that*, but—" He pressed his lips together, then tried again. "Maybe we can work something out."

The mechanic narrowed his eyes, setting his coffee down with a heavy clink. "What kind of 'something'?"

"A trade-in," Aden said, forcing the words through his teeth.

That got the mechanic's attention. His eyebrows lifted as he tilted his head, looking Aden over like he was reconsidering whether or not to bother with him at all. "A trade-in? You talking about that Camry, right?"

"It's a '98," Sammy piped up quietly, his voice small in the echoing garage.

The mechanic let out a whistle. "Right. A '98 Camry with a busted transmission and enough rust to start its own ecosystem. You wanna trade that for . . . what, exactly?"

"Something that runs," Aden said flatly.

The mechanic exhaled hard through his nose, a long, exaggerated sigh that said he'd had just about enough of this conversation. "You're lucky I don't charge you for wasting my time."

"Look," Aden said, sharper now, the edge creeping back into his voice, "we don't have time to wait. My sister's out there somewhere, and we need a car. It doesn't have to be good. It just has to move."

The mechanic eyed him for a moment, deciding whether or not he was serious, then grumbled something under his breath and gestured for them to follow.

Aden shot Sammy a look—something halfway between *Don't get your hopes up* and *Keep quiet*—before they trailed the mechanic through the service bay and out into the morning chill.

The lot was mostly empty this early in the day, just rows of dew-slicked cars waiting for attention, their hoods up like yawning mouths. The mechanic stopped near the far edge of the cracked asphalt and jabbed a thumb toward a hulking shape parked against the chain-link fence.

Aden stopped dead in his tracks.

It was an RV. Or at least, it *had* been an RV, once upon a time. Now it looked like an abandoned retro diner on wheels, a relic better left forgotten. The body was a pitiful, peeling combination of beige, brown, and faded orange, with rust blooming across its sides in jagged streaks—scars of a hard, used life. One of the headlights was cracked, and the windshield wipers were frozen mid-swipe, as if they'd given up halfway through a storm. If it'd had a logo stenciled on the side once, it was long gone. Disappeared out of shame, perhaps.

"My God," said Aden.

"Meet the Beast," the mechanic said, smirking like he'd just unveiled a prizewinning cow. "She's got character."

Aden stared at the RV, silent. Sammy blinked beside him, clutching his laptop to his chest like it might protect him from the sight.

"Is that . . . moss?" Sammy whispered.

"Adds charm," the mechanic replied with a shrug. "The inside's clean enough. Mostly."

Aden swore under his breath.

There was something almost alive about the thing, like it was staring back with crooked, shifty eyes. *You think you're better than me, kid?* it seemed to say. But Aden could already hear the protests of the suspension, the wheeze of the engine fighting for air. Someone should have put it out of its misery years ago.

"Anyway, she starts, she moves," said the mechanic, "and you won't have to push her up any hills—she never breaks down. Beyond that, no promises."

Aden raked a hand through his hair, trying to scrape together enough patience not to lose it completely. "You're telling me this is all you've got? Are you *sure*?"

"Yup." The mechanic grinned, revealing teeth almost as beige as the RV. "Oh, and she'll cost you a little extra. Call it two hundred bucks for the difference."

"Two *hundred*?" Aden snapped, rounding on him. "You're charging me money for this thing?"

The mechanic shrugged again, completely unbothered. "Hey, you're trading in scrap metal for a genuine *vehicle*." The way he lingered on the word *vehicle*, exaggerating each syllable—it was like he was referring to a shiny, bite-size Porsche and not a hunk of junk. "Frankly, you're lucky I'm offering this at all. Now, you got the title? Or are we doing this, uh, under the table, so to speak?"

Great. Aden was making business deals with criminals.

"The car belonged to my parents, but they've passed on," Aden explained, hesitating. "I'm the executor of their estate, so I have authority to sell, but I—"

Sammy tugged on Aden's sleeve. "We don't have a choice," he whispered, his voice small and pleading.

Aden glared at the mechanic, feeling his teeth grind together. He glanced back at the RV. It looked like it might spontaneously combust if the wind hit it wrong. If he was lucky, it would with him still in it. As far as deals went, everything about this one was red flags.

But Sammy was right. They didn't have much of a choice. Aliza was out there, miles away by now. Maybe more.

They didn't have time to argue. They didn't have time to search for some neat little sedan or wait for a rental place to open.

"Well?" the mechanic pressed.

A broken laugh almost escaped Aden.

"Fine. We'll take it," he said, yanking his wallet out of his back pocket and smacking his last handfuls of cash into the mechanic's grease-streaked palm. "But if this thing breaks down on the road, I swear to God—"

"Relax," the mechanic said, pocketing the cash with a smirk, as if he'd just won a bet Aden didn't know he'd made. "This thing's unkillable. Trust me. Keys are inside. Just try not to scare the neighbors too much when you start her up."

Aden didn't reply. He just stared at the RV for another long moment, feeling mildly sick. The way it loomed there—half metal, half monster—felt like a bad omen.

"The Beast," Sammy whispered beside him, a strange mix of awe and horror in his voice.

The mechanic threw them a wave over his shoulder, already retreating toward the garage.

"Pleasure doing business, boys!"

The RV sputtered to life, sounding like an old man with a smoker's cough, the engine so loud it drowned out everything else for a full thirty seconds. Aden gripped the oversize steering wheel, foot hovering awkwardly over the gas pedal, blinking at the disjointed collection of gauges and warning lights on the dashboard.

"It's fine. It's fine," he muttered.

It was not fine.

Driving this monstrosity felt less like operating a car and more like wrestling an ancient tractor. The entire vehicle shuddered as he finally eased it out of the garage lot, the brakes screeching loud enough to turn heads at a nearby gas station.

Sammy sat shotgun, his knees practically to his chest. His laptop was already out, tracking app open. He didn't look up as Aden veered cautiously onto the nearest two-lane road.

"Just keep me updated," Aden said through gritted teeth, narrowly avoiding a pothole the size of a bathtub. "If Aliza's chasing Coco, we need to catch up fast. And for God's sake, tell me if we're about to hit anything. I can barely see what's in front of me with all these damn blind spots."

Sammy didn't answer, which was fine, because Aden was too busy trying not to drive the RV into a ditch.

After about an hour, he was beginning to get the hang of it. The morning sunlight was thin and cold, stretching across open farmland that rolled endlessly on either side of the road. Telephone poles lined the horizon like tall, sleeping giants, and every so often they'd pass an abandoned farmhouse, all peeling paint and hollow windows.

Aden hated it. He hated how flat everything was, how alone they felt out here. The kind of place where you could shout and the only thing that would answer was your echo.

He missed Chicago.

"Where even are we?" he muttered, sneaking a glance at Sammy, whose face was buried in his phone.

"Ohio," Sammy said absently.

"No, I get that," Aden spat, "but where in Ohio?"

"Some place called Zanesville? But look." Sammy turned the screen toward Aden. A new Reddit thread had exploded in the last two hours:

> Champion Pink Cockatoo Coco Chanel Spotted in Ohio???

Champion Pink Cockatoo Coco Chanel. Aden's brain hurt reading that absurd configuration of words alone.

Sammy scrolled down, his voice picking up speed as excitement leaked in. "Someone posted an article about her—about all the competitions she's won. I didn't realize she was this famous. Like, people really know who she is."

Aden snorted. "People? What kind of people?"

Sammy ignored him, swiping through the article. "No, listen to this: *Coco Chanel, the legendary pink Major Mitchell's cockatoo, has won six Best in Plumage titles at the Northeastern Aviary Showcase.*"

Aden shot him a look. "Best in Plumage? The hell does that even mean?"

"I don't know, but it's real!" Sammy insisted. "And that's not even the biggest one—she came second in the Birds of a Feather Championship in '21. She lost to a parrot named Dorian Gray, but people say it was rigged."

Aden barked out a laugh. "Rigged? You're telling me there's bird competition drama?" The circuit had gotten even more ridiculous since he'd left.

"Apparently?" Sammy's eyebrows furrowed. "Oh. There's a pic of Mom and Dad here."

Aden's chest braced. He looked over at the screen.

Sure enough, there was a picture of his parents, both standing proudly behind Coco, who was perched on a stand, looking impossibly dignified. The image, taken at a competition he couldn't even remember, felt like a relic from another lifetime. Coco's feathers were so vibrant, it almost looked like they were glowing.

He felt a weird tug. He didn't have the emotional space for nostalgia—not now, not when they were in the middle of nowhere on some absurd quest to find a bird. But there it was, sneaking up on him anyway.

"You okay?" Sammy asked softly, though he wasn't looking at him, still absorbed in the phone.

Aden blinked, surprised—then nodded quickly, his fingers tightening on the wheel. "Yeah. Just—yeah."

A few moments passed, the tension simmering just beneath the surface. Sammy wasn't asking for any explanations, just tapping away at his phone—and for that, Aden was grateful.

"But this is good, right?" said Sammy finally. "I mean, look at this." He zoomed in on a comment below the article, a post that had drawn hundreds of upvotes:

> Saw a big pink bird near a rest stop off I-70 yesterday. Looked like a cockatoo. Didn't know they could get so far north.

Aden squinted at the username—something sad, like @SkyWatcher87—and groaned. "Oh, great. Now we've got amateur bounty hunters after the bird."

"People are talking about the reward," Sammy added. "Three thousand dollars. Wait, didn't we only offer a thousand?"

"We did."

Maybe the esteemed Bird Enthusiasts of Appalachia had something to do with it. On one hand, the bigger reward definitely provided incentive for people to start looking—but what if it only brought more trouble?

"If Aliza saw this, she's definitely headed for that rest stop, right?" Sammy went on. "We should head that way, too."

Aden pressed his lips together, irritation prickling under his skin. Aliza had vanished into this nothingness, probably convinced she could hitchhike her way to Coco. The thought of her—small, stubborn, alone—rattled him more than he wanted to admit.

He tightened his grip on the wheel.

"Fine," he said. "We'll check it out. But as soon as we find Aliza, we should go home."

The words hung in the air like a bad smell, heavy and sour—or perhaps that was just the RV.

Sammy paused, lowering his phone. "Go home?"

Aden braced himself for some kind of pushback, but when he glanced over, Sammy wasn't looking at him. He was staring out the windshield, his mouth drawn tight. "You think Aliza's just gonna pack it up and leave?"

Aden's jaw tightened. "I don't know, Sammy. I just—what else are we supposed to do?" He gestured, tiredly, at the empty road ahead of them. "Spend weeks, maybe months, chasing down Coco? When she might not even want to be found, when she might even be happier being free?"

Sammy didn't respond right away. He just sat there, seemingly turning the words over in his mind like he was deciding whether or not they were worth arguing against.

Finally, he said, "I don't think Coco ran away because she wanted to be free. She just got scared. There's a difference."

The words hit like a stone to the chest, sharp and unrelenting. Aden's hands flexed on the wheel, and for a moment he thought about snapping back. But the look on Sammy's face—earnest, careful, like he was trying to handle something fragile—stopped him.

Scared.

He couldn't remember the last time someone had come out and said it. People always had to dress it up as something else. Like weakness. Failure. Cowardice.

Not a flaw. Just a fact.

The thought coiled tight in his chest.

Because Sammy was probably right. Coco *could* have been scared—bolted out of panic, out of a desperate need to escape something she didn't understand. She'd been alone. The life she knew was gone, and the cage—the door—was open. Taking her chances elsewhere had probably felt like the only choice she had.

But was that the whole truth?

Coco had always been stubborn. Bold in the way that only something small and bright could afford to be. She was smart enough to know where home was. Smart enough to think, maybe, that they would come after her.

Maybe she'd *wanted* them to follow.

Or maybe lack of sleep was making Aden lose his damn mind.

The road stretched ahead of them. Wide. Empty. Trucks rattled past, their trailers swaying in the crosswind. At one point a pickup loaded with firewood honked its horn as it passed, the driver waving and laughing as if the sight of the RV had made his entire morning.

Aden swallowed hard and glanced at Sammy, forcing his voice to stay steady. “How far is that rest stop, you think?”

Sammy squinted at the phone, furrowing his brow. “Maybe another thirty minutes? If that.”

Aden snapped his gaze back to the road, trying not to grip the steering wheel any harder. The RV lurched over a pothole, and he cursed under his breath.

Their destination couldn’t come soon enough.

The Past

Coco learn big speak big word, but still A-den do not call do not answer. She sing for him later

Big Faces, they garble words like money always mo-ney no-money gone too fast

Today Big Face Ladyleaks water from her face, she garbles A-den, A-den not listen to her and she speaks fast Coco no understand, loud too loud

So Coco sings for her but Big Face Lady says PLEASE JUST SHUT UP COCO but her water grows too big and Big Face Manspeaks too he say A-den a bad boy who no help them enough, sad why A-den no love them, he has home nest he has food loud loud

Coco scared

But then Coco see water leak from A-den too

So much water he wipe and wipe and still more water he sad too

Little one watches A-den, but no speak, little one sad, but he no see her and Coco scared too, so Coco yell bad Coco

Is Coco Bad too?

But no one speak

Chapter 11

Aden veered into the Tiffin River Service Plaza, both man and RV rattling. The engine stuttered as it rolled over the uneven asphalt, and beside him, Sammy gritted his teeth, bracing for impact.

The lot was a patchwork of semis, minivans, and a suspicious number of U-Hauls—a sign, perhaps, that the plaza was an unspoken meeting point for people on the run, fleeing from failed MLM schemes or relocating a questionable amount of cats.

Aden parked near the far edge, where the RV's gasping engine wouldn't earn them more attention than necessary, and shut off the ignition.

The resulting silence felt oppressive, like the pause before someone said *Damn, you look like shit.* To be fair, Aden probably did.

"Do we look for Coco or Aliza first?" Sammy asked, already unbuckling. If he wasn't checking his laptop, he was scribbling in his notebook the entire drive, his pencil movements hypnotic in the corner of Aden's eye. Aden wondered whether their parents had known that someone in the family had some semblance of creative talent.

"Whichever one gets us out of here faster," Aden muttered, though he suspected it wouldn't be that simple. He squinted at the cracked windshield, hoping for some sign of either—a flash of pink feathers or Aliza's neon-green raincoat. Nothing.

Sammy leaned forward, scanning the horizon like an eager—ugh—bird-watcher. "Maybe she saw Coco here and stopped."

"Or if we're lucky, she's given up and gone home," Aden muttered. "For all we know, she could be on the couch right now. Eating fast food. Searching for a proper full-time job. Reflecting on her actions."

He unbuckled his seat belt and climbed out, the door hinges shrieking far, far too loudly.

The heat hit him immediately, thick and sticky. He scanned the plaza, shielding his eyes against the sun. The plaza seemed typical enough—a bleak expanse of concrete with a few tired fast-food chains and a couple of gas pumps scattered around the edges. Not exactly the kind of place that would attract a cockatoo.

Maybe he was right; maybe those people on Reddit were lying.

Sammy half fell out of the RV beside him.

"What do we do?" he asked timidly.

"I don't know, kid." Aden scrubbed a hand down his face. "We can try calling Aliza again and look around for Coco."

Sammy frowned.

"What? You got some other genius idea you're sitting on?"

Sammy hesitated, then shook his head and pulled out his phone. "No."

"I could use one," Aden muttered, half to himself.

Sammy dialed, the faint sound of the phone ringing filling the charged silence between them. Aden took in the stretch of asphalt and sun-bleached cars again, but the only movement right now was a lone seagull swooping toward a discarded fry.

He heaved a sigh, emptying more than his lungs.

That's when he saw it: a van parked diagonally across three spaces. It wasn't the kind of van you'd expect at a place like this—no rusted bumpers or peeling paint. Instead, its rear doors were plastered with—Aden's eyebrows furrowed—a bright-red decal that read "Drone-Free America: Take the Sky Back!"

"The hell is that?"

Sammy followed his gaze and read the decal on the van. "What does that even mean?"

Before Aden could answer, the sliding door of the van jerked open with a metallic clunk. Two guys hopped out, both in khakis and identical navy polo shirts, radiating the nauseating kind of energy that screamed *overconfident start-up founders.*

One of them clutched something in his hand—a bulky, absurd-looking gadget that could only be described as an unholy love child of a Nerf gun and an old-school bazooka. It was painted matte black with the words "SkyStopper X2000" stenciled in bold, futuristic letters across the side—like a child's idea of what tech innovation looked like.

Aden blinked. His confusion slowly curdled into mild disbelief.

"I'm telling you, man," the first guy said, waving the gun around the way spoiled kids did at the toy section in Target, "this is gonna change the game. *Shark Tank*'s not going to know what hit them. Mark Cuban is going to lose his freaking *mind*."

The second guy nodded enthusiastically, adjusting his glasses, giving a serious, almost reverent look to the SkyStopper. He clapped the first guy on the back. "Hell yeah, man." Then he seemed to remember something. "Wait, is Mark Cuban still with *Shark Tank* anymore?"

"Oh, shit," the first guy replied. "I don't know. I hope so, man. He's who I was banking on. The other guys don't have his *je ne sais quoi*, you know what I mean?"

Aden hadn't taken French in years, but he still winced at how violently the guy mangled every syllable.

"Doesn't matter," said the second. "Realness knows realness. We just gotta stay the course. This thing speaks for itself."

The two high-fived, and the first guy hefted the SkyStopper to his shoulder.

Aden crossed his arms, half amused, half exasperated. God, he'd been right. The plaza *was* a magnet for failed MLM schemes.

He'd known guys like this during undergrad. The ones who coasted through life on a cocktail of both privilege and audacity. They always had big plans, always thought they were the smartest guys in the room, despite having the depth of a kiddie pool. James Alderman was like that, too. Smug as hell because life had yet to lay a hand on him.

Aden knew better. Sooner or later, the other shoe would drop.

And he lived for that moment.

The guy with the SkyStopper aimed it at a seagull wheeling lazily above the parking lot, then dramatically pulled the trigger.

Nothing happened.

The seagull continued its slow, unbothered arc across the sky.

The first guy frowned and smacked the side of the device like he was trying to revive an old TV. "Hey, where'd the thing go? I swear it was working yesterday—"

Sammy leaned closer to Aden, his voice a conspiratorial whisper. "Do you think maybe it's a joke? Like a 'birds aren't real' thing?"

Aden had heard about that satirical conspiracy theory: that birds were actually just drones operated by the US government to spy on citizens. He wouldn't have been surprised if these guys had somehow missed the joke.

He was already walking away, his footsteps heavy on the pavement—he'd seen enough.

"See that, Sammy?" he called over his shoulder. "This is why we take school seriously. Any word from Aliza?"

Sammy padded after him. "She isn't picking up still."

"Of course she's not." Aden brushed his hair back. "Let's go grab some food, then—"

"Aliza!" Sammy yelled, pointing ahead.

And there she was: coming out of the rest stop, holding a white-and-red drink cup emblazoned with the Arby's logo.

Her eyes met theirs.

"Shit," she muttered.

Aden stared at her for a long moment, then at the cup, then back at her. Like his brain couldn't accept what he was seeing.

"Oh my God," he managed finally. "Oh my actual God. Were you just out here getting curly fries while we've been worried *sick*?"

"How—why—" Aliza stuttered, unable to land on a word.

Aden marched toward her, Sammy trailing behind. For a moment it looked like she might bolt.

Instead, she threw her drink in the nearest trash can like a criminal disposing of evidence, and crossed her arms defensively.

"Seriously, what is *wrong* with you?" Aden said, his voice low. "Hitchhiking? Turning off your phone? Do you *want* to be murdered by serial killers? Because if you're feeling self-destructive, I can just save you the trouble and strangle you right here, right now."

"I know what I'm doing," she shot back. "How did you even find me?"

"Coco," Sammy said simply. "We were tracking Coco."

Aliza bit her lip, visibly startled, then recovered. "Sammy, I—I told you to go home."

"How the hell are we supposed to go home?" Aden shot back. "The car was dead and you were *gone*. Did you really think we'd just leave without making sure you weren't dead in a ditch somewhere?"

"I had it under control," said Aliza, bristling. "I have my phone, I have my pepper spray—"

"And zero common sense! You're *alone*, Aliza! Anything can happen! Do you have any idea how many cases I've read about women traveling alone, only to get attacked from behind and brutally—"

"I don't need the gory details," said Aliza, looking away. "The point is, I'm fine—" She paused. "Wait, if you don't have the car, how did you get here?"

"How did *you* get here?" Aden countered. "Tell whoever brought you that you're going to leave with *us*, and—"

"Whoa, whoa, man," came an insufferable voice behind them. "What's the deal over here?"

Aden turned. It was the two guys from earlier—the one who'd spoken, the first guy, still toting the SkyStopper x2000 over his shoulder, while the other in glasses now held an open bag of Cool Ranch Doritos and an iced tea tucked into his armpit.

"Oh, Aliza," Aden groaned, rubbing his temples. "Say it ain't so."

"They're harmless," Aliza said defensively. "I think."

"You're not gonna kidnap our A-Game here, are you?" the first guy declared, stepping forward like he was prepared to duel. "Because she's with us."

Aden blinked. *"A-Game?"*

"We protect our crew. Which means you mess with her, you mess with us," the guy in glasses said.

Aden glanced at his sister incredulously. "Are they *defending* you?"

"Shut up."

For a moment Aden considered picking a fight with these clowns. But he could feel Sammy watching him, quiet as ever, waiting to see what he'd do. And Aliza, for all her bravado, looked younger. Smaller somehow.

Aden exhaled. Fine. Diplomacy, then.

"Listen," he began, his voice steady as he addressed the two start-up guys, "I get it. You're looking out for her. But she's our sister. We've been worried sick, and now that she's safe, I think it's time for you guys to head out. How does that sound, my, uh"—his eyes slid to the SkyStopper again—"entrepreneurial friends?"

"No can do," the first guy said, shaking his head. "First of all, we're not entrepreneurs. We prefer the term *disrupters*. But hey, nice of you to notice."

"Right." Aden's voice dripped with sarcasm. "Disrupters. Got it."

"Yeah, and second, A-Game here promised to invest. Said she saw huge potential. We're talking early-stage angel investor energy."

Aden's stomach dropped. He turned to Aliza, jaw clenching. "You did what?"

Aliza crossed her arms tighter. "I didn't—it's not a big deal. I just . . . said what I had to say so they'd give me a ride."

"Oh my God."

"Don't make it a thing, Aden."

"I fear *you* are the one who has made it a thing, *Aliza*."

The first guy clapped his hands together. "Point is, we took her on good faith, compadre. She said she'd invest, we gave her a ride. That's value exchange. That's legally binding."

This time, Aden laughed, even as he felt the pinch of a coming headache. How come it was always people who had no idea what they were talking about who threw around terms like *legally binding*?

"I appreciate that you feel that way, but I'm an attorney, and regrettably for you, it's not legally binding when one of the parties is incompetent."

"What the hell, Aden?"

Aden ignored her, his gaze locked on the two tech guys. "But I'll be generous, since you've taken such good care of her. How about I cut you a check right now? Let me be your investor."

The first guy's eyes went wide. "Wait, really? Twenty grand, just like that?"

Aliza had promised twenty grand? Aden rubbed at his temples. He was going to kill his sister.

"You've gotta let us do a demo or something, at least. Do you want to see it in action?" asked the second guy in glasses.

"You know what? I'd love to," said Aden. "So, what exactly does this SkyStopper thing do?"

"It's the future of aerospace security. It's revolutionizing the way people experience nature while regaining their right to privacy. It's not just a product. It's a lifestyle. An ethos. This thing could be big. Timely—"

Aliza muttered under her breath, "It's literally just a glorified Nerf gun."

"Aw, come on, A-Game!" the first guy snapped, his voice cracking. "Don't be reductive. It's a precision-engineered deterrence-and-disruption device capable of downing any perceived *and* nonperceived drone threats."

"You aimed it at a bird," said Sammy.

"You'd be surprised at how many drones are disguised as birds, man," said the first guy solemnly.

Sammy gave Aden a look.

"I'd show you how it works," the first guy went on, "but I'm just realizing we don't have any drones at the moment."

"It's easier when we're not in the middle of nowhere," the second guy amended. "Haven't seen a single drone for the past fifty miles."

"Oh, I believe you." Aden smiled tightly. "Anyway, unfortunately, I don't have my checkbook on me—I left it in the car. Why don't I go grab it and then we talk in more detail?"

The guys exchanged an excited look. "Dude, for real?"

"For real." Aden gave them a serious look. "Give me five minutes. Don't go *anywhere*."

Aliza opened her mouth, but Aden shot her a look that silenced her. He motioned for her and Sammy to follow him toward the RV as the start-up bros chatted animatedly with each other about IPOs and "disruptive scaling."

As soon as they were out of earshot, Aliza hissed, *"What are you doing?"*

"Getting us out of here."

"How?"

Aden opened the RV door and ushered them inside.

"Just trust me."

Once they were inside, Aden slammed the door, locked it, and bolted for the driver's seat.

"Aden, what—"

He didn't answer. He started the engine, threw the RV into gear, and hit the gas—veering sharply out of the lot.

In the rearview mirror, he saw the two guys standing there, mouths open, fists raised. They started shouting, but it was too late.

Aliza, sitting in the passenger seat, stared at him for a beat, then started to laugh. It was sudden, loud, and uncontainable, spilling out of her in a way Aden had never heard before. Sammy joined, too, giggling uncontrollably as the RV barreled down the road.

Aden didn't join in—he didn't know how, and he was still whirling in the adrenaline of it all—but he let the corner of his mouth twitch, a half smile he couldn't quite suppress.

It wasn't much, this ridiculous, stolen moment. But for the first time, Aden felt something unfamiliar settle over him. A tentative, fragile kind of belonging.

Ahead of them, the sky was just beginning to flush a soft shade of pink.

Like a bruise, trying to heal.

Chapter 12

For almost the past one hundred miles through Indiana, Aden had been stuck behind a dull-red pickup truck that its driver had adorned with a giant pair of truck nuts.

The balls swung back and forth—a disgusting, hypnotizing pendulum that drove Aden deeper into anger with every movement. He could kill this driver, he thought. Yes, people who drove pickup trucks with scrotums hanging off the back would not be missed. He would be doing the world a favor. He could simply follow the driver until they stopped somewhere—a gas station, a rest stop, a diner—and lie in wait. Then he'd strike. Rip off their stupid red baseball cap before shoving the greasy, road-dusted balls into his mouth.

You like how that tastes, huh? Aden would say. *The taste of your own fragile masculinity? HUH?*

Unfortunately, he was almost 100 percent certain that this kind of driver would carry a firearm. And as annoyed as he was being stuck behind this human toilet, he did not love the idea of murder.

But he could at least imagine it in vivid detail.

"There should be an intelligence exam you have to pass before getting a driver's license," he muttered.

"That's ableist," Aliza chimed in from the back. "A lot of people wouldn't be able to drive."

"Exactly," said Aden, gesturing to the truck nuts on the pickup ahead of them.

He was losing his mind, he was sure of it. Had he ever driven so much in his life? No, of course not—not since the twelve-hour slog to Chicago for law school. He barely remembered that trip. He'd listened to a lot of music. Cried a bit, if he was being honest.

"So Sammy says you exchanged Mom and Dad's car for this junk?"

Aliza slid into the passenger seat; she and Sammy had been whispering together, gossiping about him, maybe, just out of earshot. But he was too tired to interrogate her.

"Didn't have much of a choice," Aden said, rubbing his eyes with one hand. "It was going to take a few more days for the right parts to come in, and we didn't want to wait. The car was ancient, anyway."

"Because this RV is a spring chicken in comparison," she said.

"'Spring chicken'? What are you, eighty? You sound like Mrs. Lowell. Anyway, it is what it is. At least we don't have to sleep on skeezy motel beds anymore."

Aliza didn't answer. She was flipping between tabs on her phone: the Reddit thread about Coco and some blog post that read "It Girl Gift Guide." *It Girl*—what the hell was an "It Girl"? The image of Cousin Itt from *The Addams Family* popped into his mind, only wearing a pink bow and holding a tiny handbag. But that couldn't be right. Was this the kind of stuff women her age were into? And who was she shopping for?

Maybe Aliza had other friends—friends he didn't know about, a whole It Girl life he wasn't privy to.

Whatever. At least Sammy wasn't glued to a screen like she was. He was nose-deep in his notebook again, sketching at the rickety table in the back. His small hands pressed down to keep the pages steady, though the motion of the RV kept jostling him. Aden had half a mind to pull over just to sneak a look at the drawings, but he figured Sammy would be one of those squirrelly artists who wouldn't let anyone see his work until it was finished.

"You really worried Sammy, you know," said Aden after a while.

"Yeah," Aliza replied softly. "I know."

"I thought the poor kid was going to break down. He's really attached to you."

"Goes both ways," Aliza said with a small smile. Then, after a pause: "What about you?"

"What about me?"

"Were you worried?"

The question caught him off guard. He shot her a quick glance, but her face was turned toward the window, her expression unreadable.

He smirked. "Nah."

Aliza let out a huff of a laugh. "*Nah?* Really?"

"I mean, I *did* wonder if you were going to end up dead."

"Killed by a serial killer, you mean?"

"Shit's dark out there. You never know."

"God, you're bleak."

For a moment Aliza seemed to sink deep into her own thoughts. Then she murmured, "I hope Coco's okay."

Aden didn't reply right away. The sound of the engine hummed through the cabin, steady and low, and his chest buzzed with it.

"She's tougher than you think," he said finally.

"I don't know," Aliza said. "I think she's really sensitive. Like how she didn't like it when Mom and Dad would argue, so she'd squawk real loud. But what she does have going for her is . . . persistence."

Aden thought of Coco prying at her foraging toy puzzles just to get a piece of mango. Tearing through paper towel rolls, chipping at the kitchen doorframe, or chewing through drywall to make herself a hidey-hole. It was true that she never gave up, even when they wished, *begged*, that she would.

Part of him almost envied her for that.

Aliza shifted in her seat, and her phone dimmed in her lap. She pulled her legs up to her chest, her bare feet resting on the edge of the seat. "I want us to visit Mom and Dad's grave," she said suddenly. "With Coco. When we find her."

Aden flinched, just slightly. *Mom and Dad's grave.* Right—because that was what their parents were now. Two plots in the dirt.

But the idea of standing above them—it didn't give him the pleasure he'd thought it would.

"It's not . . . a bad idea," he said.

Aliza nodded, chin dropping to her knees. "I've been thinking about it. It's been too long since we were all together. You know they would've wanted that. Seeing all of us together, one last time."

". . . Sure," Aden said, though he didn't know whether he believed it. Their parents had wanted a lot of things. Things he hadn't been. Things he couldn't be.

"I just want to make sure Sammy's ready, too," she added. "Before we visit Mom and Dad."

"I get the impression he'll be ready if you are."

Aliza sighed. "I'm worried about him, too. He really doesn't want to go back to school. I think something's going on."

"It's normal for kids like him to hate school," Aden said. "I'd be more worried if he *did* love school. Those are always the people-pleasing type A kids who develop anxiety disorders later in life."

Aliza gave a small laugh, but it faded quickly.

"Maybe I should homeschool him."

Aden almost slammed on the brakes.

"Jesus, Aliza—no. That's a *terrible* idea. He needs to interact with other kids his age. And homeschooling isn't just some side project you wing between shifts."

He glanced over. "You're clearly maxed out as it is, especially now that Mom and Dad are gone. Just focus on getting your own life back."

Aliza's eyes darkened. "I *do* have a life, you ass."

"Yeah," he muttered. "You're a part-time vet tech. Fine."

He paused, just long enough for the silence to sting.

"But that's not what you really wanted, is it?"

He could still picture her at thirteen, crashing into his room to rattle off animal facts no one had asked for. *Octopuses have three hearts.*

Axolotls can regrow their limbs. The first endangered species cloned in the US was a black-footed ferret named Elizabeth Ann.

I want to be like Jane Goodall, but for elephants, she'd told him, eyes glowing. *They have matriarchal herds. They grieve together. They mate for life. Even captive elephants can recognize their families after thirty years apart.*

Not birds? he'd asked, half listening.

Occasionally birds, she'd said, smiling. *I'll always love birds, too.*

"Sometimes things just don't work out, I guess," Aliza said now.

"Giving up that quickly?" asked Aden, though he regretted it as soon as he'd said it. He already knew what Aliza would say: He didn't know her, didn't know what she'd been going through. And he knew going to vet school was easier said than done. After all, it wasn't as if law school had been a walk in the park.

But Aliza said none of that.

Instead, her shoulders tensed, as if she was clenching every bone in her body. Bracing.

"Like I said," she murmured, "sometimes things just don't work out."

Ah.

Aden also knew heartbreak when he saw it. And he wasn't just looking at it. He could *feel* it, like secondhand grief. The ache of a life rerouted. A dream abandoned so slowly, it stopped feeling like a choice and more like an inevitability.

He felt something soften in him.

"You know, I had a . . . good friend in law school," he began slowly. "She has connections to people working in environmental law, protecting wildlife and all that." He could picture her so clearly that it hurt: walking Sẹ̀yí to class, their shoulders nearly touching. Her laughter like music at his embarrassment; he loved it when she laughed at him. Her love slipping into his life like an unwelcome guest. "Her name is Sẹ̀yí. You'd like her."

"You had friends?"

Aden laughed. "Yeah, I know. But Sẹ̀yí was really cool."

"That's even more surprising." Aliza's lips twitched into a smile.

For a moment it looked like she was going to say something else, then thought better of it.

Instead, she asked, "Is she here?"

"Here?" Aden frowned.

Aliza pointed out the window at the highway sign they were passing.

WELCOME TO ILLINOIS

The words landed like a punch to the gut. Aden was back—home? Could he call it home?

He thought being in Illinois again would tempt him to floor the RV back to his apartment in Chicago, to safety. Instead, something in his chest squirmed painfully raw.

"No," he said at last. "Maybe. I don't know, she travels a lot." She could be in Denver; work had often brought her there. Or she could be with her parents and brother in Minneapolis. Or maybe—

Maybe she had started seeing other people, and she was with someone new now. She could have found someone who could give her everything she deserved, everything he couldn't. Someone better.

"It's getting pretty late, huh?" Aliza said quietly.

He glanced at her again, startled.

But she was still looking out the window, her face carefully neutral—though her fingers were gripping the hem of her hoodie.

Aden felt a flare of warmth in his chest. "Yeah," he said, after a moment. "How about we find someplace to eat, then park up for the night?"

"Can we go to Arby's?" Sammy piped up from the back.

"God, no," Aliza shot back immediately, horrified.

Aden snorted. "See? Failed parenting in action."

As if the first night spent sleeping in an old RV wasn't bad enough—with Aden claiming the lumpy couch and Aliza and Sammy crammed together on the pullout bed in the back—Aden was jarred awake by a violent banging on the door.

"Sheriff's Department! Open up!" a gruff voice barked.

Aden shot upright, heart pounding. He blinked at the low ceiling, disoriented. The tiny RV smelled like stale chips and old socks. His mouth was bone dry, and there was a pooling ache between his ribs.

"What the hell . . ." Aliza's groggy voice came from the back, followed by the creak of the pullout bed as she sat up.

Sammy groaned. "Is this a dream?"

"If only," Aden muttered. He swung his legs off the couch, grimacing as his joints protested. The stale air clung to his skin like an extra layer.

Through the tiny window, he glimpsed a man in uniform, wide-brimmed hat pulled low. The sharp glint of a badge caught the rising sun.

His breath caught. Great. Just great. His sleep-fogged brain replayed too many stories of roadside encounters like this that ended horribly.

"Stay here," he hissed over his shoulder to his siblings.

Aliza tensed. "What? Why?"

"Just—stay." Aden pushed aside his nerves and cracked the door open.

The morning air swept in, brushing his face like sandpaper. The sky hung low and orange, and the parking lot stretched around them, empty except for a few stray shopping carts.

Aden met the officer with a tight smile, forcing a professional tone. "Morning, Officer. Can I help you?"

The sheriff gave him a hard once-over. "Step outside," he said curtly.

Aden's fingers tightened on the edge of the door. "I'm not sure that's necessary," he began. "I'm an attorney, and—"

The sheriff held up a hand. "Sir, I said step outside. Now."

Aden hesitated, feeling a fresh wave of unease. He was a lawyer—he knew his rights—but he also knew better than to test them here, in a deserted parking lot, with no witnesses.

With a sharp breath, he stepped outside into the cool morning air. The sheriff's eyes scanned the RV behind him.

"Are you traveling alone?"

His voice was clipped. No room for pleasantries.

Aden's fingers squeezed the edge of the door.

"No," he said carefully. "My younger siblings are with me."

The sheriff's expression didn't change. "Mind telling me what you're doing here? You're aware this isn't a campsite, right?"

"We just stopped to sleep for a bit," Aden explained, keeping his tone measured. "We've been on the road for a while, and it was late—"

The sheriff cut him off. "And you wouldn't happen to be transporting anyone else, would you?"

Aden blinked. "Excuse me?"

"Any . . . unregistered passengers."

It took a moment for the words to sink in. Aden stared at the man, almost too stunned to respond.

"I'm sorry, are you asking if we're *trafficking people*?" he said finally.

Behind him, the RV door creaked open, and Aliza stepped out, barefoot and furious, her arms crossed tightly over her chest. Aden caught a glimpse of black lines peeking out from under her sleeve. Her tattoo.

"What's going on?" she demanded.

The sheriff's gaze shifted to her. "Ma'am, I need you to step back."

"Seriously?" Aliza snapped. "We're not criminals. We just happened to park in an empty parking lot. What's wrong with that?"

"Ma'am, I need you to calm down," the sheriff said, his hand inching toward his belt.

"Excuse me? I am *very* calm—"

Aden stepped between them, his heart thudding. "Whoa, whoa, there's no need for that," he said quickly. "Look, Sheriff"—he glanced at the badge—"Bowden, right? We're just passing through. We've been searching for our lost pet."

The sheriff's eyes glinted with something between doubt and confusion. *"Pet?"*

"Our cockatoo," came Sammy's voice, startling both Aden and Aliza. He was leaning out of the RV door, his hair a messy halo around his face. "Her name's Coco."

The sheriff's stern expression finally cracked. His hand fell away from his belt. "Wait . . . Coco?" he said. "You're the ones looking for that fancy bird?"

Aliza's eyebrows shot up. "You've . . . heard of her?"

The sheriff chuckled under his breath. "Yeah. My daughter's been showing me updates online. She's been pretty invested—something about a pretty pink bird flying halfway across the country." He shook his head. "Didn't realize it was real."

"Oh, it's real," Aden muttered.

"Well, I'll be damned," the sheriff said, stepping back and shaking his head. "Don't know if you kids know, but you've gone pretty, uh, viral."

"Huh." Aden's mind spun. He'd been so certain he was about to be taken into custody—and yet, Coco being lost had somehow caused an officer to *pity* them.

"Well, you're not doing anything illegal," said the sheriff, stepping back, "so I'll let you off with a warning. But maybe don't camp out in parking lots unless you want more wake-up calls like this."

"Noted," Aden said, tension slowly ebbing as the sheriff sauntered back to his patrol car.

The rumble of the engine broke the silence as the car pulled away, leaving the siblings standing in the still, orange-tinged dawn.

"Viral," Aliza whispered.

"I heard him the first time." But it made no sense. Their scrappy little Reddit post—how could it possibly have gone viral? Why would people care that much? Then again, maybe it shouldn't have been surprising. Coco always had a way of commanding attention. But *still.*

Sammy's face lit up like he'd been waiting for this moment. "It worked!"

Aden spun toward him. "What are you talking about?" he demanded, just as Aliza asked sharply, "What did you do?"

With a triumphant grin, Sammy pulled out his phone. He navigated to the now-familiar Reddit thread and held it up.

"I've been posting updates," he said, scrolling down the screen. "Sometimes a few a day. People seem to really like them."

On the screen, the text read: Day 3 of Finding Coco. Below the title, Sammy had posted a doodle—a rough sketch of Coco perched smugly on a tree branch, looking down, her feathers fluffed out like a queen's robe.

"That's . . ." Aliza blinked. "Was that in Michaux State Forest?"

"Yep."

Aden thought the tree had looked familiar. He remembered trudging toward it with a pounding headache, aching feet, and his (still) ruined loafers.

It was a pretty good drawing for a thirteen-year-old.

"So you've been documenting *everything*?" he asked.

"Most of it," Sammy mumbled, suddenly self-conscious. "I figured if people knew what we were doing . . . maybe they'd help."

Aliza grabbed the phone from his hand, eyes narrowing as she scanned the screen. "God, someone even posted a video about her—this one has half a million views. I guess they were trying to boost your post on Reddit."

"Great," Aden muttered under his breath. "I *love* having an audience."

Sammy's grin faltered. "I just . . . thought it might help." He shifted his weight. "Was I wrong?"

Aden's first instinct was to snap, to remind Sammy how unpredictable people could be, how this whole viral mess could turn into something bigger and worse. But when he looked at

Sammy—thin shoulders slumped, eyes darting nervously between him and Aliza—Aden swallowed the words down.

Sammy had tried. After weeks of feeling powerless and overlooked, he'd found his own way to help.

And it had worked.

"No," Aliza said, ruffling his hair. "No. It was good thinking."

Aden wasn't sure turning Coco into a meme qualified as *good thinking*, exactly. But as they climbed back into the RV, he felt something stir beneath the usual static in his chest.

This whole thing was absurd. She was just a bird, for God's sake. Not a person. Not family.

And yet, even he couldn't deny that shift within him.

It wasn't hope he felt—not exactly. It was quieter than that. The subtle but unmistakable tug of momentum.

Like Coco was pulling them forward.

The Past

Coco does not like big screaming but two Big Faces do big scream at little one at A-den make big river big sad and Coco scream too louder louder make them stop SAD COCO NO make louder STOP *they put big dark over Coco cage say* go sleep now *Coco but Coco hear small one sad no sleep Coco no see*

A-den friend little one gone no see where A-Den go Coco hear they say he's not answering his phone anymore *where A-den fly where A-den why he leave Coco*

Did we do something wrong? This isn't like him.

But we are flock I sing we are flock where A-den where SHUT UP COCO

Chapter 13

It happened like this:

The post Aliza made on the birding subreddit—with a picture of Coco and the promise of a $1,000 reward—had gotten off to a sluggish start. Most of the comments came from Marcy's group and the occasional "Birb really said ✌" troll.

Then Marcy had upped the ante with a $3,000 reward.

And once Sammy began posting daily updates under the theme of "Finding Coco," complete with his sketches, people began to—Aden grimaced—*flock* to the thread.

That bird's gorgeous, damn.

What kind is she?? I've never seen a bird like that!

Oh my God, how many awards has this freaking bird won? lol.

yo $3,000 ain't bad, brb.

Aden scrolled through the comments in a daze, phone in one hand as he filled the RV's tank.

The thread had truly blown up, reposted across a dozen social media sites. And it had been Sammy, quiet but persistent, who'd pushed it past the tipping point, somehow making people feel connected to their story.

Aden wasn't sure how he felt about it. Relieved, sure. But also . . . frustrated. Like the whole thing had slipped out of his hands.

And then there was Marcy. Well on her way to becoming the nosiest woman he'd ever met, she'd started a GoFundMe to boost the reward even further—and had called Aliza to share the good news.

"Marcy, you didn't have to do all that," Aliza had murmured, glancing uneasily at Aden.

"It's my pleasure, hon. We're all worried for Coco. I can tell she means a lot to you kids," Marcy had replied warmly. Like they were family.

Aden had stayed quiet during the call, biting his tongue.

Marcy's voice always sounded like she was smiling—like maybe she was waiting for the perfect moment to call her local paper and spin this whole thing into some kind of PR stunt. *Local Woman Funds Viral Search for Missing Bird Out of the Goodness of Her Heart.* Aden could already see the headline. Or, worse—the GoFundMe could be just a thinly veiled grift, a way to pocket the money herself.

And yet . . . underneath all that cheer, there'd been something else in her voice, too. A softness. Like she wasn't doing this for attention, but because she'd heard the exhaustion in Aliza's voice and couldn't help but want to ease their burden.

Trusting that—trusting *anyone*—felt dangerous.

Because this wasn't just about finding Coco anymore. It was about bracing for what would happen if they failed.

That was what people were really watching for, wasn't it? Not the happy ending. Not the miraculous reunion. People didn't follow these stories because they hoped it would end well.

They followed because they wanted to see the moment it *didn't.*

When the gas pump clicked off, Aden shoved his phone into his pocket and climbed back into the driver's seat—only to find Aliza on the phone again.

"It's Reema," she mouthed, her face tight.

Aden's stomach plummeted.

He'd completely forgotten to tell Reema about Coco.

To be fair, he hadn't been in touch with Reema khala in years. Their conversations, when they happened, were polite and perfunctory, orbiting around birthdays or obligatory Eid greetings. Surely she didn't expect him to keep her updated on *every* little thing.

But this felt different. They were long gone, chasing Coco halfway across the country, as if that made any sense. Reema would've wanted to know—if not about the trip, then at least about Coco missing. This wasn't just another one of Aden's disappearing acts, slipping away from a house that barely noticed he was gone. It involved all of them.

"You three can't just leave without saying something! You know how worried I was when I got a call from the Lowells?" Reema's voice crackled over the speaker.

Aliza frowned. "The Lowells?"

"They said they hadn't seen the lights on in your house for the past three days. No car in the driveway. They even tried looking through the windows. You were just gone."

"I'm sure they were just trying to figure out how to kidnap Coco," Aliza muttered.

"That's not the point. You should've told someone, okay? You have work—and doesn't Sammy have school tomorrow? Sammy's your responsibility now, both of yours, and I'm trusting you to take care of him."

"It's *fine*," Aliza said, though Aden noticed the vein twitching at her temple. "I let his school know. I took off work. Aden's with us. It's okay."

Reema heaved a long sigh. "You can look for Coco a little longer, but you need to come home. Tomorrow, ideally. It's not safe to be out in the middle of nowhere, looking for her on your own."

"But we're already in Indiana!" Aliza's voice climbed, exasperated. "And Coco's still on the move!"

"Tomorrow," Reema repeated, sharp and unyielding. "Promise me. Is Aden there?"

"I'm here," Aden said, leaning closer to the phone.

"Good. *Tomorrow*, okay? You're their big brother. You need to step up and take charge."

Aden took a breath. Reema khala didn't technically have any authority over them, given that he and Aliza were adults now. But it was obvious, even to him, what this was really about. After all, he'd heard it in her voice before, back when she'd tried to talk their parents out of their obsession with Coco.

She was worried. For them. For Sammy.

"Understood." Aden ignored the knife-edged glare Aliza shot at him.

"Love you. Give Sammy a hug for me."

Aliza hung up and let her head fall into her hands. For a moment, the RV was silent, the only sound the faint chug of the cooling engine, punctuated by the occasional creak of its aging frame.

The silence stretched, weighted by Reema's words. Sammy broke it first, his voice barely above a murmur. "So . . . what's the plan now?"

Aliza didn't look up, her gaze now focused on her phone, on the app tracking Coco's chip. "We keep following her signal. Same as before. Reema can wait another couple of days. Coco can't."

Sammy glanced at Aden as if waiting for him to contradict her.

Aden stared at the dashboard, fingers drumming lightly against the steering wheel. He knew Aliza wouldn't budge on this; if he tried to convince her otherwise, she'd probably just sneak off again and try to find Coco on her own. He needed to approach this from a different angle.

"Look, I do think Reema has a point," he said carefully. "We can't keep chasing Coco forever. At some point we'll run out of road—or gas money."

Aliza's eyes narrowed, her lips pressed tight. "Don't start again."

Aden put his hands up defensively. "I'm not, I'm not. I'm just bringing up some considerations." He leaned forward, resting his arms on the steering wheel. "I'm also worried about this post going viral. Not everyone out there is going to help Coco out of the goodness of their hearts. Someone could beat us to her and keep her for themselves. Or worse."

Sammy hesitated, his brow furrowed. "Did I make things worse for Coco?"

"No, no, Sammy." Aliza turned to face him, her voice soothing. "You meant well. Aden's just a very sad cynic. You can't take what he says to heart."

"Damn, okay, I didn't mean—"

"The point is," Aliza interrupted, "we're staying on course." She paused her scrolling and added, more to herself than anyone else, "We just need to keep moving."

Aden took a breath, his gaze flicking to her. Her posture was tense; she was clenching her jaw the way she did when the weight of it all pressed too hard. He could tell she was closing herself off, slipping into that familiar single-mindedness she always adopted when something mattered too much to her: Like when she was in high school and went on a food strike for two straight days after Mom and Dad informed her that vet school was too expensive to justify. Like the way she'd scratched his face when he kept his hoodies from her. Like the way she'd tried to sneak an abandoned kitten in her room for a straight week, knowing their parents would never allow it.

She'd cried for days when they forced her to put the kitten up for adoption.

Aden didn't want to argue anymore. Not with her. Hell, he wasn't even sure where he stood on all this anymore. Aliza was simply too determined, and he'd gotten caught up in it.

But there was also frantic, frenetic energy to her, a panic that simmered just below the surface. It worried him. It was as if Aliza wasn't just searching for Coco anymore; she was chasing the last piece of something. Something that couldn't be found just by tracking Coco's chip.

How much further could Aliza push herself before something cracked?

"Look, I get it," said Aden quietly. "You want to find her. But you can't push yourself into the ground in the process."

She finally looked up at him, her eyes sharp, defensive. "I'm fine. What are you talking about?"

Aden's lips thinned. "No, you're not. You ran off on your own. Left Sammy behind. You think pushing harder is going to fix things, but it's just making you reckless."

Sammy shrank back in his seat behind them, looking between them nervously. But the fact that he didn't speak up to defend Aliza spoke multitudes.

That was the funny thing about silence—it didn't take sides, but it had a way of making you look like you had. Aden knew that all too well. He'd learned it in different ways: from the quiet in his parents' house when things went wrong, and from the quieter spaces he'd left between himself and Sẹ̀yí.

A held breath that could suffocate you, if you weren't careful.

Aliza's jaw clenched, and for a long while she didn't speak. Then, finally, she let out another shaky breath, her shoulders slumping. "I just—we have to find her, Aden. We have to. I don't care how."

"Sure," Aden answered gently. "Just prepare yourself in case things don't work out the way you want."

Aliza turned away again, her face unreadable as she checked the app on her phone. Sammy, as per usual, remained quiet. Observing.

Aden felt his discomfort rise again, something gnawing at him that he couldn't put into words.

What happened if they *did* find Coco?

What would happen when they returned home? Would Aliza go back to pushing herself into the ground? Too frantic, too eager, to fix things on her own? Would Sammy just . . . fade into the background again, quiet and overlooked?

And him? Would he just retreat to his own life in Chicago, like before?

Don't think about that yet, he told himself. One thing at a time.

He turned the key, and the RV groaned to life. The engine rumbled, and the familiar hum of the motor filled the air as he backed the RV out of the gas station.

"All right," he said before clearing his throat. "Where to next?"

The park was peaceful at first glance—green grass dotted with dandelions, a few scattered benches, and the faint hum of city life just beyond the trees. It was a gorgeous August day. A few people had spread towels for sunbathing; others sat on picnic tables, catching up with friends while mindlessly pushing strollers back and forth. Aden passed a man playing Frisbee with his dog.

It all felt so . . . normal, when lately everything in their life had been anything but.

The only thing out of place in this park was a small group of five or six people—maybe in their early twenties—lingering near a cluster of trees with their phones out. Occasionally, one of them would glance up at the sky.

Something about them made Aden uneasy.

Aliza was out of the RV before he could even throw it in park. Her eyes were locked on her phone, tracking Coco's location. Sammy trailed behind her, hands buried in his pockets, his face unreadable.

"Where is she?" Aliza asked, louder than she'd probably meant. A couple of heads turned their way.

Aden caught up. "A lot of people here," he said quietly. "Let's just . . . take a breath. Take it easy."

But Aliza didn't answer. Her gaze was already locked on the group by the trees.

"I think she's over there," she said, pointing toward them, her phone clenched tight in her grip.

A young woman in the group—wearing the tiniest sunglasses Aden had ever seen—gasped and pointed up at a nearby tree. "Oh my God. Look!"

Aliza's pace quickened. Her back was rigid, shoulders tight, jaw set. Aden could feel it—the urgency bleeding off her in waves. Desperate to do something. Anything.

He hurried after her, pulse kicking faster. Something about this didn't feel right. There were too many people, too many phones. And Aliza—she was too wired, too raw.

"Excuse me," she said, unapologetically breaking up the group to stand by the tree trunk. Aden and Sammy were by her side in a moment, ignoring the dirty looks from the others.

Aliza's breath snagged.

"Oh, *Coco*," she said, the name splintering in her throat.

"Do you see her?" Sammy asked, scanning the bushes with frantic urgency.

And then Aden saw her, too: Coco, perched once more on a high branch, a small silhouette against the branches.

But something was wrong.

Her feathers, once bright and iridescent in the light, looked faded now, dull and bleached by time and weather. Patches were missing altogether, exposing delicate pale-pink skin beneath. Her body trembled with nervous energy, each movement twitchy and erratic, stripped of its usual grace—and her eyes flicked past them with a kind of empty detachment, like she couldn't quite place who they were anymore.

A sick twist knotted in Aden's gut. He'd never seen Coco look so . . . weak.

One of the guys—tall, with a camera slung around his neck—stepped forward. His eyes lit up as he tilted his lens. "Is that her? Coco Chanel?"

The girl gasped. "Oh my God, are you guys her owners? We saw all the posts about her!"

"There goes the reward," another muttered.

"Stay back, please," Aliza snapped. "She's obviously scared."

But the tall guy with the camera was already grabbing a low branch, testing its strength, starting to hoist himself up.

Aden's blood pressure spiked. *No, no no.* This was bad.

But Aliza didn't hesitate. She grabbed the guy's arm, eyes blazing. "I said *back off.*"

Above them, Coco's neck puffed in alarm.

Aden's stomach lurched. He yanked Aliza back before anyone could start yelling about assault charges. "Don't," he said, his voice low. "You'll scare her."

Aliza turned on him, eyes wild. "*I'm* not the one scaring her, Aden."

"I know." Aden turned to the guy with the camera. "Hey, man—get down. Coco's not going to like it if we keep crowding her."

The guy scowled but let go of the branch. "We're just trying to help."

"Then help by giving us some space, all right?" Aden said tightly.

For a beat, the guy backed off, grumbling. Aden let out a breath, but the tension in Aliza wasn't easing. If anything, she looked more brittle, more volatile, by the second.

She stepped toward the tree again, raising the bag of lucky birdseed that Marcy's friend Bill had given them. Her voice softened but her hands were shaking.

"Coco, it's okay. It's okay. Please, Coco. It's me."

Coco hesitated, then inched forward, her ID band catching the light.

The woman with the tiny sunglasses snorted. "She's not going to come down like that. Don't you people have a net or something?"

Aliza ignored her, but Aden didn't miss it—the sharp twitch in her jaw, her white-knuckled grip on the seed bag. The wrong word, the wrong noise, and she was going to snap.

And if she did, he wasn't sure he'd be able to bring her back.

"Coco, come on," Aliza begged. "Please. It's me. I'll take you home."

Sammy's voice came from beside Aden, small, worried. "Maybe you should try."

"No," Aden said, gaze fixed on his sister. "Coco's far more likely to go to Aliza than me." Though truthfully, he didn't know if Coco would come to anyone anymore.

Coco inched closer. For a fleeting moment, Aden thought—maybe. Maybe it would be fine.

But . . .

The woman abruptly pulled out her phone, angling it straight at Aliza. "Well, I hope you don't mind if we record. People should see this."

Aliza looked over her shoulder. "Actually, I *do* mind. This isn't content. I'm trying to save my bird."

"It's a public park," the woman singsonged, thumbing her screen. "We can do whatever we want."

"Aliza . . ." Aden started, a warning edge in his voice—but it was too late.

Aliza lunged.

She swatted the phone from the woman's hand. It hit the dirt with a sharp crack.

The whole group gasped. One of the guys kneeled to pick it up, inspecting the screen. "Hey! You broke it!"

"Good!" Aliza hissed. "Maybe next time you'll mind your fucking business."

Aden's stomach jumped to his throat. *Shit.*

He'd been right after all: This was *exactly* what he'd been afraid of when the posts about Coco had gone viral.

He grabbed for Aliza, pulling her back, but the damage was done. The raised voices, the sharp movements—it was too much.

Coco startled. Wings flaring. Body jolting.

She flew. A clumsy, frantic launch into the sky.

"No!" Aliza's voice broke.

But she was gone.

The group fell silent. Even the guy with the camera looked awkward, scuffing his sneaker in the dirt.

Finally, the woman with the sunglasses sneered as she brushed off her phone. "Serves you right. You're lucky we don't tell everyone how you treat the people helping you. Your little internet sob story? Over."

Aliza rounded on her. Her whole body was shaking now. "Screw you. You didn't want to help. You wanted a fucking video—"

"Okay, okay," Aden cut in, stepping between them.

He yanked out his wallet and shoved a Target gift card—one he'd won at a work raffle—into the woman's hand. "There's like a hundred bucks on it. Just . . . don't post anything. Please. We're all just . . . stressed."

Aliza's head whipped toward him, mouth open like she was about to yell.

But nothing came out.

She just stared, furious and shaking. Then turned away.

The woman blinked. "Seriously? You think this is gonna cover a new—"

"Please," Aden said again, gritting his teeth.

A pause. Then the group drifted away, muttering and shaking their heads.

Aden let out a long, heavy breath, his heart still hammering. They'd lost another shot at catching Coco—had nearly gotten into a fight—but by some miracle, he'd actually done something. Stepped in before things got worse.

And yet . . . it wasn't enough.

Aliza stood frozen, staring at the empty tree branch, her face bone white.

"She was right there," she whispered. *"She was right there."*

Then, with a raw, furious motion, she kicked at the dirt, sending pebbles skittering.

Aden's throat tightened. He wanted to comfort her. To say, *We did everything right. It wasn't your fault.* To be the big brother, for once.

He almost wanted to believe it would help.

But would it even matter coming from him?

Was it too late to try?

And that familiar voice returned, curling at the dark edges of his mind.

Coward, Sẹ̀yí whispered.

His fists clenched, the words lodged uselessly in his throat.

Then Sammy spoke up, small but steady. “She hasn’t gone far.” He pulled out his phone to show the tracking app, the blinking dot still in range.

Aliza wiped her face with a sharp jerking motion, like she didn’t want either of them to see. “Let’s just go,” she said, her voice clipped.

But Aden caught the defeated slump in her shoulders as she turned away.

He followed her back to the RV, Sammy trailing behind. The air felt heavier now, like the sun had leaned too close to the earth, and the weight of it pressed against his chest.

Aden climbed into the driver’s seat and turned the key without a word.

Maybe he didn’t need to say anything.

The silence, as always, said enough.

The Past

Little one Aa-liza sing to Coco like pretty bird Coco like her she small warm soft like A-den and Coco sing too A-den come to Coco he come yes he show teeth but no bite nice sound pretty sound like song Coco like

Where you learn song he garble and Coco sing Coco dance so Aa-liza dance too

A-den make pretty sound with us happy happy A-den

Pretty bird Coco he garble Good girl

Little one Aa-liza make pretty sound again and A-den pets her too

Yes yes

Coco sing forever

Chapter 14

The day after Sẹ̀yí broke up with him, Aden had looked at engagement rings online.

It was too late—at least several months too late, based on Sẹ̀yí's parting words. But after he'd managed to roll himself out of bed with all the effort of a three-hundred-year-old boulder, weathered by time and glued in place by hard soil, he dragged his body to his computer and typed in the search bar *designer rings for women.*

Within minutes, he was overwhelmed. Pear shaped, princess cut, gold, platinum, custom, sizing. His eyes had softened to jelly, and now decision fatigue was crusting them shut beneath the weight of a million unmade choices.

But the truth was, Sẹ̀yí would look beautiful in any ring, in anything—he'd imagined it countless times, weeks into dating her. In a wedding dress. In her sweatpants at home, with a mug of chamomile and honey, a smile playing on her face as they sat on the couch and talked. Looking at him like he had something worthwhile to say.

He'd imagined attending holiday parties together at work, too, squeezing her hand beneath the table. *This is my wife,* he'd introduce her. Then she'd take the reins of the small talk he always fumbled through, her laugh filling the room as his eyes stayed glued to her face, to the way their fingers intertwined beneath the dim light.

But even if he'd gotten her the perfect ring, what would it have mattered? It wouldn't have changed the fact that it was *him* putting it on her. The one who left things unsaid, unread, unfinished. The one who'd spent the past ten years convincing himself that staying gone was noble, when really, he just couldn't bear to come back and let anyone, including his own siblings, see what a mess he still was.

If he couldn't even face his own family, how could he ask Sẹ̀yí to believe in him? He had no steady ground to stand on, no long-term plans. Just him: offering her a life that could collapse at any second.

I wish you'd fight for me, she'd said to him once. *I just wish you'd try.*

Except he didn't know how. The hardest he'd ever tried was leaving home—and that had gutted him. He wasn't sure he had anything more to give.

So when she left, he didn't stop her. Didn't fight. Didn't run after her. Didn't even call.

Instead, he sat in his apartment, staring at his reflection in the darkened window. Telling himself it was better this way. She'd find someone who deserved her.

But the thing about telling yourself you were doing the right thing was that it didn't make you feel any less like shit.

Which was why he was the last person anyone could go to for advice. The last person Aliza should hear from right now.

"Aden?"

Sammy's soft voice was a gentle shake that brought him back.

"What's up?" Aden croaked, his throat dry.

"Are you okay?"

It never got any less strange, having his little brother *worry* about him.

Aden rubbed a hand down his face, like that could wipe away the last ten years. "I'll be all right after I get some sleep."

He glanced into the RV's rearview mirror. His reflection looked worse than he felt, which was saying something. "You're a good kid, Sammy. You know that?"

Sammy didn't blink. "Yeah, I know."

Aden snorted, shaking his head.

But Aliza didn't laugh. She hadn't said a word since they'd failed to catch Coco again, and the silence felt louder than anything she could have yelled.

By the time they pulled into the RV campground, the sun had started its descent. The campground wasn't much: a gravel lot with faded signs, a few crooked picnic tables, and the faint smell of burning.

Missouri. They were already halfway across the country. Just how far was Coco planning to go?

Aden parked in what looked like an acceptable spot and killed the engine. "All right, this is it. I'm starving, so I'm going to heat up some Easy Mac." He gestured toward the gas station stash he'd grabbed back in Illinois; instant mac and cheese wasn't the most sophisticated meal, but his stomach wouldn't protest. "Want anything?"

Aliza opened the passenger door, already stepping out. "I'm fine," she said, slamming it behind her.

"Okay, then." Aden turned to Sammy. "Mac and cheese? We don't have propane for the stove, but the microwave works."

"Yes, please."

Inside the RV, the smell of powdered cheese and boiling water filled the cramped space. Sammy ate quietly, his fork scraping against the disposable bowl in a way that set Aden's teeth on edge. He took a few bites of his own, the macaroni gluey and lukewarm, but the uneasy feeling gnawing at him dulled his appetite.

"Is Aliza usually like . . . this?" Aden finally asked, breaking the silence.

"Sort of," Sammy mumbled around a mouthful of macaroni. He swallowed, then added, "There's been a lot going on."

A lot, indeed, thought Aden. Mom and Dad being gone. Her older brother waltzing back into their lives.

And now Coco on the run, no matter how hard they tried to bring her back.

"I got that." Aden sighed, leaning against the kitchenette counter. Through the small window, he could see Aliza pacing by a weathered picnic table, her phone clutched tight in one hand like it might explode. Her movements were sharp, restless. Like a cracking statue.

"It's just—I don't know," Aden muttered, almost to himself. "Something feels . . . different."

"She's been stressed for years," Sammy said, his tone matter-of-fact. "Maybe it just caught up to her."

"What do you mean?"

"She said no to vet school."

Aden blinked. "Wait, what? She got in?"

Sammy nodded, his gaze fixed on his macaroni. "Yeah, but she'd have had to go to Colorado. UPenn wouldn't give her a scholarship."

The words hit Aden like a stone in his chest. He remembered now: how Mom and Dad had tried to talk her out of vet school, as useful as it would be for Coco. Said it was too expensive. Not realistic unless she got full aid.

He sat up straighter, trying to process. "So . . . she just didn't go?"

"She said she couldn't." Sammy swirled his macaroni with a spoon. "Too much money. And she . . . didn't want to leave me."

Of course. *Of course.* She must've applied hoping something would work out—a scholarship, a loophole, maybe a miracle. Something that wouldn't force her to choose. But in the end, she did what she always did: put Sammy first.

He could picture it too clearly now: Aliza weighing her future against his. And deciding that her dreams weren't worth the price. So she'd graduated from college, stayed home. Took a part-time vet tech job. Stayed close, stayed useful.

Then Mom and Dad had died.

"Jesus." Aden ran a hand over his face.

"She didn't tell you?"

"No." Aden let out a bitter laugh. "Guess that's on me, though."

Sammy looked up at him. "She doesn't like to talk about it."

"Yeah," Aden muttered, his voice thick. "I think I get why."

Outside, Aliza's pacing had stopped. She stood still now, staring at her phone like she was trying to will it to solve something. The orange glow of the setting sun caught in her hair, outlining her like a figure from a dream, or a memory.

Aden's jaw tightened. He'd left her to carry all of it alone. And Aliza had, without complaint. Like it wasn't a sacrifice—just something that had to be done. Like flossing.

She was a better older sibling than he'd ever been.

Aden was halfway through a now-lukewarm gas station kombucha—Sẹ̀yí used to drink it all the time—and was scrolling through an article on his phone titled "10 Humane Tips for Capturing Escaped Birds" when Sammy looked up from his sketchbook and glanced out the window.

"I think Aliza's hanging out with some guy."

Aden didn't respond immediately, distracted by the article's suggestions of "offering favorite treats" and "calling their name." As if those weren't obvious to anyone with half a brain. Who even *wrote* these articles?

"What do you mean 'some guy'?" Aden asked finally, still squinting at his phone.

"She's over by a firepit," Sammy said, nodding toward the window. "I guess she made a friend?"

That got Aden's attention. He set the phone down and hopped over to the window Sammy was peering through, almost spilling his kombucha.

Sammy was right: Through the glass, Aden could make out Aliza sitting by a roaring campfire about fifty yards away. Stranger still, she was next to some guy perched on a log, all thick black hair, trimmed beard, and blue flannel—straight out of a Brawny ad. He had the kind of easy confidence that came from splitting logs for fun or bench-pressing 225 without breaking a sweat.

God, when was the last time Aden had seen the inside of a gym?

"Huh," he muttered.

The guy said something, and Aliza laughed—actually laughed. The sound was distant, faint through the window, but it caught him off guard, like hearing an old song he'd forgotten.

Sammy shifted in his seat, sketchbook balanced on his lap. "Should we do something?"

"Why would we do something?"

"Because Aliza has terrible taste. Her last ex got engaged on her birthday."

"Fair point." Aden stared out the window again, watching Aliza as she tilted her head toward Brawny Man. She looked . . . relaxed. Almost happy.

"But no. She's allowed to talk to strangers. She's an adult." Even if she didn't always act like it.

"But . . ." Sammy frowned.

"Look," said Aden, turning back to Sammy, "she deserves a break. And frankly, so do I." He picked up his kombucha and took another swig, grimacing at the vinegary aftertaste. "Besides, what the hell am I supposed to do? March out there and ruin her fun? She already hates me. Accusing her new friend of being a serial killer isn't going to win me any points."

Sammy didn't answer. He just fixed him with that steady, unblinking gaze that made Aden feel vaguely like an ant under a magnifying glass.

"I'm serious," Aden insisted, though it sounded weak even to him. "She can handle herself."

Like when their parents yelled at him for forgetting to make Coco's vet appointment, Aliza had jumped in without hesitation. *Actually, I told Aden I'd take care of it, but I forgot. It's my fault.*

And just like that, their parents had dropped it.

The guilt still stuck with him, that heavy, useless feeling he couldn't shake. He'd told himself he'd make it up to her somehow, that he'd step up next time. But somehow, Aliza would always beat him to the punch.

And now, watching her through the window, sitting next to some stranger, Aden felt that same useless stuck feeling curling in his gut. Because this should have been another opportunity to step in. But maybe Aliza was right—he'd forfeited the right to protect her years ago when he'd left. Whatever instinct he felt now was too little, too late.

Aden picked up his phone again, scrolling through the article on bird-catching tips. He tried to focus, but his eyes kept drifting to the window, to the stranger's annoyingly broad shoulders and Aliza's unguarded laugh.

"You don't think she's fine, do you?" Sammy asked.

Aden rubbed his face, trying to ignore the tight knot in his chest. "There's just *so many* serial killers, Sammy! And we're at an RV campground, for God's sake. It's practically a murderer *breeding* ground!"

For a moment the corner of Sammy's mouth twitched in a smirk. "You sound like Dad."

"Take that back," he said.

A sound from outside caught their attention.

Aliza had stood up abruptly, shaking her head. Brawny Man stood as well, towering over her, too close. And his hands were tense, twitching at his sides. Like he was considering grabbing her.

"Shit," Aden said, jumping out of the RV.

Sammy was right behind him, scrambling out of the door just as Aden's feet hit the gravel.

They jogged over to the firepit, but before they could get close enough, Aliza's voice rose, cutting through the air.

"Don't touch me."

"What's going on here?" asked Aden, trying to hide his breathlessness.

"It's fine, Aden," came Aliza's answer, though she didn't spare him a look. Her eyes remained locked on Brawny Man, who looked wholly unbothered. Up close, Aden could see that his beard was peppered with flecks of gray, the beer can resting on the log behind him.

"We were just talking," he said. "Friendly chat, that's all."

"Screw you," Aliza growled.

Aden cleared his throat. "Well, it's clear she's not interested."

Sammy stayed quiet behind him, phone in hand; he'd already typed in 911. He just needed to press the call button.

The man gave a slow, lazy smile. "Whoa. No need to freak out. Let's not blow this out of proportion."

"I don't think we are," Aden replied, his fists balling up at his sides. He wasn't sure where this surge of protectiveness was coming from, but it was here now, solid and immovable.

Brawny Man's gaze flicked to Aden, then back to Aliza. "Come on, you really gotta call backup for this?"

Aliza let out a sharp laugh. "Please. I don't need backup."

Brawny Man chuckled under his breath, swaying a little as he stepped closer—hand lifting, loose and sloppy. Like he wasn't quite in control.

"Seriously, buddy," Aden said, stepping forward, too, "do yourself a favor and walk away. Now."

He felt Sammy tense up beside him, thumb hovering over his phone.

The man tipped his chin, eyes glassy. "Relax," he slurred. "I'm not doing anything." But even as he said it, he leaned in—just enough for the shift to feel deliberate. Invasive.

Aden's heart hammered, but his protective instincts roared to the surface. He took another step forward—

But Aliza had already swung first.

She landed a clean shot right to the guy's gut.

His breath whooshed out, and he stumbled back, eyes wide. Aden barely registered the look of shock on his face before Aliza followed through, her foot snapping into the guy's knee in a quick, decisive move.

He toppled like a tree.

Aden's mouth fell open, Sammy's expression a mirror.

Aliza rubbed her fist as she stood over him, her chest heaving. "*God*, I hate men sometimes," she said. She wiped her hands on her jeans and glanced up at Aden. "What?"

Aden blinked. He wasn't sure what to say.

The little sister he'd left behind didn't need his protection after all. It stung more than he wanted to admit.

Still, he managed to find his voice. "Serial killers. See?"

"Oh my God, Aden. I don't think he's a serial killer. Just an idiot."

Sammy stifled a laugh beside him, but Aden ignored it, his focus still on Aliza. He hesitated, then asked, more softly, "You okay?"

Aliza's sharpness faltered for a moment, her shoulders sagging slightly. She let out a breath, the firelight catching in her eyes. "Yeah," she said. "I'm fine."

"Good." Aden swallowed. "But . . . how did you—"

"Four years of kickboxing." Aliza smirked. "Thanks for coming, though."

Her tone wasn't warm exactly, but it wasn't cutting, either. Just a simple acknowledgment. It was the closest thing to an olive branch he'd gotten from her in years.

For once, Aden didn't try to deflect or make a joke. He just nodded. "Anytime."

Behind him, Sammy cleared his throat. "Uh, should we, like . . . call someone?"

They all turned to look at the man still groaning on the ground.

Aden sighed, rubbing the back of his neck. "Yeah. Probably."

As they walked toward the RV, Aden couldn't help but glance at Aliza again, watching the way she carried herself—steady, strong. And for the first time in a long time, he felt an unfamiliar emotion: pride.

"You know," he said, smirking despite himself, "we're so lucky to have your leadership in these trying times."

Aliza rolled her eyes and murmured, "Shut up"—but he could have sworn there was the faintest smile in her voice.

Chapter 15

Coco was trending on the internet, and Aden did not like it.

What had started as Sammy's Reddit thread and a few viral posts had snowballed into a full-blown social media explosion. Aden blamed Marcy. Of course she had a famous bird-watching friend—with his own Emmy-winning show—who'd blasted the story all over Instagram.

> US friends: Spotted a pink bird in the sky recently? That might have been Coco Chanel, a Major Mitchell's cockatoo native to Australia. Her family is looking for her. If you have any sightings to report, let us know so we can reunite this gorgeous bird with her loved ones.

Aden snorted. *Loved ones*. Coco's "loved ones" had been dead for nearly a week now. But if she had any sense left—if she wasn't too stubborn for her own good—she'd settle for the three of them.

Except Aden couldn't shake the feeling that she wouldn't come back. Not if she had a choice. Because that was the thing about Coco: She'd *always* had a choice. And more often than not, she hadn't chosen him.

He remembered the late nights spent fixing her favorite toys, or the hours he'd spent trying to coax her down from the ceiling fan when their parents weren't around. He'd been the one to calm her during thunderstorms, when his parents couldn't be bothered.

And yet, somehow, she'd always loved their parents more. Maybe that was why she mimicked their mother's voice so perfectly, even the cackling laugh.

But Aden's voice? When she mimicked *him*, it always came out wrong. Too thin, too flat. Like his voice wasn't worth remembering.

He knew it wasn't fair—that cockatoos mimicked the sounds they heard most often, not whom they loved most—but that hadn't stopped him from feeling like an afterthought. Like no matter how much time he spent looking out for her, Coco would always be waiting for someone else.

Still, he couldn't get the image of her out of his head. The Coco they'd seen at the park, her feathers hanging limp, her eyes dulled.

Aden rubbed at the space between his brows.

He didn't know why he was thinking about this. It was just a damn bird.

"I think we need a new game plan," said Aliza, finishing chugging her first cup of coffee for the day.

The three of them had crossed the border into Kansas and were now grabbing breakfast in a little diner called Petunia's off I-70. It was the kind of place that had a fake vintage vibe, where the neon sign flickered a little too much and the waitstaff acted like they'd been there for decades. The cracked Formica tables and the coffee that tasted like it had been brewed just to keep the machines running had started to feel strangely comforting.

Aden glanced at Aliza. Her eyes were already sharp with focus, caffeine sparking behind them.

"I'm not saying it's going to be easy," she said, setting the cup down with deliberate precision, "but we need to start thinking bigger. This isn't just about tracking Coco anymore, hoping she just conveniently shows up on some street corner. It's about"—she paused, as if calculating the best way to phrase it—"flushing her out."

Aden raised an eyebrow. "I'm listening."

"I think we need to hit the bird-watching communities harder," she continued. "We've been relying on Marcy's connections and random sightings, but clearly that's not cutting it. We need to be more strategic instead of just—you know—flying blind."

Sammy, who had been quietly listening, finally spoke. "There's a big bird-watching convention coming up in Denver."

Aliza turned to him, surprised but pleased. "Yes, that's *exactly* what I'm talking about." She turned back to Aden. "We could head there, network, connect with more people who know what they're doing. People who can actually help us properly track Coco's flight patterns and get some real leads, instead of just chasing after her."

"Hmm." Aden scrolled through his phone. Seventeen new emails from work. No one at the office cared that one of their associate attorneys had taken off for his parents' funeral. Corporate law waited for no one.

More to the point, he was due back in Chicago in a *week*, and he still hadn't had his meeting with Abigail. Nothing was going right. As usual.

He flagged a waitress for more coffee—his one true solace.

"Maybe what we need is an animal tranquilizer," he offered.

"Aden."

"What?"

"We're not doing that to Coco. In any case, we'd need a vet for that," said Aliza, pursing her mouth.

A vet. Which Aliza should have been studying to become right now.

Aden cleared his throat. "Okay, but you really think if we just show up to some bird convention, people will drive around with us to track Coco for who-knows-how-long? I think we need to be realistic."

"What if we also take advantage of how viral she's becoming?" asked Sammy. He'd ordered the Hungry Trucker plate, which included three eggs, three turkey sausages, three pancakes, and a side of home fries. Aden had blinked and it was already half gone. He envied the kid's metabolism.

Aliza chewed on some buttered toast. "What are you thinking?"

"Hashtag, maybe. Or we post a video somewhere telling people about Coco and how much she means to us."

Aden frowned. "Didn't you already do that on Reddit?"

Sammy shrugged. "Kind of. But it's just updates—sketches, sightings."

"Right, that's the problem," Aliza cut in. "Right now people are just watching. But if we tell a real story—the *full* story—it could make them feel invested. They won't just scroll past another 'lost pet' post. They'll care enough to want to find her. So we need to show them why Coco matters."

"We're already offering a reward. How else do you make people care?" asked Aden, savoring a slow sip of coffee.

Aliza tapped her fingers against her mug. "We talk about Mom and Dad—about how Coco's all we have left of them. We tell people what she's been through, all the competitions and training. How she even sounds like our mom. We make her more than just a viral bird. We make her *our* bird."

Aden set down his mug and exhaled. "And if it blows up in our faces? If it brings the wrong kind of attention, like with those assholes at the park? What then?"

Aliza sighed and leaned back in the booth. "We won't know until we try. It's the only shot we've got to reach more people, get more eyes on her. Sammy's right, we should take advantage of Coco's fame. People will care."

"Right. Maybe people will care, until the next big thing comes along. Then Coco's just another lost pet in a sea of . . . viral junk."

Aliza's eyes narrowed. "You think I don't know that? It doesn't matter. We can't do this all alo—" She took a deep breath, steadying herself. "We need all hands on deck. Doesn't some small part of you at least want her back? Don't you want to try *something*?"

Aden winced at the bluntness of her question. He knew she didn't mean to, but it hit somewhere deeper than he'd expected. Somewhere vulnerable.

His jaw tensed. "I'm driving you guys around in an RV halfway across the country. I *am* trying."

"No, I didn't mean—" Aliza stopped, biting her lip. "I'm just . . . I'm scared she's running out of time."

Aden looked between his siblings as they stared back at him expectantly. He opened his mouth. Hesitated.

"Fine," he muttered, tossing a crumpled napkin onto his finished plate. "But don't come crying to me if we end up with a hundred freaks showing up at our RV offering to 'help' and then trying to recruit us in a cult. Also, you got crumbs all over your mouth. Wipe it off, you animal."

Aliza smiled as she smeared a napkin around the edges of her lips. "Deal."

"And you two are making whatever pity post—or video, whatever—by yourselves. I want no part," he added.

"No part of what?" croaked a woman behind them, in a voice Aden knew all too well.

He turned around slowly, disbelief stiffening his every joint. And there they were—a smiling Carol and Peter Lowell: Carol, in a pink knit sweater—handmade, probably—her whitish-blond hair perfectly coiffed at the edges that only old-fashioned rollers could bring, and Peter, standing slightly behind her in his usual brass-rimmed glasses and air of vague befuddlement always about him. Today he'd opted for a tropical-themed button-up, as if he'd just stepped off some island resort.

Aden blinked once, twice, as if that might banish the apparition. Carol and Peter in Kansas—or were they even in Kansas anymore? He could hardly say with certainty. It was far more likely they were in hell.

"Why?" he asked finally, stupidly.

Carol's laugh rasped like a lawn mower on gravel. "Why, Aden, what a question! We're on our way to the convention in Denver, of course. And when we saw Marcy's post about Coco on Birders United, we thought, *Oh, wouldn't it be something if they were on the same route?* And wouldn't you know it? We pulled into Petunia's, and there you were."

"How . . . nice," Aden said flatly.

"When we saw Marcy's post, we *knew* it had to be your Coco. And we thought—well, what are the chances?" Carol's grin widened as she leaned closer, dropping her voice as if sharing a great secret. "It's fate, don't you think?"

"You weren't . . . *tracking* us, were you?" Aliza asked, eyes wide.

"Oh, no, no, nothing like that." Carol waved a hand dismissively. "We just connected the dots. Marcy's post, the timing, the route—pure coincidence, really. But a happy one! We're all on the same team here, after all."

"Are we?" Aden asked, leaning back in his seat. "Because *we're* out here to make sure Coco gets back home. You know, *with us*."

Carol's smile tightened, but her tone remained syrupy. "Aden! You know that incident at the Eastern Regionals was a simple misunderstanding. And here I thought time might've softened your perspective. Carrying that kind of bitterness—it's not healthy, honey."

"Not bitter," muttered Aden. He reached for his water, taking a sip to avoid looking directly at them.

Peter stepped forward then, adjusting his glasses with the same earnest precision he applied to everything. "We're not here to rehash old wounds. We thought we could help, that's all. Birds like Coco"—he hesitated, glancing at Carol for reassurance—"they don't always make it back. She's special. And she's in danger out there. We've seen what happens when rare birds go missing."

Aden leaned back in his seat, glancing at Sammy, who was refusing to look up from his half-eaten Hungry Trucker plate. Aliza beside him, though, seemed to be gearing up for a fight, her shoulders tense, her fingers wrapping tightly around her fork.

"How convenient that you're here, then," he said.

"Oh, but we're worried about you kids, too," said Carol softly, as though she hadn't heard him. "We've seen Coco grow up, but we've also watched all three of you grow up, too. I remember you and Aliza playing in the yard—oh, do you remember, Peter? Aden, with that old red bicycle? And the day Sammy came home from the hospital?" Her voice wavered, and for a moment she looked genuinely stricken. "You've all been through so much. Losing your parents, losing Coco . . . it's a lot. Too much for anyone."

Aden studied her face, searching for an angle, because there was always an angle with the Lowells. But strangely, her sadness didn't appear manufactured—the way some people looked at a tragic headline, muttered "What a shame," and moved on without a second thought. When he looked at Carol, her eyes glistening, she looked . . . genuinely upset on their behalf. And for a disarming moment, he thought she might cry.

He hated that it made him pause.

"We might not be family," Carol continued, her voice steadying, "but we'll always be here for you. If you need assistance, you know how to reach us. We've got migration routes, contacts with birders in the area. And if Coco ever becomes too much—especially on top of everything else you've been dealing with—well . . ." She hesitated, glancing at Peter, who nodded faintly. "We'd be here for that, too. Not to take her, but to make sure she's cared for."

Aliza made a sharp sound, part scoff, part disbelief. Aden reached over, gently pressing his hand to her arm.

It wasn't worth fighting. Not here, not now.

"That's awfully generous of you," Aden said finally.

"We mean it," Peter said. "This isn't about us. It's about Coco. And about you three. You've been through enough already."

Normally, Aden would scoff, too. Brush it off as another calculated move. They were pretending to care, to soften them up in the hopes that they'd finally get their hands on Coco.

But as he glanced at Carol again, he couldn't shake off the sincerity that clung to her words—clinging like a new rash. The Lowells were never exactly good people. More often than not, they were overbearing and meddling and self-righteous. The kind of people he'd learned to write off, and had.

And yet, there was no mistaking the care in their voices. The way Carol's face softened when she looked at Aliza or Sammy. Even him.

It wasn't the kind of care his parents had given—conditional and flawed, littered by neglect—but it was . . . something.

And maybe it would be easier. Easier to let go of a bird that had always felt like more burden than blessing. Caring for Coco wasn't just work; it was a responsibility that would follow Aliza and Sammy for the rest of their lives.

The Lowells, though—they had resources, experience. Hell, they probably had a detailed five-year plan for Coco's enrichment.

"You really do want to help, huh," he said, surprising even himself.

Carol blinked, taken aback. She glanced at Peter, then back to Aden. For a moment no one spoke.

"We do, Aden," she said at last. She smiled sadly. "That's all."

He looked past them, out the window, where the RV gleamed faintly under the harsh midday sun.

They'd traveled almost 1,500 miles from New Hope, he thought. All the way to freaking *Kansas*, or wherever the hell they were now. And for what? Even if they did find Coco, they couldn't afford to keep her, not with everything else hanging over their heads.

The Lowells—for all their smugness—could probably give her a better life. And taking the easy way out . . . well, that was what Aden did best. Cutting his losses. Walking away.

But this felt different.

Maybe it was how far they'd come—the miles, the dead ends, the mess they'd made just trying to keep moving forward. Or maybe it was just the way Aliza kept looking at him, like she was counting on him to stay. For them to be a team.

Letting the Lowells take Coco now—the thought settled on the back of his neck like a cold hand.

It would feel like proof he hadn't learned a damn thing.

"I guess we'll see," he muttered to himself.

Chapter 16

Aden stopped just inside the main doors to the Colorado Convention Center in Denver, a towering sprawl of glass and stainless steel.

The moment he stepped in, the noise hit him like a slap: a thousand overlapping conversations, the hum and blare of sound systems, the occasional scream of a mechanical birdcall. Rows of booths stretched out before him, gaudy and glittering—many promising to revolutionize birding in ways he doubted were necessary.

And the people. So many people. A dense, churning crowd of binoculars and bird-print vests.

"Wow," Sammy murmured, eyes wide as they roamed the massive hall. A banner overhead proudly proclaimed **DENVER BIRDING EXPO 2025: FOR THE LOVE OF THE BIRDS!**

"Yeah," Aden muttered, not quite as taken by it.

It'd been a long, long time since he'd gone to a bird expo—though not long enough. Trying to navigate the crowds with Coco in tow had been *hell*; he and his parents would get stopped every two seconds by weirdos gawking at Her Majesty, to be entertained by all her tricks. *God, is she real?* they'd say, eyes glazed in awe. *Her feathers aren't dyed pink, are they? Hey, kid, can you take a picture of us with the bird? You must be so proud of her!*

Even remembering it all was giving him the chills.

Beside him, Aliza was quiet, staring past the booths and crowds as if trying to find an exit already. Maybe she was overwhelmed—their parents had never dragged her to these conventions the way they had with him.

"So you think they sell capes for actual birds here?" he asked, gesturing toward a nearby vendor hawking "flight-enhancing" bird-wing covers.

Nothing.

"Aliza?" he tried again, nudging her shoulder lightly.

She blinked, finally turning to look at him.

"What?"

"Hey, we don't have to be here if you don't want to. It was your idea," Aden said, keeping his tone light. But he was starting to get worried. They were standing in the heart of birding Mecca—heaven for someone as animal obsessed as her—and she looked *lost.* Like someone who wanted to run away from it all.

"Sorry," she said, her voice barely audible over the crowd. She shoved her hands into her pockets and nodded toward Sammy, who was already inching toward a booth displaying incredibly detailed miniature birdhouses. "Let's just grab our tickets and get this over with."

Aden tugged at her shoulder, bringing her back. "No, spill first. What's going on?"

Aliza avoided his eyes. "What do you mean?"

"You've barely said two words since we got here. And I know it's not because you're overwhelmed by the nerdy-ass Birding Comic-Con." He gestured toward a man strutting past in a vest plastered with patches that read "Birding Is My Superpower."

"Hey, don't hate on Comic-Con."

But her shoulders sagged, as if she were emptied out.

For a second, Aden thought she was going to change the subject, brush him off like she usually did. Instead, she muttered, "It's just, I can't stop thinking about it. What if the Lowells are right?"

He blinked. "What?"

She looked up at him, her jaw set in that stubborn, determined way she got when she was about to say something she didn't want to admit.

"What if . . . Coco *would* be better off with them? Let's face it, Gus is healthy. There's a reason they keep winning second place. What if . . ." Aliza exhaled sharply, forcing her words out like they were stone. "What if we're being selfish?"

Aden stared at her, struggling to process what she was saying. Sure, he'd had a similar thought earlier, but this was Aliza. *Aliza*—the same Aliza who had spent hours fighting him to prove her independence, who was ready to trawl through woods and highways to bring Coco home. *She* was considering giving Coco up?

"But we hate the Lowells," he said, because it was all he could think to say.

"I know," she said tiredly. "But look what happened when we were in charge of her."

A flare of guilt erupted in Aden's chest. He quickly cleared his throat. "Well, that was, uh, all my fault. Technically."

"Yeah. But let's be real. It could've happened to any of us. And Coco requires so much care, it's—" She chewed on her bottom lip. "I don't know."

Aden's mouth pressed into a thin line. He was used to Aliza's relentless, annoying levels of conviction. This sudden switch-up—it felt wrong. It wasn't *her*.

Before he could find the words, Sammy reappeared at their side, his face lit up.

"Guys, look!" he said, grabbing Aliza's sleeve and pointing.

Aden and Aliza both turned to see what he was pointing at: a sleek display booth showcasing a small black contraption called the QuickCatch Net, glowing beneath the fluorescent lights. The black-and-silver banner above it read: "The Ultimate Tool for Humane Wildlife Capture."

Sammy was more animated than Aden had ever seen him. "I think that could actually help us catch Coco."

Aliza looked at the booth, then back at Aden. He saw something flicker in her expression—hope, maybe, or at least a shadow of it.

"Let's check it out," she said.

After buying their tickets—Aden swiping his credit card with a painful hiss—the three of them shouldered a path through a gaggle of enthusiastic birders ogling a display for a robotic bionic bird from some robotics conference before finally approaching the booth.

Aden immediately clocked the vendor: a man with spiked blond hair and a pair of cheap tinted sunglasses around his neck. With an orange skin tint representing far too many trips to the tanning bed, he looked more like an Ozempic Guy Fieri than an inventor.

He was adjusting a row of pamphlets when they reached his table, and his teeth gleamed unnaturally white. "Oh, welcome, welcome! You kids here to witness the cutting edge of wildlife capture?"

Aden glanced sideways at Aliza, whose arms remained crossed. He shrugged. "Sure."

The vendor brandished the QuickCatch Net, grinning. Aden squinted at the baton-size contraption, which looked far more like something you'd use to fend off an overenthusiastic dog than catch a bird. Sammy, at least, had a glint in his eye—the kind Aden now recognized as the one he got when he was deep in his sketchbook.

With a sharp snap, the vendor extended the baton, revealing a tightly coiled net inside. "See, this little beauty uses patented spring-loaded technology to deploy a humane, ultralight net that's strong enough to catch your feathered quarry, but gentle enough for even the most delicate of wildlife. Perfect for researchers, conservationists, veterinarians"—he gave the baton a clumsy twirl—"you name it."

He turned to a small windup bird toy perched on a fake tree branch that Aden had assumed was part of the booth decor. He pressed a small button on the baton, and the net shot out with a soft *fwip*, enveloping the plastic bird mid-flap.

Sammy's mouth fell, his fingers tightening around the edge of the table. "Whoa."

"'Whoa' is right," said the vendor, grinning. "With a range of up to thirty feet, the QuickCatch is the future of wildlife rescue. Compact and so easy to use, even a little guy like you could do it."

Sammy turned to Aden and Aliza, his eyes wide. "We could use this."

Aliza frowned, her arms still folded. "I don't know. I don't like the idea of using a net on Coco. Something like this could really stress her out. And we'd only get one shot. If we miss and she bolts, it's over."

"You got a better idea?" asked Aden. "Because I'm all ears."

The vendor looked between them. "You kids missing a bird?"

"A cockatoo," said Sammy.

The vendor nodded sagely. "Ah, yes. Beautiful creatures, but definitely sensitive. I can tell you this, though: Catching them, no matter what it takes, may be the safer option than letting your bird fly off into danger."

Aden hesitated. The contraption looked ridiculous, but he had to admit it could be useful. And Coco—every day she was out there was another day something else could happen to her.

"I don't know if we have much of a choice," said Aden.

Aliza's brows furrowed.

Sammy gave her a pleading look. *"Aliza."*

"How much is it?" asked Aden.

"Two hundred and ninety-nine dollars and ninety-nine cents, plus tax."

"Two ninety—" Aden ran a hand down his face, biting back a scream. His salary could take a couple of hits, but between the gas, the motel, and the snacks and takeout that Aliza insisted she'd "help cover" with her "next paycheck," this trip was proving far more expensive than it was worth.

And their inheritance—what little there was—wasn't for things like this. He'd already decided that whatever scraps his parents had left behind would be for Aliza and Sammy, while they got back on their feet. For school. For emergencies. For *them*.

He let out a long sigh and pulled out his wallet with all the enthusiasm of someone being robbed at gunpoint. "Fine. We'll take it."

"Excellent choice!" The vendor's grin grew, if possible, even wider as he processed the transaction.

As they walked away from the booth, Sammy cradled the box like it was a holy relic, his eyes scanning the instruction manual printed on the side.

Aliza fell into step beside Aden, her lips pressed into a tight line. "You think this'll actually work?"

"I don't know," Aden admitted. Then, lowering his voice, he added, "But it's better than nothing."

She gave him a wary look but didn't argue.

Ahead of them, Sammy stopped to adjust his grip on the box. "Guys, this thing is so cool. It even has a safety release, just in case!"

"Silver linings, I guess. Knowing Aden—" Aliza began, but Aden stopped dead.

Across the hall stood a booth lit up like a fucking Christmas tree, completely out of place beside the ones touting humble binoculars and handmade stuffed birds. Neon strips framed the display, pulsing obnoxiously in sync with a digital banner that screamed **SKYSTOPPER X2000: DEFEND YOUR SKIES!** The words flashed in alternating colors, each more aggressive than the last.

There they were: the tech bros, identical in their black branded hoodies, gesturing animatedly at a small crowd of attendees. One of them was demonstrating the SkyStopper prototype—probably the same one Aden and his siblings had seen earlier. The other was mid-pitch, pointing to a laminated poster plastered with meaningless buzzwords like *AI-Integrated Targeting* and *Disruption-Free Zones*.

Aden muttered a curse under his breath and ducked his head. "Stop," he whispered sharply, stepping closer to Aliza and Sammy. "Stop and turn around slowly."

Aliza paused, frowning. "What? Why?"

"Just trust me," Aden said, his tone clipped. "Casual, like you're browsing."

"Browsing what?" she asked, but Sammy obediently pivoted, cradling the QuickCatch box in his arms.

Aden angled his body to shield Aliza's line of sight. "Don't *look*."

Aliza squinted past him. "What is your *problem*?"

"They're here," Aden hissed.

She blinked. "Who's—"

Then she saw them. The black hoodies, the buzzing neon lights, the leaf-blower-rifle thing. Her expression darkened immediately. "Oh, no."

"Oh, yeah," Aden said grimly, already turning toward the exit. "Your best friends in the whole entire world."

"They're not looking this way," she said, trying to sound hopeful.

"Not yet," he muttered, steering her toward the nearest aisle. "But the moment—"

"A-Game!" The shout cut through the hum of the convention like a lightning bolt.

Aliza froze. Sammy clutched the box tighter, his eyes darting between his siblings.

"What do we do?" he whispered.

Behind them, the tech bros were abandoning their booth; one hopped over the table with ease while the other stumbled and chased after him.

"Run," replied Aden.

The three of them broke into a clumsy sprint, dodging through the crowd, weaving between booths and displays. The tech bros were undeterred, though, their shouts growing louder with every step.

"You promised you'd invest!" one of them hollered, hefting the SkyStopper like a weapon.

"We did not!" Aliza yelled over her shoulder.

"It was legally binding!"

"No, it wasn't!"

Aden grabbed her arm and quickened their pace, weaving between rows of displays. Sammy's sneakers squeaked on the polished floor as he tried to keep up.

“Jesus Christ, they’re persistent,” Aden said, breathless. Other attendees shuffled out of the way, some outright gawking.

“Stop running!” one of the tech bros yelled, equally out of breath, but still determined.

“This is harassment!” Aliza shouted back.

“It’s business ethics!”

Aden’s eyes darted around the hall, searching for an escape. His gaze finally landed on a glowing red EXIT sign halfway down a side corridor. He nudged Aliza and Sammy, and they bolted toward the exit, dodging past a fan in a feathered hat and skirting a booth selling artisanal birdseed—the kind Coco would love. Sammy clutched the QuickCatch box tighter, his eyes half closed.

As they neared the exit, though, salvation came in the form of a security guard—a broad-shouldered man in a navy uniform, standing with a posture that brought Aden to shame. He stepped directly into the tech bros’ path.

“Sirs,” the guard said, his voice steady but firm, “do you have a permit for that, er . . . weapon?”

The first tech bro stopped so abruptly that his partner nearly crashed into him. “What? No!” he said, his voice an octave higher than usual. “It’s a drone deterrent! Completely harmless! We’re selling them at our booth.”

“It looks like a weapon.” The guard crossed his arms. “I’m going to have to ask you to let me inspect it.”

“But we’re in the middle of—”

“Now.”

Aden didn’t stick around to watch the fallout.

He shoved the exit door open, and the siblings spilled out into the cool afternoon air, coming to a halt in a quiet corner of the convention center’s parking lot.

Sammy leaned against the wall, chest heaving. Aliza bent over, hands on her knees, muttering something about “absolute clowns” and “need more cardio.”

Aden caught his breath, straightening and glancing back at the door they'd just burst through. For a moment all he could hear was the distant hum of traffic and their collective panting.

"Man, you see this shit?" he said. "This is why people say tech bros ruin everything."

Aliza shot him a tired glare, too exhausted for his jokes. Sammy, though, slid down the wall to sit on the asphalt, groaning. "Why does this keep happening to us? Does this kind of thing happen to normal people?"

"Nothing about our family has ever been normal."

Aliza straightened, brushing her hair back from her face. "Let's just go," she muttered. "Before someone else decides to chase us. Or worse."

"Like we bump into a serial killer?" offered Sammy.

Aden grimaced. "At this point? Preferable."

Chapter 17

Sammy was drawing again, perched in the passenger seat while Aliza dozed in the back beneath a crumpled blanket. Her steady breathing filled the quiet gaps between the hum of the RV engine and the scratch of Sammy's pencil.

It was almost 10:00 p.m., and the exhaustion was beginning to hit Aden, too. But they couldn't slow down; their detour to the Denver Birding Expo had put too much distance between them and Coco. She'd barely stopped to rest in the past three hours; stress seemed to only fuel her journey west. Crazy freaking bird.

At the very least, Aden discovered that the ancient radio in the RV worked. A classic rock station, the volume low, helped fill the silence.

He sneaked a glance at his brother's sketch pad but couldn't make out what he was drawing. Just dark lines, rough and jagged but deliberate, leaving behind the faint, silvery smell of graphite. Sammy worked with quick, sharp strokes, then paused to smudge the lines with his fingers, giving them depth. Occasionally his phone would light up on the dashboard, revealing updates from the various social media sites where they'd posted about Coco. Possible sightings. Updates on her location. Comments from strangers wishing them luck. Sammy would check the screen, his face unreadable, then go back to his sketch pad.

The quiet between them stretched, comfortable but taut, like a string waiting to be plucked. Aden finally broke it. "Have you always been into drawing?"

Sammy didn't look up. His pencil scratched steadily across the page. "Mm-hmm."

"You, uh, like it?" Aden asked, wincing at his own awkwardness.

"Yeah."

Aden ran a hand through his hair, grimacing at the grease. They'd have to stop at another motel soon—he was overdue for a proper shower. He gestured vaguely toward the notebook. "What, uh, do you draw?"

"Anything. Mostly things I see." Sammy's voice was soft, like he was halfway lost in his own world. "My fourth-grade teacher said it could help me think when I have trouble finding the right words."

"So you draw instead of writing in a journal?"

"Yeah. It's easier for me."

"Finding the right words is tough," Aden murmured.

"Yeah. It's hard making friends because of it."

"Is that why you don't want to go back to school?" Aden asked, his voice careful so as not to startle him. Sammy, he was learning, could close up as fast as a shy clam if one said the wrong thing.

But Sammy said nothing for a few long seconds. His pencil slowed, like he was in thought.

"Mm-hmm. People don't like me there," he said slowly.

Indignation flared in Aden. Granted, he was no stranger to being bullied; kids were merciless, and he'd always had a target on his back—not just because he was, in their eyes, a weird little brown kid, but because his parents were *the bird people*. While normal families went on their camping trips or vacations to Europe, Aden would be dragged to bird competitions in the middle of nowhere, forced to carry Coco's suitcase and keep her feathers pristine.

Who would want to go to his house when it smelled funny—of feathers and birdseed and bird poop—with Coco hollering her head off whenever there was a new guest? Who would ever want to associate with *him*?

But if Sammy was experiencing the same thing—if their parents and their ridiculous life choices had forced *him* to live through that, too—Aden could've happily dug up their graves just to kick them in the throats. Sammy was a kid, for God's sake. A good kid. He didn't deserve it.

"Well, I'd like to see your drawings sometime," Aden said, his voice a little softer. "If you're cool with it."

Sammy hesitated, his pencil hovering over the page. "Maybe. If you promise not to sell the house when we get back home."

"Bargaining, huh? You might have a future as a lawyer." Aden checked the rearview mirror; Aliza was still fast asleep. As successful as their trip to the Colorado Convention Center had been, it had clearly drained her.

The road ahead was empty, stretching out toward the dark silhouettes of mountains in the distance. The night cloaked the highway in inky blue, broken only by the steady beams of the headlights. The air outside felt thinner here—colder too. The kind that scraped your lungs with every breath.

"What about moving somewhere new? Getting a fresh start at a new school?" asked Aden, deliberately casual.

"Maybe. But Aliza will be sad."

"Sad? Because she'll miss the house?"

"Sad because she'll miss home. Miss what it represents. Where things were still . . . normal." Sammy's eyebrows furrowed. "One more thing to lose."

Aden chewed the inside of his cheek. Home. That house had never been home to him. When he thought of it, he didn't picture warmth or stability; he pictured the cracked kitchen tiles where Coco had once flung a ceramic mug, the peeling wallpaper—like raw skin over old wounds—his parents arguing about Coco, voices rattling the walls like a storm.

It had been a holding pen. A place where they were all crammed together, suffocating under the weight of their parents' expectations and Coco's endless demands.

The place where childhoods went to die.

But Aliza had never felt the same. Maybe because Aden had been the one to take the brunt of their parents' behavior. He was the oldest; he was the one expected to lead by example. And his resentment, over the years, festered beneath the surface.

Aliza, with her rose-tinted memories of occasional family dinners and even rarer, once-a-year game nights, couldn't—or wouldn't—see what Aden saw. What he remembered. It was probably why they would never see eye to eye. Not on this. Maybe not on anything.

Aden exhaled slowly, his gaze flicking to the rearview mirror. Aliza was still curled up in the back seat, her face half hidden under the blanket. Even in sleep, her brow was slightly furrowed, as if she were holding on to something too tightly to let go.

"What's this music?" asked Sammy, gesturing at the radio with his pencil.

Aden blinked. "It's Led Zeppelin. 'Kashmir.'" When Sammy didn't react, Aden's face fell. "Don't tell me you don't know *Led Zeppelin*."

"The song is called *'Kashmir*'? Are they Kashmiri?"

"Oh my God." Aden kneaded between his brows. "Mom and Dad really taught you nothing of value, did they?"

Though, as Sammy's older brother, perhaps *he* was partly to blame.

Suddenly, the RV rattled violently beneath them, and outside, a sharp pop pierced the hum of the tires on asphalt. Sammy jumped in his seat, startled, his sketchbook sliding off his lap. Aden swore under his breath, yanking on the wheel. For a moment everything tilted—the RV listing uneasily to one side—before he regained control, guiding it shakily onto the shoulder.

The RV groaned to a stop, the engine sputtering as Aden killed it. The silence that followed was heavy, almost suffocating.

"What happened?" Aliza's voice floated from the back, thick with sleep. A shuffle of movement, then she appeared, hair rumpled and face half buried in her hoodie.

"Tire popped," Aden muttered, rubbing his temples. "Cheap piece of junk."

"Where are we?" She yawned, leaning forward to peer over his shoulder, one hand ruffling Sammy's hair in a half-conscious gesture.

"Still in Colorado," Aden said, flicking on the hazard lights, though he wasn't entirely sure they'd work. The ancient dashboard seemed to operate on faith and duct tape. He grabbed his phone, his fingers already flying across the screen. *How to change a tire.* The search results blinked back at him: neat, sterile instructions completely detached from the chaos of real life.

Aliza leaned closer, reading over his shoulder. "You don't know how to change a tire?"

"No, Aliza, I don't," Aden snapped, dragging a hand down his face. "I actually take care of my car back home, so believe it or not, this is a . . . novel experience for me. Do you know how?"

"Isn't that why we have Triple A?"

Aden groaned. "I didn't exactly have time to sign up for Triple A when I bought this rust bucket in a panic, Aliza. And even if I did, they'd take hours to show up. Meanwhile, every second we're sitting here, Coco's putting more miles between us."

Panic sparked in his chest like a live wire, sending up little bursts of heat. He leaned back against the seat, trying to steady his breathing.

Aliza tapped thoughtfully on the back of Sammy's seat. "I mean, we could probably figure it out. Do we have a wrench?"

"It's an RV," Aden shot back. "We're going to need more than a wrench."

Muttering about the universe's personal vendetta against him, Aden slid out of the driver's seat, slamming the door behind him. Sammy followed, a silent shadow, while Aliza trailed after them, rubbing the sleep from her eyes.

"Let's at least look at the damage, I guess," said Aden, circling the RV. He stopped short when he reached the back right side, a grim laugh escaping his throat. The tire sagged pitifully against the rim, a clean split running along the sidewall like a fatal wound. The rubber looked intact otherwise, but the RV leaned precariously toward the flat.

"Well," said Aliza, crossing her arms, "this is . . . bad."

"No shit." Aden crouched to inspect the wheel. He gave the damaged tire a tentative nudge with his leather loafer, as if hoping it might miraculously reinflate. "Looks like we hit something sharp. Maybe a nail."

Sammy squinted at the road behind them. "I didn't see anything."

"Exactly. This is why I hate driving at night."

Aliza scoffed. "Well, if you just let *me* drive, maybe we wouldn't be in this mess."

"Driving an RV on a highway is very different from driving a car to the grocery store."

"Oh, as if *you're* such an expert."

"I'm older, which means I've been driving longer. I've got more experience."

"God, you're so annoy—"

"It's going to rain," Sammy interrupted them, looking up. His voice was soft, but it carried a certainty that made both of them pause.

Aliza sucked in a breath. *"Coco."*

"She's a bird; she can handle some rain. I think we need to worry about ourselves here," said Aden. "You wouldn't happen to know anyone in Colorado, would you?"

"No," Aliza answered stiffly.

Aden wondered whether he was being insensitive—just because Aliza had applied to vet school in Colorado didn't mean she'd magically built a Rolodex of Colorado connections. And she probably didn't need the reminder that in some better, alternate version of her life, she might've belonged here.

He sighed and pulled out his phone again, thumbing through Google searches with a growing sense of futility. He could figure this out—probably. People on YouTube made changing a tire look simple enough, though none of them were working with a rusted hulk of an RV in the middle of nowhere.

His mind wandered. They weren't far from Boulder, were they? That was where Sẹ̀yí's family lived. What if she was there?

His finger hovered over the screen, his stomach curling. He hated that he'd never deleted her number. Hated that he'd remember it even if he did. Hated that he always would.

Except nearly six months had passed. Over *180 excruciating days* since their last conversation—tears on her end, and stupid, dead silence on his. He should have called her when his parents died. She would have wanted to know. Except he'd told himself not to, over and over. Told himself that dragging her into his mess would hurt her more.

Aden scrubbed a hand down his face. If he was being honest with himself, he wanted a good excuse to call. To hear her voice. To make sure she knew he was still here.

"She's not going to pick up," he muttered.

"What?" Aliza asked, turning toward him.

"Nothing."

No, he couldn't call her. Not for something as stupid as a blown tire. That wasn't fair to her. But it didn't change the fact that they were stranded out here, and Sẹ̀yí would know what to do. She'd always find a way, because she was the kind of person who turned obstacles into puzzles, and puzzles into victories.

Except him. The one problem she couldn't solve, no matter how many times she'd tried.

The sky rumbled overhead, a low, growling threat that made Aliza glance upward and mutter under her breath. Sammy stood, brushing dirt from his jeans and frowning at the horizon like he could will the storm away.

Aden took a deep breath. His hand hesitated over his phone screen, then opened his contacts. He scrolled past names he hadn't thought about in years—college acquaintances, law school classmates, his old landlord. Then there were work colleagues. His boss, Richard. He stopped at hers.

Sẹ̀yí.

The line rang. Once. Twice. He almost hung up.

Then:

"Hello?" Her familiar honeyed voice—hesitant, soft—was like a balm to his ears.

Aden swallowed, his throat tight.

"Hi," he said, his voice barely above a whisper. "I, uh, need your help."

Almost two hours later, a red sedan rolled in behind them, its headlights slicing through the misty rain. Aden straightened, brushing his palms against his damp jeans.

The car door opened, and there she was.

"Ṣẹ̀yí," he said, breathless.

"Aden." Her mouth twitched, almost a smile, though her eyes stayed guarded. "It's good to see you."

"You—you too."

Rain streaked her face, glistening on her skin. Even in the dim glow of the cloudy sky, she looked . . . impossible. *Unreal.* Her hair, a soft cloud of loose curls, framed her face, and the line of her jaw was as sharp as ever. She wore a practical jacket, zipped just high enough to show the silver chain she always wore. Aden hated how the sight of her made him feel like the ground beneath his feet wasn't solid anymore.

"You look great," he said, almost choking.

"Can't say the same for you. Rough time of it?" Her lips curved slightly, a hint of the playful Ṣẹ̀yí he remembered. "Nice shoes."

Aden looked down at his feet, at his destroyed loafers. Behind him, Aliza snorted.

He laughed awkwardly, rubbing the back of his neck. "It's a long story."

Ṣẹ̀yí's gaze shifted past him, her brow lifting slightly. "I take it you're his siblings? Or are you stuck babysitting him?"

Aliza grinned. "I'm Aliza. This is Sammy. Aden's babysitters-slash-siblings."

Sẹ̀yí smiled warmly, her entire face lighting up. "It's so nice to finally meet you. I'd say I've heard so much about you, but your brother's *very* secretive."

"Yeah, he suffers from a condition called 'having a stick up his ass,'" Aliza said, her tone matter-of-fact.

Sẹ̀yí laughed, a sound that seemed to pierce straight through Aden's chest. His fingers curled tightly around his phone, as if that might somehow ground him.

"What are you guys even doing out here?" she asked. "Weird spot for a family vacation."

"We lost Coco," Sammy chimed in. "Our pet cockatoo. We're tracking her down."

"A cockatoo?" Sẹ̀yí tilted her head, one brow arched. "I didn't know you had a cockatoo."

"Miss Coco Chanel," Aliza corrected with mock seriousness. "An *award-winning* cockatoo. She was our parents'—their pride and joy."

"But not anymore?"

Of course she caught that—Sẹ̀yí never missed a thing.

Aden swallowed hard, the words sticking in his throat. "My, uh, parents passed away. About a week ago."

Pain fluttered across her face. "Oh, Aden," she said. "I'm so sorry."

He nodded but didn't respond. How could he tell her that he wasn't sorry? That his parents were likely the reason why he couldn't let people in, couldn't keep people close? That loving her had always felt like trying to hold water in his hands?

The silence stretched between them, heavy with words he'd never learned to say.

Sẹ̀yí broke it, shifting her focus to the RV. "You've got the parking brake on?" she asked, crouching beside the broken tire.

God, he ached to touch her. To reach out and bring her close enough to smell her rose perfume, and trace his fingers along her arm, the back of her neck, just to prove to himself that she was *real.* That this wasn't some half-formed daydream symptomatic of a psychotic break.

But she wasn't his to hold anymore. Hadn't been for a long time.

"Aden?"

"Uh—yeah," Aden muttered finally, his voice rough. "I think so."

"Good. I've got some wheel chocks. Looks like I'll need a screwdriver and a breaker bar . . ." She trailed off, already pulling out tools with practiced ease. Seconds later, she'd removed a silver plate from the wheel.

Aliza hovered behind her, clearly fascinated. "Need a wrench?"

Sẹ̀yí nodded, taking it from her without missing a beat.

Aden watched helplessly as the two of them worked. "How are you, uh—how do you lift the RV?"

Sẹ̀yí glanced at him, a small smile tugging at her lips. "My dad let me borrow his bottle jack."

"I don't know what that is."

"You don't need to. Why don't you sit somewhere and relax?" She didn't wait for his response, turning to Aliza instead. "Want to help me with this? Sammy, you can watch, too, if you're interested."

"Hell, yeah," Aliza said, already crouching beside her.

Sammy hesitated, then moved closer, his wide eyes fixed on Sẹ̀yí's hands as she explained what she was doing.

Aden suddenly felt like an outsider, standing uselessly in the rain. He drifted to the shoulder railing, sitting down heavily. His phone was a cold weight in his pocket, and he pulled it out, scrolling absently through nothing at all.

The memory came unbidden, sharp as the rain biting against his skin: Sẹ̀yí, curled into his chest, her voice soft and certain as she'd whispered, *I want to marry you.*

His body had gone rigid at the time, every muscle locking in protest, even as a small, fragile part of him soared at the idea. He'd said nothing. And in the silence that followed, Sẹ̀yí had pulled away. Looked at him like he were a stranger.

You don't want to?

He could still remember the hurt in her voice—the disbelief that had bloomed into something colder when he couldn't find the words.

He told himself he'd done it for her, that walking away was an act of love. She deserved someone whole, someone unafraid. Someone who didn't carry the shadow of his parents' marriage like a curse.

Because Aden's parents had called what they had love, too—but that wasn't what it had felt like. It had felt like drowning—a constant tug-of-war between their bitterness and their need to be needed. They'd clung to each other so tightly that no one else could breathe. Not their kids, their friends. Just them and Coco.

Coco, who'd been their greatest excuse, their endless project: something to pour their twisted devotion into. Proof that their obsession wasn't destructive, but purposeful.

Aden had spent his entire life walking on the edges of that mess, desperate to avoid getting pulled in.

And yet, when Sẹ̀yí had said those words—*I want to marry you*—he'd seen it: the same desperate attachment waiting to take hold of him. He'd seen himself suffocating her, dragging her down with him.

He would fail her. Just like his parents had failed each other.

So he'd let her go—convinced himself it was mercy. A clean break before he could ruin her, too.

And it had worked, hadn't it? She looked happy now, standing there in the rain. Whole. Bright. Like time had healed her in ways it hadn't touched him. And yet, it was like she hadn't changed. She was still light-years ahead of him, still solving problems he couldn't even name.

But watching her work with his siblings, he felt the ache of something lost. Not just her. But the life he'd refused to let himself imagine. She handed Sammy a wrench, and her laughter carried faintly through the rain. Aliza said something that made her grin wider. Brighter.

And for a moment—just one reckless, impossible moment—he let himself imagine her not as someone he'd loved and left, but as *family*. A family he didn't have to walk on eggshells around. A family that stayed together because they wanted to—not because they were too tangled in guilt or obligation to walk away.

Quiet. *Steady.*

He imagined those lazy mornings in bed with warm light filtered through half-open curtains. Being teased for somehow burning the toast, *again*. Mornings spent driving Sammy to school, both of them half asleep and grumbling about traffic. Aliza stealing his jacket because she couldn't find any of her own—like nothing had changed.

And Sẹ̀yí, curled up beside him on the couch, resting easily against his side.

But that kind of life wasn't meant for people like him. People who knew better than to get too comfortable. Because that was the other thing about family—the thing no one liked to admit: Sometimes it fell apart, no matter how badly you wanted it to stay whole.

It *sucked.*

"So Aden said you two were friends in law school?" asked Aliza, leaning casually against the RV.

Sẹ̀yí had busied herself by removing the last lug nut; against Aden's better judgment, his gaze traced the hint of the captivating curve of her back through her rain jacket.

"Friends? Is that what he told you?" Sẹ̀yí glanced back then, her eyes catching Aden's like a spark before she turned away.

A smirk broke across Aliza's face. "Ohh. I see. Now it all makes sense."

"Oh?" asked Sẹ̀yí as she worked. "What makes sense?"

"It makes sense that you two are clearly no longer together. Because, frankly, you're too good for him."

Sẹ̀yí threw her head back and laughed—a full, unguarded sound that seemed to cut through the gloom. "Oh, I like you."

"Great. You can date me instead."

"Aliza," Aden warned sharply, unable to watch any longer.

"What? She's cool. It's your mistake for not locking her down first."

"Can we not do this?"

"No, no, *let's,*" Aliza shot back, still smirking, but her voice was a little too pointed, her teasing a little too sharp. Like she'd been holding something in for too long and couldn't help herself. "Because it seems to me you've left out some very important details about your *friend.* For example, why did you break up? Was it because he did something stupid? I bet it's because he did something stupid."

There it was: frustration creeping in beneath her grin. Because Aliza *knew* Aden too well. Knew how often he walked away from things, from people. And how easily he pretended it didn't matter.

Sẹ̀yí positioned the jack under the RV. "My lips are sealed," she said.

"And it's none of your business," said Aden tightly, glaring.

"Okay, so he did something stupid and then had the audacity to call you to fix our tire. You're the *worst,* Aden."

Aden's jaw clenched. "Please stop."

Sammy, oblivious to the tension, pointed at the jack. "Is it supposed to do that?"

Sẹ̀yí shifted her focus, making a quick adjustment. "Good catch, Sammy. You've got an eye for this."

The rain had softened to a mist, but the air felt heavy with things left unsaid. Aden watched as his siblings huddled around Sẹ̀yí, her easy laughter threading through the night like it belonged there. He didn't.

But then Aliza's voice broke through the haze. "Sẹ̀yí, you should totally come with us. We could use someone competent."

Aden's chest tightened. "Aliza—"

Sẹ̀yí shook her head, laughing softly. "As fun as it would be to go across the country to find a bird, I have a day job that won't let me take off."

Aliza mock-pouted, her arms folding across her chest. "Really? You don't want to waste all your time with the three of us?"

Sẹ̀yí smiled but didn't answer right away. Instead, she glanced toward Aden, her expression flickering. "I just don't think Aden would particularly love it if I joined."

Aliza now turned to her brother, her eyes narrowing as if daring him to deny it openly. Aden opened his mouth but found himself stuck in the flytrap of Sẹ̀yí's implication.

He didn't know what he wanted to say.

"No? Nothing to add?" Aliza said, eyebrows raised.

"I—" Aden rubbed the back of his neck, focusing on the ground. "It's . . . complicated."

Sẹ̀yí stepped back, wiping her hands on her jeans. "It always is."

The rain had started up again, a soft patter punctuated by the occasional clink of tools as Sammy tucked the wrench into its spot. Aliza studied Aden for a long moment, her smirk fading into something softer, almost . . . worried.

"Well," she said finally, turning back to Sẹ̀yí, "next time you should come over to our place in New Hope. Meet Coco. We can hang out properly."

"Maybe one day," Sẹ̀yí said quietly, her smile tinged with something sad.

The new tire was in place, the crisis over. "Just make sure you get all the other tires replaced soon, too!" Sẹ̀yí called out to Aliza. "They don't look like they're going to last much longer."

"Got it," said Aliza, before she and Sammy climbed back into the RV, leaving Aden standing in the rain.

But Aden lingered, awkwardly shifting his weight as Sẹ̀yí leaned against her car.

She said nothing. Only stared at him with the endless depths of her eyes, the ones that had always undone him. The ones undoing him again as she waited for him to gather himself.

He cleared his throat.

"Sẹ̀yí, I . . ." The words stalled somewhere beneath his ribs, and he rubbed the back of his neck. What was he trying to say? That he missed her? That he wished things had been different? That he wished he hadn't screwed it all up?

God, how fucking melodramatic. Even if it was true.

"How's . . . the family?"

"Fine," said Sẹ̀yí, folding her arms across her chest in that measured, graceful way of hers. "Mom and Dad are upset with you, obviously. Aunty Chima said if she sees your face again, she'll skin you alive."

She said it lightly, but there was weight behind it. Because even if *she'd* been the one to break up with him, even if *she'd* been the one to finally say she couldn't wait around for him to figure himself out, her family still blamed *him*.

And honestly? Aden knew they were right.

He winced. "Ah." He'd met Aunty Chima once, during the Thanksgiving holidays in their 3L year. Aunty Chima, Sẹ̀yí's mom's older sister, was the kind of woman who loved hard, but held grudges harder.

"But otherwise, they're fine. Same as always."

Aden could only nod, dry lipped. "And—and you?" he asked tentatively.

"Fine now." Sẹ̀yí's lips curved in a wry smirk. "Seeing you squirm like this certainly helps." She stood straight—she always had impeccable posture from all the ballet she'd taken since college. "So you're a big brother, huh? I know you mentioned having siblings, but here I thought you had younger-brother energy. I wish you'd told me more about them. Your family."

Aden felt his own shoulders sag, tension and exhaustion twin weights on each arm. "It was . . . hard," he admitted. "My parents and I—we had a big falling-out. Before I came to law school. I didn't exactly have a great childhood, so there's a lot of unresolved . . ." He faltered, searching for the word.

"Anger?"

"Yeah."

Anger. Hate. But it also felt like drowning. Because that was the scary thing about drowning—it could be so quiet, so unnoticeable. Water filling your lungs, making you unable to scream for help. The same way it had almost done to Aliza when they were kids. It was why no one had noticed, except for him.

"So what—you decided it was easier to just pretend they didn't exist?" Sẹ̀yí let out a small, quiet huff. "I'm sensing a trend here."

"I deserve that," muttered Aden.

"Yeah. You do."

"I'm sorry. You deserve—"

"I know what I deserve," Sẹ̀yí interrupted calmly. "The real question is, Why couldn't you give it to me?"

Aden said nothing. He couldn't. His head was barely bobbing above the water. Choking.

Sẹ̀yí sighed. Looked away. "Not that it matters now."

"I'm sorry," Aden muttered. "It's . . . not that simple."

Sẹ̀yí raised a brow. "When you actually open up to the people who care about you, you might just find that it really, really is. And stop saying you're sorry. That doesn't do anything for me. At least say thank you. You owe me that, at least."

Finally, Aden looked up at her, let his eyes alight on the soft angles of her face. Strands of wet hair stuck to her cheeks, the cold leaving a light flush.

"You're right," he said, the words falling short of everything he meant. *"Thank you."*

Sẹ̀yí studied him for a moment, her expression unreadable. Then she gave a small nod, brushing a strand of hair from her face. "Of course. But if you're going to ever call me again, maybe do it when you aren't just asking for a favor."

Aden blinked, the words hitting him like a slap and a lifeline all at once. Of course. She was right, she always was. But was she . . . was she saying he could call her?

Did he dare think she'd given him another opening?

"Get—" He swallowed. "Get home safe, Sẹ̀yí."

Sẹ̀yí, who'd gone very still, suddenly let out a breath. "Yeah." She looked over her shoulder as she walked back to her car. "And for what it's worth, I don't know what your parents did to you. How your life might've looked before. But from what I'm seeing"—she nodded toward the RV—"they at least gave you something good."

Before he could respond, she climbed into her car and drove off, her headlights cutting through the rain until they disappeared completely.

Aden stood there for a while, the rain soaking through his jacket, the silence closing in.

When Aden finally climbed into the RV, he found Sammy in the back seat, scrolling through his laptop, getting an updated location for Coco. As they pulled back onto the road, Aliza glanced at him from the driver's seat. "So . . ." she said, her voice careful, testing the waters.

"Not now, Aliza," Aden said, his gaze fixed on the window, watching the rain streak past.

"Then when? Because it's clear you still love her. Don't you?"

The question hung there, weightless and heavy all at once. Aden's jaw tightened. He stared back at his empty reflection in the glass, like a ghost in the night.

"It's none of your business."

"Oh, okay. So, what, you're just going to keep it all to yourself? That's real healthy, Aden. Do you even have friends you can talk to about this?"

"Shut up, Aliza."

"Let me guess. You guys dated for a while, but then it got too serious and you chickened out because you're afraid of commitment? You probably convinced yourself you were doing her a favor, didn't you? That breaking it off was noble somehow?" Aliza let out a short, bitter laugh. "Typical. Did you ever once think about how not saying anything, how running away, hurts the people who care about you? Or are you so selfish that you didn't once stop to consider—"

"I said SHUT UP!" Aden yelled. The eruption was searing, cauterizing; it made Aliza flinch.

Sammy had stopped. The stillness in the back seat was palpable. The only noise now was the low, scratchy drone of the radio. Another Led Zeppelin song. Sẹ̀yí had never been much of a Zeppelin fan, but she'd hum along anyway, always with a small, teasing smile. *I'll listen to anything. I love jazz, though.*

He stared hard at the rain-streaked window, his breath coming fast. His reflection looked as hollow as he felt, his face hovering before him like a phantom. Carefully, focusing on his breath, he exhaled, dragging himself back from the edge.

"Please," he whispered.

Aliza didn't say anything for a moment, but he could feel her gaze flicking toward him, a mirror of his own, like she was weighing whether to push further or let it drop.

"From the looks of it, though," she said at last, softer now, "I think she still loves you, too."

Aden stayed silent, gripping the edge of the seat. The road stretched out ahead, dark and endless, but her words lingered, sinking deep into his chest.

Chapter 18

During one of the last Eid dinner parties Aden could remember, at one of Mom's friends' houses, his dad had summoned him to the living room, where the adults were sitting. As soon as he walked in, he felt the uncomfortable, thorny weight of a dozen pairs of eyes, probing. Dissecting. He was only thirteen at the time, and his parents had recently thrown themselves full throttle into Coco's competition circuit. It hadn't gone unnoticed.

"Aden, beta," said Tasleem aunty, the host of their Eid dinner. Her smile was soft, but her eyes were sharp, assessing. "Your mom tells us you're doing such a good job taking care of Coco."

"I . . ." Aden glanced at his parents, who nodded for him to continue. "Yes. I try."

"Oh, but you look so tired." Tasleem aunty tilted her head, the gold bangles on her wrist jingling. "Are you sleeping enough? Are you able to keep up with school?"

"Yes . . . ?"

"You know, beta, if it gets too much, I do homeschooling for my kids. Amir's around your age. You could always join us," she added, her voice light, almost teasing. But there was something else there—a flicker of concern Aden wished he could grab and cling on to.

His parents shifted in their seats. His dad gave a subtle shake of his head. His mom smoothed the crease of her salwar.

"It's okay," Aden answered quickly. "I can keep up with my schoolwork just fine."

"Are you sure, beta?" Another aunty, Nura, piped up. "Because with all that travel—"

"I like taking care of Coco," Aden said, forcing a smile. His cheeks burned. "And when my parents get older, I'll have to be the one to take care of her anyway. So . . ."

"Exactly," his mom said, her hands slapping her thighs as if to put a period on the whole matter. "This is good for Aden. He gets to see parts of America most children his age will never see. And spend time with his family."

"Ah," Tasleem aunty said, though the word was heavy with doubt. A few of the adults exchanged looks.

"We were just worried about you, beta. But it's clear you're happy," Nura aunty added, her smile too kind, too knowing.

"Can I go now?" Aden asked his mom.

She smiled, satisfied. "Go."

Aden left the room, ignoring the hushed conversation that followed. *But you know it's important for a child to spend time with children his own age. To have a normal childhood . . .*

Part of him wanted to run back in there. Beg them to stop his parents' madness, to give him the normal childhood he so desperately craved. But he knew better than to hope for the impossible.

It was why Aden had always been good at lying. To his parents. To other adults.

Mostly, to himself.

Aden leaned against the RV's peeling vinyl upholstery, sipping his third cup of burned motel coffee. The caffeine was working, though, and he'd finally taken a good, long shower, sharpening his senses just enough to notice Sammy hunched over his tablet at the RV's wobbly dinette. His little brother's brow furrowed, a sure sign he was deep in bird-world computations.

"Anything new?" Aden asked, mostly to fill the silence.

Sammy didn't look up. "She's still heading west, toward the Utah border, but she's slowing down. Her patterns are getting shorter. I think she's getting really tired."

Aden frowned. Was that good or bad? What was going through Coco's mind?

As much as he hated to admit it, Coco wasn't some oblivious goldfish; she was smart, uncomfortably so. Annoyingly so. That was what made the whole thing harder. She'd been on the move for weeks now, surviving rain and cats and who knew what else.

But why was she still going, even now? Did she even know what she was looking for anymore?

He wasn't sure what scared him more: the idea that she didn't, or the idea that she did.

Aden stared out the window at the sunburned landscape. "Good," he said. "Although I refuse to believe Coco gets tired, ever. That bird is fueled purely by spite. At this rate, she'll see the Grand Canyon before we do."

Sammy's lips twitched, almost a smile. Almost. "I've always wanted to see it."

Across the RV, Aliza was cradling her phone like it was a holy relic. Her expression was pure caffeine: jittery, awake, slightly manic. "If Coco's slowing down," she said, "that means we're close, right? We're close."

"Sure," Aden said. "All we have to do is drive across the Rockies in a van older than all of us."

Aliza ignored him, her focus locked on the screen. Then her expression shifted—sharpened, almost. "Oh my God."

Aden raised an eyebrow. "What? Did Coco shoot you a text? Nay, a tweet?"

Aliza rolled her eyes. "You're *such* a loser, Aden. No wonder you're single."

Since their argument in the RV last night, Aden was determined to pretend it had never happened. For now, at least, Aliza seemed to comply. She turned her phone toward him, the glow of the screen casting faint shadows on her face. "For your information, a reporter from a local news station just emailed me. Apparently the Lowells told them about us. They want to do a story."

Aden blinked at the email. "Just what we need—our family dysfunction turned into a human-interest piece. *Look at the sad brown kids traveling alone through the American heartland. Is this the new Americana, or is this what the American dream has been reduced to?* So? Are they paying us in exposure or pity?"

"They think the story could help get even more people looking for Coco. We're in a pretty rural area. Word of mouth will be important. It's not the worst idea."

"You know they're going to make us look stupid, right? What's the outlet?"

"Dunno, I've never heard of this one. Kind of reminds me of BuzzFeed, though."

"So the headline will be something like 'Three Siblings, One Bird, and a Cross-Country Chase.' Cheap clickbait shit. You can't possibly be seriously considering this."

Sammy finally spoke up, turning his laptop toward Aden to show the tracking app. "Coco is slowing down, but the terrain is too open here. The app doesn't give an exact location, just a range. So even with the QuickCatch Net, we're not going to spot her here without some help. People help."

"People help," Aden repeated blankly.

He stared at the maps, at the small blinking point Sammy had marked as Coco's last known location. Somewhere out there, she was sitting in a tree, or maybe pacing along a ridge. Waiting? Resting? Deciding?

He sighed. "She's not going to stop for good until she has to."

"Exactly," Aliza said, taking it as agreement. "This interview could be what gets us to her before anything bad happens. So, are you in?"

He rubbed the bridge of his nose, feeling the weight of her gaze. "Fine. But we need to make it quick. And if they ask anything about the second-gen immigrant experience, I'm out."

It all went wrong the moment Lorraine, the journalist, opened her mouth.

The three siblings sat awkwardly in the cramped booth of a roadside diner. Aden had insisted they stop somewhere with Wi-Fi, and this turned out to be the only place for miles, its walls lined in faded photographs of cowboys and wild horses.

Aden was getting sick of diner food.

Before the interview started, Aliza had taken charge, propping her phone on an upturned sugar dispenser and testing the angle of the camera. Sammy had fidgeted next to her; he clearly regretted letting Aliza comb his hair into submission. Aden sat across from them, leaning back against the cracked vinyl seat, arms crossed, his face a mask of reluctant participation.

Then the reporter's face had popped up on the screen—a perky brunette with a glossy smile and the kind of manic brightness that suggested she'd had one too many energy drinks. "Hi, Aliza! Hi, Aden! And you must be Sammy. I'm Lorraine. Great to meet you all."

Aden couldn't help himself; something about her just rubbed him the wrong way. "Yeah," he replied. "So *great* to meet you, too, Lorraine."

Aliza shot him a warning look but quickly turned her attention back to the screen. "Thanks for having us. We *really* appreciate the opportunity to talk about Coco."

The reporter's smile faltered for a fraction of a second before bouncing back. "Of course! Your story is so inspiring. Three siblings on a mission to reunite with their family's cockatoo—it's like something out of a movie!"

Aden fake-chuckled. "You could say that again!" This earned an elbow into his ribs from Aliza.

The interview stretched on longer than Aden had expected. Lorraine asked about their route, their timeline, their interactions with locals. Aliza answered most of it, calm and composed, while Aden tried not to fidget. But the longer Lorraine pressed—asking about their parents, about the future, about what Coco really meant to them—the more Aden could feel the tension creeping in.

"One last question, and I know it's a big one: What happens when you find Coco? Do you have plans for what comes next?"

The question hung like a live wire no one wanted to touch.

This was why Aden hated journalists, especially good ones: They knew how to find someone's weakest points and jab right into them with pencils and cutting questions. He knew Lorraine was just doing her job, but God, couldn't she see this wasn't just about the bird? It wasn't that simple. Nothing was.

Aden opened his mouth to respond, to deflect, but Aliza spoke first.

"Right now, I think our focus is on finding Coco. I don't think we have the capacity to think about anything else until then," she said, steady and deliberate. "But after we do find her, we'll figure things out. Together."

Aden nodded faintly. "Right," he muttered. "We still have a lot of pressing legal matters to deal with. A lot of . . . housekeeping, including possibly rehoming Coco—"

"Well, let's not get ahead of ourselves, Aden."

Aden's eyes narrowed. "Wait, so you're changing your mind again? What—" He shook his head. "As you can see, some things are still up in the air. Either way, we just want to focus on doing what's best. For everyone."

Aliza's jaw twitched. "Assuming we can actually agree on what 'best' actually means."

"Well, best is best, regardless of whether we agree or not."

"I don't know. Feels pretty subjective to me."

Sammy shifted slightly between them, shrinking back like a cornered rabbit.

"Is it, though?"

"Of course it is," said Aliza. The smile didn't leave her face, but it was too tight, too deliberate—like the seams were showing and she was desperate to hide them. "For example, *you* might think it's best to sell the house and then ditch us for Chicago like none of this ever happened. But *I* still think it's best to keep the house so Sammy and I have *some* semblance of normalcy."

He should have seen this coming.

"Sure. But I *also* think that's bullshit because the taxes on the house aren't cheap, and I hate to break it to you, but it's not like Mom and Dad had much by way of savings." Aden leaned back in his seat. "And like I thought we both agreed, Coco's expenses aren't exactly pocket change. Sentiment doesn't pay the bills."

"I know, Aden. But some things aren't that simple. I'm not heartless like you. It's just hard to make those kinds of big important decisions, and I'm not sure how you can sit there and act like it isn't."

The words landed like a gut-punch.

God, was that how she saw him? Like all of this was somehow *easy* for him?

"That's not fair. *Someone* has to make those hard decisions," Aden said. "How many times do we have to go over this? I'm not the bad guy here."

Aliza scoffed. "That's exactly what a bad guy would say."

Lorraine glanced between them, her fingers flying across the keyboard. "It does sound like Coco has been a big part of your family's history. I'm sure you'll find the right answer for her—and for you."

Aden clenched his fist. The right answer wasn't the problem. It was getting Aliza to see it.

The silence stretched just enough to be uncomfortable.

But it was Sammy who broke it with quiet certainty. "We'll figure it all out eventually."

Aliza turned to him, her posture softening almost imperceptibly. She reached over and brushed his arm—a fleeting, instinctive gesture that might have gone unnoticed if not for the tension lingering in the room.

"Yeah. We will," she said gently.

Aden shifted in his seat, staring out the window to where the neon diner sign flickered against the encroaching dark. He didn't need to look at Aliza to know she was watching him. He could feel it: frustration layered with something harder to pin down, something that wasn't quite disappointment but wasn't far from it, either.

Lorraine's cheerful voice cut through the haze. "Thank you all so much for sharing your story. I know our viewers will be rooting for you—and for Coco!" She typed at her laptop. "I'm looking at my schedule—I should have this piece published in the next two weeks."

Aliza's jaw fell. "*Two weeks?* That's—that's way too late. Coco could be *gone* by then. We need help getting the word out now."

Lorraine's expression was only half sympathetic. "I understand. I'm sorry. I'll try my best to get it out sooner, but unfortunately, that's just the reality of my schedule. My boss is already not happy with me doing another bird piece. I already did one on the world of bird shows two years ago—that's how I met the Lowells and Gus, by the way. *Fascinating* stuff. Anyway, that's just the way things are panning out. So two weeks, give or take. I'll shoot you an email, Aliza. When it's published."

"All right." Aliza's gaze wavered. "Thanks, Lorraine."

They said their polite goodbyes. Sammy leaned forward to turn off the webcam, not sparing either of his siblings a glance. Instead, he pulled up the tracking app on his laptop screen, wordlessly checking Coco's location again.

But Aliza's heavy glare landed on Aden. "What the hell is your problem?"

"What? What'd I do?"

Her exhale was more of a hiss. "You're so *clueless*."

Aden frowned, running a hand over his face, his exhaustion settling into his bones. "Great talk. Are we done here?"

"We're never done, Aden," she shot back, sliding out of the booth. "That's the problem. You think you can just coast through anything without a thought, pretending like none of this matters. Like none of us matter."

"I know you're pissed because the piece isn't being published fast enough for you, but don't take it out on me," he said, his voice taut. "Don't go putting words in my mouth."

"I don't need to!" Aliza snapped. "You say it every time with your actions, all your unresolved *issues*! I know how you think selling the house is your way of washing your hands of all this. Erasing Mom and Dad's memory like it'll somehow fix things. And I know how you're desperate to get rid of Coco and go back to Chicago and leave us behind. *Again*."

Aden was this close to snapping. She'd pushed him, again and again—Aliza just didn't *let up*. He opened his mouth to respond, to push back, to tell her some hard truths so she would leave him alone—

But the look in her eyes stopped him.

It wasn't anger. It wasn't even just grief. It was something smaller, quieter—like she'd been bracing herself for him to prove her right.

His chest squeezed. He'd seen it before—after their parents' funeral. But he hadn't realized what it was until now.

She wasn't yelling because she wanted to fight.

She was yelling because she was scared.

"Aliza—" he said, softer this time.

But she was already turning, her steps sharp and purposeful as Sammy followed her out the door, leaving Aden alone at the table.

He stayed seated, staring at the empty screen of the laptop. Lorraine's voice still echoed faintly in his ears: *What happens when you find Coco?*

The truth was, he still didn't fully know.

Maybe he didn't want to know. Maybe Aliza was right about him. Maybe he was heartless. Maybe he was always running away, willing to leave yet another thing behind, escape yet another responsibility, abandon those who depended on him and leave them to fend for themselves.

But at the end of the day, Coco was family, too. After everything, did she deserve to be left in the past? Was that really his answer to everything: Leave and forget?

For a moment, guilt was a sharp stab in his solar plexus. But as quickly as it came, it was gone, replaced by something that froze him over, numbed him to the core.

Aliza didn't understand why he had to leave, but he'd done it to survive.

She didn't know what it had been like. Being treated more like an unpaid assistant than a son. Always expected to do the heavy lifting. Not just with Coco, but everything. Taking Aliza to doctors' appointments when they forgot. Printing out his parents' flight itineraries for Coco's competition circuits. Managing Coco's medications and supplements.

They'd counted on him like clockwork—right up until the one day he'd needed something from them.

Maybe Coco knew. If anyone knew, *she* did. After all, Aden used to sit beside her. Talk to her. Sometimes he'd even sing whatever song came to mind. Anything to make the house feel less heavy.

Of course, that was a long time ago. But *Aliza*—she'd grown up under the same roof. How had *she* not seen how their parents had treated him?

Tell her, some part of him whispered. *Tell her what happened.*

But he didn't know if he could—or if he should.

Didn't know if it would even change anything.

The Past

Little one A-liza make big river in Coco's nest. Big sad.

Where A-den? Coco no know. Coco sing for her. Still big sad. Coco big sad too. Home feel different now. Flock broken. No A-den. A-den give Coco treats. Coco get less treat now.

New little one here too. Small. Featherless. Look like A-den but no A-den. Like but he no sing back. Too small.

Coco sing for A-den. Maybe he hear.

Maybe he come home.

Chapter 19

The drive was silent except for the low rumble of the engine and the occasional rasp of Sammy's pencil against his sketch pad. Aden kept his eyes on the road, the coffee cup he'd insisted on bringing still untouched in the console. Lorraine's pointed questions still clung to him like static, sharpening the edges of Aliza's parting words.

And I know how you're desperate to go back to Chicago and leave us behind. Again.

He'd spent the past thirty minutes trying not to think about it, but the desert horizon stretched endlessly ahead, offering nothing to distract him. Occasionally, though, he'd catch a glimpse of himself in the sideview mirror and blanch. He'd need a lawn mower for the thick stubble on his face—he hadn't exactly had time to shave this past week, hadn't even thought to pack his shaving kit—and he was certain the two or three white hairs on his scalp had quadrupled while he wasn't looking.

He'd aged ten years since his parents' funeral.

And for what? It wasn't like he'd even mourned them. Not in the usual way, at least. He didn't miss them, didn't lie awake at night wondering how he'd survive without their guidance. No dramatic sobbing in the shower.

But lately it felt like the past had been creeping back in—his parents' silences, Sẹ̀yí's voice breaking on the phone, Coco's head bobbing along while he sang. Memories he'd tried so hard to bury, surfacing again and again. Like some twisted part of his brain had decided he didn't *get* to forget.

For so long, his anger had been his scaffolding—something to keep him upright when everything else caved in. But now that scaffolding was crumbling, and there was nothing underneath. Just a hollow ache that slowly devoured everything in its path.

Without his parents to fight against, without his anger to brace himself on . . . he didn't know what was left. And worst of all—what gnawed at him no matter how hard he tried to shake it—was the fear that maybe Aliza was right.

Maybe he'd spent so long running that he'd forgotten how to stay.

From the back seat, the laptop chimed, cutting through the quiet. "Whoa," Sammy said suddenly, sitting up straighter.

Aliza leaned over from the passenger seat, her arms crossed tightly over her chest. "What is it?"

Sammy tilted the screen to show her. "The thread's still getting traction. Someone just posted a picture . . . of a bird." He paused. "A cockatoo. An actual cockatoo this time. Not a pigeon or a cloud."

Aden glanced at them in the rearview mirror, his stomach tightening. "And?"

Sammy hesitated, scrolling. "It's . . . at a gas station. Near the Grand Canyon." He turned the laptop to Aliza, who snatched it from his hands for a better look.

"That's her," she breathed. "That has to be her."

Aden frowned, flicking his turn signal as if it might help him process what he'd just heard. "You're sure? I mean, it could just be some random bird—"

"I have eyes, Aden. It's definitely Coco," Aliza said sharply, her voice cutting through the rising doubt. She turned the screen to face him for a second, her expression daring him to challenge her certainty.

The photo wasn't crystal clear, but the bird perched on the man's arm was unmistakable. Her pink feathers were vivid against the backdrop of an old truck-stop sign, her eyes a sharp black that pierced through the screen.

The caption beneath the image read: "Found this gorgeous bird at our gas station! Anyone missing her? She's friendly, but we can't keep her for long."

Aden exhaled heavily, gripping the wheel tighter. "All right. So I take it we're heading there next?" Guess he was getting that family trip to the Grand Canyon after all. This wasn't exactly how he'd imagined it going, though.

"What do you think?" Aliza shot back, already typing a reply on Sammy's laptop. "We need to hurry. You got that QuickCatch Net ready, Sammy?"

Sammy nodded.

Aliza's eyes had that wild, unrelenting edge again, the same look she'd had when she'd insisted they keep searching through the night back in Ohio; she hovered over the laptop, clinging to it like it was a life raft.

"Good," she said. "This is it. We're bringing Coco home."

Aden said nothing, just pressed his foot harder on the gas.

The road to the Grand Canyon stretched endlessly, the RV rattling and groaning with every mile. Aden had long stopped lamenting, loudly, about its questionable condition, but the RV's smell of burned oil was getting harder to ignore.

Sammy sat on the floor in the back, his pencil sketching steadily as he drew the jagged cliffs visible in the distance. In the passenger seat, Aliza gripped her phone tightly, staring at the screen with an obsessive focus. She was checking the Reddit post every minute, waiting for the man at the gas station's response.

"Staring at the screen isn't going to make him magically respond," Aden said dryly.

Aliza didn't even glance at him. "Well, it's not like I have anything else to do. Anyway, pay attention to the road. I don't want us to miss any turns."

"Right, because we have *so* many turns here in the middle of fucking nowhere." Aden glanced at her. "How sure are we that this is even the right gas station? There could be fifty in the area, who knows."

Sammy looked up from his sketch pad. "There's only three. I checked. And based on the picture he posted, it has to be the Desertview Fuel."

"At least *someone* has some foresight. Good job, Sammy," said Aden.

"You're not driving fast enough," muttered Aliza.

"I'm going fifteen over the speed limit, you criminal," Aden retorted. "Chill, we'll get to Coco in time. Trust me, that guy's going to want the reward money. Just listen to music or something." He reached for the volume dial on the radio and increased it.

Aliza folded her arms across her chest. "I don't even know what this is," she muttered.

"*The Rolling Stones?* You don't know the Rolling Stones?" Aden gave her a disgusted look. "God, Mom and Dad really failed you guys in *so* many ways."

"They weren't exactly known for their great taste in music, Aden. Sorry I don't have the same music tastes as a seventy-year-old white retiree with sciatica and a Harley."

"That's not even—" Aden stopped himself with a groan. "Okay, smart-ass, what kind of music do *you* listen to?"

"Billie Eilish. Sufjan Stevens. Mitski. Searows. Phoebe Bridgers, Ethel Cain—"

"I know maybe two of those."

"Oh, trust me, it shows."

"Are you going to fight again?" asked Sammy.

"No," replied Aden at the same time that Aliza said, "Probably."

The road to the Grand Canyon stretched before them, flanked by sparse desert shrubs and a horizon that seemed to melt into the sky.

As they climbed higher in altitude, the jagged cliffs Sammy had been sketching came into view, their sharp edges cutting across the distance like a promise. The Grand Canyon itself remained just out of sight, hidden behind the plateau.

Sammy pressed his face to the window, his sketch pad forgotten in his lap. "I think we're getting closer," he said, his voice tinged with excitement.

Aliza was already out of her seat, phone in hand. "He finally replied to my message. He still has Coco; they're at the station right now. But he says she's making a racket, so we need to get there *now*."

"Well, shit. It's a miracle," Aden said, glancing at the cracked clock on the RV's dashboard. "Coco might just be sitting here with us in the next hour."

"She will," Aliza said, her voice sharp. "I'm not letting her get away again."

She stared at the map on her phone, zoomed in to the road. "Turn right up ahead."

"Right? Are you sure?" Aden squinted up ahead. The road on the right narrowed into a dirt path marked with a faded wooden sign: **SCENIC OVERLOOK—1 MILE**.

"Yes, I'm sure. It'll get us there faster."

"Is that what Google Maps says, or is that what *you're* saying?" Aden gripped the wheel tighter, the RV rattling louder with each bump.

"I know how to read a map," Aliza shot back, practically vibrating with impatience. "Just shut up and keep going."

The dirt path twisted toward the edge of a ridge, offering a dizzying glimpse of the canyon far below. The late sun burned orange against the jagged cliffs, shadows stretching like fingers across the expanse.

"Aliza," Aden said tightly, as they bumped along the narrow road, "this does not look like a shortcut."

"The road's a little rough, but I'm not taking any chances. We need to get there ASAP."

The dirt road became thinner, bumpier, and increasingly unforgiving.

"So, friendly reminder, Aliza, but this isn't *Mario Kart*," Aden said as he drove, the RV lurching over a deep pothole, sending a fresh wave of rattles through its frame. "This is real life. We could die."

The dead end came up fast—a rusted fence cutting across the road, its jagged edges sagging under its own weight. Beyond it was a rocky drop-off, the canyon looming like a warning. Aden slammed on the brakes.

ROAD CLOSED, a white sign on the fence read, hanging slightly crookedly.

"Great. End of the line," he said, throwing the RV into neutral. "Congratulations, navigator. Where's your genius plan now?"

Aliza was already unbuckling her seat belt, phone still clutched in her hand. "There has to be another way around," she said, ignoring Aden's glare as she shoved the door open.

"Mm, yes, because historically there's always convenient ways to just drive an RV across a cliff," Aden said, stepping out after her. The late-afternoon air was sharp and dry, carrying the faint metallic scent of sunbaked rock. "How'd that go for Mom and Dad?"

"That's not funny, Aden."

Sammy climbed out last, his arms wrapped around the folded QuickCatch Net protectively. "The road's too narrow and the cliff is . . . close. If we can't turn around here, how do we—"

"We'll figure it out," Aliza barked, cutting him off. But something in Sammy's expression gave her pause. She let out a strained breath. "Sorry, Sammy. It's just, this can't be it. It can't. We're so close."

Aden could feel his patience fraying. "Surprise, some shortcuts aren't actually shortcuts."

Aliza paced near the edge of the ridge, her arms crossed tightly over her chest. The canyon yawned below, indifferent to their panic. "We could walk," she said finally, turning back to Aden. "It can't be more than a couple of miles to the station."

"Walk?" Aden echoed, his tone edged with disbelief. He leaned against the RV, arms folded like a human barricade. "We're in a literal desert. I'm not going to leave all our stuff behind and hike through a desert."

"The only thing that matters is getting to Coco," she countered. "She's waiting for us. She's probably scared to death right now."

Sammy clung to his QuickCatch Net, his eyes darting between them. "Guys, I don't think we should be fighting—"

"So you want us to walk there, get Coco, and then what—walk back here, where our RV will still be stuck?" Aden let out an incredulous laugh. "You sound nuts. Do you know how nuts you sound? I know how badly you want to find her, but you need to calm down and think."

Aliza's shoulders sagged for a moment, the fight in her voice replaced by something rawer, sharper. "Do you have any idea what it's like to be left behind? To feel like you've been forgotten?"

Aden's breath caught, his easy retort dissolving into silence. Of course he knew. He knew too well. But as her words hung in the air, heavy and undeniable, something twisted in him, a flare of anger sparking where guilt should have been. She couldn't possibly mean—

"You don't get it," she added, more to herself than to him, shaking her head. "You never had to."

Before Aden could respond, the RV groaned—a low, mechanical sound like the earth shifting beneath them. Aden snapped his head around just in time to see the RV lurch forward, its bulk pitching with an unsettling jolt, like something had given way beneath it.

"What the hell—"

"The brake!" Aliza shouted, scrambling toward the door. "Aden, did you forget to put on the parking brake?"

The RV picked up speed, the loose gravel underneath it giving way. "Sorry, I got a *little* distracted, thanks to someone constantly arguing with me!" he said, chasing after her.

Aliza leaped onto the RV's step, yanking the door open. She disappeared inside just as the RV hit a particularly large rock, jolting violently. The groan of metal echoed as the popping sound of a tire rang out—a sharp, dreadful noise that caused the vehicle to tilt ominously to one side. The tires—they'd forgotten to change the rest of the tires, like Sẹ̀yí had warned.

Dust kicked up in frantic clouds around Aden as he scrambled alongside the RV, the soles of his loafers slipping on loose gravel. "Aliza!" he shouted again, his voice cracking. The road sloped downward here, and the RV was veering dangerously sideways, inching closer to the crumbling edge of the road. The open canyon yawned beside it—a terrible promise just waiting to swallow it whole. "Hit the damn brakes already!"

Inside, he heard the desperate clang of her fumbling with the controls.

"It's not stopping!" she shouted back, her voice muffled but laced with rising panic. "I think it's stuck!"

Aden reached for the handle near the driver's-side door, desperate to slow it down, but it slipped from his sweaty grasp as the RV jolted over another rock. The tilted tire ground audibly against the dirt. His heart pounded in his ears, and every nerve screamed at him to do something—anything—to stop what was about to happen.

The RV groaned again, tilting farther, and for one horrible moment, Aden thought he was about to watch it tip over entirely. He froze, hands trembling uselessly at his sides, before a voice cut through the chaos.

"Can—we—use—this?"

Aden turned to see Sammy running up behind him, out of breath, holding the QuickCatch Net like a lifeline. His face was pale, but his eyes burned, determined. The net, its poles folded tightly, glinted in the late sunlight, absurdly flimsy against the hulking mass of the RV.

"It's not a damn magic wand, Sammy!" Aden snapped, his frustration spilling over—but his hands were already reaching for it.

He unfolded the net with shaking fingers, cursing under his breath as the RV jolted again, its frame listing dangerously to one side. Dirt cascaded over the edge of the cliff—a grim preview of what would happen next if he didn't stop it.

Aden darted faster toward the rear of the RV, where the back bumper jutted out like a taunt. He braced the net against the soft, dry ground, angling it to catch against the bumper's edge. His muscles screamed as he pushed down, hoping the metal poles would hold.

For a moment it worked—the RV slowed, its frame groaning as though protesting the indignity of being stopped. Aden's breath hitched, his grip tightening.

Then came the sound he dreaded: a sharp, metallic crack. The poles buckled, the net snapping in two like a dry twig, and the RV surged forward, its momentum unchecked.

"Damn it!" Aden yelled, throwing the broken pieces aside as he stumbled backward.

His mind splintered in every direction. Aliza was in there.

Aliza, who never backed down. Aliza, who'd dragged him into this ridiculous mess. Aliza, who could die, just like their parents did, flying over the edge of a cliff.

The RV's nose tipped closer to the drop, and Aden's heart plunged further with every inch. The seconds stretched unbearably long, the roar of the engine fading into the hum of the canyon wind. His mind raced, his body locked in that awful space between action and failure.

He couldn't let it end here—not with Aliza still inside.

Aden had never been a religious man. What was the point of praying to an all-knowing being who always seemed to have their proverbial fingers in their ears whenever he'd asked for help? Sẹ̀yí had shaken her head at him when he'd told her as much.

Sometimes praying isn't just about reaching God's ears, she'd said. *Sometimes it's about hearing yourself say the thoughts you're too afraid to share with anyone else. It's the first step to understanding what you really want. Or what you're willing to fight for.*

He didn't understand how that would help anyone, least of all him. He didn't know if it could help, if anything could help. But for Aliza—for Aliza, in this moment, he'd pray.

Please, God, he thought, the sentiment strange, rough. *I'll do whatever you want. Just help me save her. Please.*

Despite the heat, the exhaustion that had long settled in his bones, he gained speed—his weak heart hammering in protest as he scrambled toward the RV door. His loafers—*his damn loafers*—squeezed his toes painfully. But eventually he grabbed the handle with both hands and slammed the door open with a force that made his shoulder jar.

"Aliza!" he shouted again, gripping the doorframe like a lifeline, his legs burning. "Get out of the RV—now!"

She didn't answer at first. Inside, he saw her hands frantically moving over the dashboard, her fingers slipping across every button she could, her face contorted in concentration.

"I can stop it." Aliza's voice was strained, almost frantic. "I can—I just need to turn the wheel more. If I can just angle the RV correctly, I—"

"Aliza!" Aden shouted, panic scraping his throat.

"Why can't you just trust me, Aden?" Aliza's eyes never left the dashboard, but her voice cracked. "I can save the RV. Why can't you ever just believe in me?"

The words struck home. *Trust. Believe.*

For years those words had felt like a joke—empty promises tossed around by people who never followed through. Like his parents, who were supposed to show up when he needed them most. Who were supposed to love him.

And every time, they'd failed.

But Aliza wasn't them. If anyone deserved his trust, it was her. She was the one who'd stayed—the one who had no choice but to pick up the pieces after he'd left.

He still didn't know exactly what she'd gone through. He hadn't asked. But he knew enough. He knew how she'd given up vet school. How she'd dealt with the bone-deep emptiness of that house. He told himself she was strong enough to handle it all. That she didn't need him.

But now—watching her fight to save the damn RV, like it was proof she could still hold everything together—he realized just how wrong he'd been.

She was strong, yes. But no one was strong enough to carry all that alone.

"I don't give a shit about the RV, you idiot!" Aden's breath came fast, the words tearing out of him. "It's you! None of this matters if you get yourself killed. We can walk to the gas station. We can walk all the way back home for all I care!"

For a moment everything stood still. The RV, the cliff, the canyon below—it all felt like it was frozen in place. Aliza's gaze flickered toward him, her lips trembling.

"Aden!" Sammy cried out. "Hurry!"

Aden didn't wait. He clambered into the RV, stepping toward his sister. "I'm not abandoning you again, Aliza. Okay? So either you get out, or we both die in the stupidest way possible." His eyes bore into hers. Scared. Pleading. *"Please."*

This time, Aliza didn't resist. Her face crumpled, and she allowed Aden to pull her out of the RV, her hands trembling in his.

Their feet skidded across loose gravel as she collapsed into his arms, her breath coming in uneven, stuttering gasps. Everything else melted away as Aden felt the warmth of her trembling frame against his, the flood of relief and leftover fear tightening in his chest like a fist.

They hadn't held each other like this in years—not since a much weaker, tinier Aliza had nearly drowned in the pool and Aden almost lost—

He didn't let the memory finish. Just held her, steadying her weight as her breathing slowed.

And then he saw it: the edge of a tattoo peeking from under her sleeve. He'd noticed it at the funeral but hadn't asked. Didn't feel like he had a right. Just another sign of how much had changed since he'd been gone.

But now, up close, the design was unmistakable: delicate wings etched in black ink, lines precise but soft—like they might lift off at any moment.

Aden nearly laughed. Wings. Of course.

He could picture Aliza standing in front of some grimy tattoo parlor, jaw set, deciding, of all things, to give herself wings.

Maybe it was because of Coco. A way of holding on to something solid, something familiar, when everything else felt like it was slipping away. Or maybe it was more than that. Maybe it was because, for years, she'd been stuck: trapped in a house with parents who forgot she existed, trapped under the weight of keeping things together.

A flightless bird, trying to fly anyway.

Because Aden had left.

And she couldn't.

His throat tightened. He wanted to ask her about it now—about all of it—but before he could find the words, the RV jolted again, metal grating against rock, the sound snapping them both to attention.

Aden whipped around, bracing for the worst—but instead of plunging over the edge, the RV stopped. Just . . . stopped.

It had snagged on a jagged rock jutting out from another pothole. The front tires sank slightly into the loose earth, tilting the RV at a precarious angle, but the groans had quieted to a low, metallic whine.

No one said a word. The only sound was the canyon wind, a hollow rush that seemed to echo the disbelief between them.

God, it seemed, had a twisted sense of humor.

Aliza wiped her forehead with the back of her hand, her cheeks flushed, her breath uneven. She looked at Aden.

"Do you think . . . do you think Mom and Dad saved us?"

Aden let out a sharp snort. "Who knows. God, Mom and Dad—at the end of the day, I think *I* saved you, thank you very much. That and a poorly maintained American road."

"Well, technically, you didn't save me," she muttered. "Since I was never in any actual danger."

"Oh, okay, in that case, how about you go back in the RV and I just push you off the edge, you ungrateful little—"

Sammy appeared beside them, hands on his knees as he tried to catch his breath. "Is it . . . stuck? Is it over?"

Aden got back to his feet.

"Looks like it," he said, glancing back at the RV. It was still tilted but blessedly still. He exhaled deeply, the tension easing slightly from his shoulders. "Aliza, send the guy at the gas station another message and tell him we're going to be late. And if he has a tow truck, tell him we'd be much, *much* obliged."

The Present

A-den home. A-den come back to nest! He come to Coco, big now, bigger than two Big Faces, but also small. Coco! Say hi, Coco! I sing but A-den no sing. Maybe A-den forget song so Coco remind. Pretty girl, pretty girl. A-den look at Coco but no see. Coco sad. A-den open door. Coco look, head tilt, feathers puff. A-den let Coco out? Why? Coco good girl, stay in nest. Coco safe.

Fly, *A-den say. Voice big, like wind in storm. But no soft. No warm. Fly? Where fly? But A-den no smile, no sing. A-den forget Coco? Pretty girl, pretty girl. But A-den turn. A-den no stay. Coco small now, smaller than smallest worm.*

Wind come in door, brush feathers. Whisper to Coco: Fly. *Fly!*

Coco look at nest. Quiet now, empty. No Big Faces. No A-den song. Just wall. Dark.

Coco step to edge. Look at sky. Sky big, bigger than nest, bigger than A-den. Coco fly. Sky big. Sky soft. Coco think maybe A-den small now because A-den forget song. Coco find Big Faces.

Make nest big again. Make nest home again.

Because that was what birds do.

Chapter 20

"Sounds like you kids have had quite a trip!" John's friendly voice rang out over the engine of his rusted red pickup truck, a beast rivaling the RV.

John was the man who'd found Coco. A serendipitous encounter and, from the looks of it, one of the most exciting things that had happened to him in years.

"You wouldn't believe it," he'd explained as soon as he'd finished hitching the RV to the back of the truck. "I was checking the old dried-up creek just outside town—it's a good spot for a smoke, don't tell the missus—and there she was, sittin' all puffed up on a rock, lookin' like she'd seen the end of days."

Aliza's face softened with concern. "Is she okay?"

"I'm no bird expert, I'll tell ya. But I think she's fine, other than some missing feathers. Just tired. Real tired," John had reassured her. "She let me pick her right up. Took her back to the garage. Now, I didn't have any cage on me or anything, but she went right to sleep on my old coatrack." He chuckled, patting the steering wheel as everyone piled into the truck.

Aden, squished in the passenger seat, leaned back, trying to get comfortable. The seat belt cut into his chest, and he shifted, trying to ignore the faint smell of gasoline and leather. "Well, we're grateful, John."

"Of course! Your bird's got some spirit. Reminds me of my old hound, Tank. Lost him, too, when I was about your age," John said, gesturing toward Sammy, who looked up from his notebook, intrigued.

The truck bumped along the road, its tires crunching over loose gravel. Outside, the desert stretched wide and golden, broken only by the jagged edges of distant cliffs.

"How'd you find him?"

"Well, it was a whole song and dance. Tank wandered off one summer, middle of a heat wave. Didn't have much hope findin' him, but the whole town came together to help. Folks I barely knew started pitchin' in—making flyers, posting 'em up everywhere. This old man who owns the general store, Rob Dorsey—he spent half the summer combing through roads with a flashlight, lookin' for Tank. Didn't even ask him to. Mrs. Hendricks kept sendin' me cookies. To cheer me up, she said."

John had a wistful smile pulling at the corners of his mouth. "Ended up marrying her daughter."

"That's . . . kind of incredible," said Aliza. "So did you—did you find Tank?"

The truck rumbled on in silence for a moment. John's grip on the wheel tightened, his knuckles going white. "Not the way I would've liked to find him," he said finally.

Aliza sank back into her seat, her face falling. The weight of John's words filled the cab, thick and heavy, like the desert heat pressing against the windows.

Aden stared out at the endless expanse of sand and shrub, his jaw clenched. All those people helping, only for Tank to end up dead. Sometimes that was just the way things went.

But he couldn't stop imagining the eerie similarities to Coco's story. Sammy's and Aliza's phones were constantly buzzing with possible sightings of Coco, with unsolicited emails from experts and "experts," advising them on how best to lure a cockatoo, with texts from the Lowells, desperate for updates. What if they found her and she wasn't perched on some guy's coatrack? What if her familiar pink body was limp on the floor, lifeless?

A-den!

He could see Aliza's face crumpling, Sammy's silence turning into something deeper. Darker. It would destroy them. And as much as he didn't want to admit it, it'd mess with him, too.

The gas station came into view, a squat building crouched at the edge of the road, its neon sign buzzing faintly against the twilight. Aliza straightened in her seat, her hands gripping the door handle.

"There it is," John said, his voice brightening. "She'll be right there in my office, I'm sure of it. Let's get your girl home."

John's office was inside a small garage connected to the gas station, a homey place that smelled like motor oil and old leather—far more quaint than the auto shop where Aden had bought the RV. John led them to the back, to a dusty coatrack near the door, its branches bare except for an oil-stained rag and a battered trucker hat.

There was no sign of Coco.

"Where—" John's confident stride faltered as he looked around. "She was right here." He spun in place, his eyes scanning every corner, as if expecting Coco to materialize on command. "I—I swear, she was right here!"

Aden glanced at Aliza. She was already scouring every corner of the garage, looking behind tires and mobile storage cabinets, her face tight with frantic focus. Sammy had already pulled out his phone, fingers swiping across the screen.

"I'm checking," he murmured. "She couldn't have gone far."

John began pacing, running his hands through his thinning hair. "I didn't think she'd go anywhere! Poor thing was so tuckered out. I—I didn't have a cage or anything, and I figured—hell, I don't know what I figured! I'm so sorry, kids. I thought I was helping, truly."

Aden crouched near the coatrack, his eyes scanning the floor. Something metallic caught the light, nestled among a scattering of white fluff. His stomach dropped. Slowly, he picked it up—a small, familiar cuff, its latch snapped clean off. Coco's ID band.

And with it, their only way of tracking her.

"Dammit," he whispered under his breath.

"What?" Aliza's head snapped up.

Aden held out the ID band, its broken hinge dangling in his fingers. "Her band. It's off."

The color drained from Aliza's face. Sammy froze mid-swipe, his phone hanging limply in his hand.

"Shit," she whispered. "Shit!"

John stopped pacing, his eyes darting between the silver band and their faces. "I—I didn't realize she had that thing on her. I promise, I didn't touch it. I just—oh, hell, I'm sorry, kids. This is all on me."

Aden pocketed the ID band. "It's okay."

Aliza's fist met a metal toolbox, rattling its contents.

"It's not okay!" she snapped at John. "You couldn't have just, I don't know, kept her in a room? Or watched her? You left her all by herself! And now we can't even rush out to chase her because our RV's tires are completely blown, and—"

"Aliza," Aden cut in, firm. "Come on, I know you're upset, but it's not John's fault."

"I know!" She cupped her face in her hands, taking ragged breaths. "I know. But *why*? Why does this keep happening? Every time we almost have her, she flies off again, and at this rate, we're *never* going to get her back." Her breath hitched. "I'm sick of it! I'm so fucking sick of it!"

"So what, you want to give up? Go home?"

"Of course not!" she choked out. "That's the problem! I don't want to give up. I *can't*—"

"Then there's your answer." Aden sighed. "We just have to suck it up and keep looking. Figure out some other way to find her. Right?"

Aliza's lip quivered, and for a second Aden thought she might argue. What he was suggesting—it was an impossible thing. There was no other way to find Coco. They both knew it.

But then her shoulders sagged. She swallowed hard.

"I'm sorry, John. You didn't deserve that."

"It's all right, darlin'," John said, his voice as warm as the oil-scented air around them. "I'll go get your tires fixed up right now, all right? We'll get you three on your way."

Aden dug through his pocket for his wallet, bracing himself. "How much is that going to be?"

But John waved his hands. "Not a dime. It's the least I could do for losing your bird again."

"John, that's not—"

"There's some chairs out under the awning. You kids sit tight," he answered, already jogging off toward the RV, boots echoing on the concrete floor.

When the three of them were alone again, Aden glanced at Aliza.

"You good?" he asked.

"No." She turned away. "But I don't have a choice, do I?"

"We do what we have to." Aden walked out to the garage entrance. "Speaking of which, come on. I need a nap."

But Aliza didn't follow. Instead, she lingered near the coatrack, staring at the floor like Coco might just magically reappear if she stood there long enough.

Aden sighed and turned back. "Aliza . . ."

"I just don't get it, Aden," she said quietly. "How does this keep happening?"

"What else can you expect? She's a bird," he offered flatly. "Birds fly."

"Yeah," Aliza said with a bitter laugh. "Birds fly."

She rubbed her arm absently, fingers tracing her sleeve like she was trying to soothe something beneath it.

It was where her tattoo was, Aden realized.

He hesitated. "Your tattoo . . ."

Aliza blinked, caught off guard. "Oh. Yeah."

"You got that after I left, right?"

"I did. Why?"

"I just . . ." He trailed off. "I was curious, I guess. What it meant."

Aliza shrugged. "It's not some deep metaphor, if that's what you're thinking."

"So why wings?"

For a moment, she looked like she might brush off the question. Then, almost reluctantly, she pushed her sleeve up, revealing the dark outline.

"I told myself it was about freedom," she said. "Or resilience. Or whatever the hell you're supposed to say when you get a tattoo after a mental breakdown."

"Yeah?"

"Yeah." She flexed her arm like she was showing it off, but her smile faltered. "But honestly . . . I don't know. I think I just wanted something permanent. Something that couldn't leave."

The words lingered, heavy between them.

Aden licked his dry lips. Slipped his hands in his pockets.

"I mean . . . it's a cool tattoo," he said weakly.

"It's stupid," Aliza muttered. "Honestly, I got it because my therapist stopped taking insurance."

That startled a laugh out of him. "Yeah, well," he said, smiling faintly, "could be worse. A lot of people do far worse things."

"True." Her face sobered. "You know, though, sometimes I look at it and I don't think about freedom at all."

Aden frowned. "Then what do you think about?"

She hesitated. Met his eyes.

"I think about you," she said. "How much I missed you. After you left."

Her voice was so quiet, Aden almost didn't catch it. For a moment he thought maybe he'd imagined it—that his brain was just filling in the silence with something he wished she'd say.

But no. She was looking at him, her face drawn tight, hand still absently tracing the tattoo on her arm.

She'd missed him? After everything he'd done?

"Me?"

"Well, yeah," she muttered. "You know, when I think back to when things were—you know, like, actually kind of normal? You were always there. Even when Mom and Dad were being impossible, or Coco was screeching her head off . . . you were there. And I just . . ."

She took a shaky breath. "It felt like you cared about us more than anyone else did. I just wished you knew that."

Aden's chest felt tight—like someone had cinched a belt around his heart and kept pulling.

All this time, he'd been drowning in his own bitterness. And she—she'd been quietly, desperately trying to keep everything together. Holding the family. Holding him. Even if it was just ink on her skin.

Her eyes flicked away, like she regretted saying it the second the words left her mouth. She rubbed her arm again, fingers skimming over the tattoo like she was trying to smooth out a wrinkle.

"Anyway," she said briskly, too quick, "you still need that nap, right?"

"Aliza—" Aden started, but she was already turning away, walking toward the garage entrance.

"Come on, old fart," she said over her shoulder. "I'll wake you if John finishes early."

And just like that, the door swung shut behind her, leaving Aden alone in the quiet garage.

He exhaled slowly, running a hand down his face.

I just wished you knew that.

The words kept stubbornly looping in his head—like one of Coco's little songs she'd sing over and over again.

He just wished he'd heard it sooner.

About an hour later, when the late-afternoon sun had begun casting long shadows across the concrete, John emerged from deep within the garage, his boots scuffing against the cracked floor. He wiped his hands on a rag.

"She's all set, kids. I added a little air to the spare, too, just in case."

Aliza, leaning against the RV, straightened. Her earlier frustration had softened into something closer to gratitude. "Thank you, John. For everything."

"Seriously," Aden added, his voice sincere as he stuffed his hands in his pockets. "We owe you."

John gave a crooked smile, the kind of expression that seemed both hopeful and resigned. "Y'all be careful now, all right? Be vigilant. I wish I'd seen that tracker on her. Could've saved y'all a heap of trouble." He glanced at the cuff in Aden's hand, now dangling by its broken hinge. "Shame it's busted. She's a clever bird, though—I know you'll find her."

Aliza bit her lip and nodded, her hands clasped tightly in front of her. Sammy offered John a small, shy wave before climbing into the RV.

The vehicle rumbled to life, the tires humming against the asphalt as they pulled out of the station. Aden gave a final wave to John through the driver's-side window. In the rearview mirror, the squat gas station and its neon sign grew smaller, swallowed by the wide expanse of the highway.

They were back on the road, I-70 stretching endlessly westward, the horizon shimmering with heat.

But the earlier excitement that had filled the RV was gone, snuffed out like a candle, replaced instead by the occasional creak of the RV and the question they dared not speak aloud: *What now?*

Sammy, perched on the edge of the passenger seat, stared at the screen with all the intensity of a hedge fund manager on a drug-fueled bender. His fingers tapped relentlessly, his gaze locked on the tiny red dot that represented Coco—or, rather, *had* represented her. Now the red dot remained frozen in one spot, a cruel reminder of what they'd lost.

Aliza, too, looked no better. She sat curled into the corner of the bench seat, her arms wrapped around her knees, staring blankly out the window. She looked both so young and so *drained*, her earlier spark dulled by disappointment after disappointment. But still she clutched the photo he'd given her, the one of her and Coco.

Aden exhaled sharply, turning his attention back to the road. Sometimes Aliza reminded him too much of himself. Hadn't he been like this once? Eyes too wide for his years, carrying a weight no one had prepared him for, facing disappointment after disappointment until it wore him down. He knew all too well how the constant dashing of every hope could drain a person's soul until there was nothing left.

It was no wonder he was the way he was.

Aden reached for the radio, twisting the knob with the idle idea of cutting through the dejection. Static crackled, followed by snippets of distorted voices and fading melodies. Then, a familiar riff broke through the noise, sharp and unmistakable.

A grin tugged at the corner of his mouth. He cranked the volume.

From the back, Aliza lifted her head, frowning. "What's this? More old-man rock?"

"Led Zeppelin," Sammy said without looking up, his tone almost clinical. "It's that band you mentioned before, right, Aden?"

Aden chuckled, pleased. "Yeah. 'Immigrant Song.' What, you recognize it now?"

Sammy shrugged, a faint smirk creeping onto his face. "I guess so."

"Good man."

"Huh," Aliza muttered, her head bobbing slightly to the beat. "The guitar riff's kinda . . . catchy, I guess."

"Do you not have ears?" Aden replied, indignant. He turned it up louder; the relentless wail of Robert Plant's vocals filled the RV, the steady thrum of drums reverberating through the walls.

Aden mouthed the lines—about a stormy voyage, oars sweeping forward, the wild call of the west—then howled the chorus scream: *"Ah-ahhhh, ah!"*

"God, you're such a loser!" Aliza yelled over the music.

Sammy giggled, almost shyly, before throwing his head back. *"Ah-ahhhh, ah!"*

"Yes, Sammy! My man!"

Aliza's lips twitched upward. "What is *wrong* with you guys?"

"Come on, you've never done karaoke?" Aden shot back, pounding the steering wheel like a drum.

"I have, but not—" She gestured toward him, snorting. "Not like *that*."

"It's fun," said Sammy, his smile wide.

But when the chorus came around again, Aden glanced in the rearview mirror and caught her mouthing the words, almost absentmindedly.

"Mm-hmm, I see you," he said, smirking.

"Shut up."

The song played on, their voices overlapping in something that was more noise than music: obnoxious and tuneless and all over the place. Alive. When it finally ended, Aden reached for the dial, fingers lingering as static crackled softly through the speakers. He thought about finding another track but let it be.

No one spoke. The RV rattled faintly on the asphalt. The silence wasn't the uneasy kind that begged to be filled. It unfolded between them like the road ahead—unbroken, steady, holding them together in its quietness.

Aden glanced in the rearview mirror. Aliza had her chin propped on her hand, gazing out the window, her expression somewhere far away, but peaceful. And Sammy was slouched in his seat, struggling to keep his eyes open, like he was finally letting the exhaustion hit.

Watching them, Aden felt something unfamiliar stir in his chest.

He didn't reach for the radio again. For once, the silence here felt . . . enough.

Chapter 21

The reply from Aden's boss at Farley, Richard Albert—who was a walking asshole—came swiftly:

> I'm sorry for your loss, Aden, but I need you back here Monday.

Aden stared at his phone screen. Unfortunately for him, he could imagine his boss's face clearly—too clearly: his peppered hair, the tight set of his jaw, the permanently scrunched-up expression. His ridiculously expensive tie, so cinched around his neck it was a miracle his head didn't pop right off like a cork.

Aden sighed and raked his hand through his hair. It was Thursday evening; that left less than three days to pull off the impossible. Finding Coco by tomorrow would barely give him enough time to drive back, let alone catch a last-minute flight to Chicago. Even if he did manage it, he'd still need to convince Abigail Harper to accept a Zoom call for the estate meeting. He could already hear her clipped voice insisting that these matters were best handled "in person."

But none of that mattered if they couldn't find Coco.

If this were Sweden or some other sane country that wasn't a total capitalist hellscape, he might've gotten at least two full weeks to grieve. Not that he *needed* two weeks, but still. It was the principle of it all. Was asking for a sliver of humanity really so outrageous?

His eyes drifted to the small pile of Coco-related gear they'd amassed on the counter: an empty bag of almonds, the pitiful remains of the QuickCatch Net, and a couple of half-crushed energy drinks that Aliza had sworn would *keep them sharp*.

And, of course, the latest addition to the pile: Coco's broken silver ID band, their only means of tracking her.

How the hell were they supposed to catch her now?

Aden set his phone down and tried to get comfortable on the driver's seat, which he'd put as far back as he could to create a makeshift bed. He'd parked the RV in a rest stop in the corner tip of New Mexico, and even though Sammy had politely asked whether it were possible to make a stop to Roswell, they simply had no time to spare, especially when they had to take sleep and bathroom breaks into account. They'd have to rely on random sightings of Coco, who, as far as they knew, had seemed determined to keep heading west—at least before she'd lost her band.

Now the soft snores from the back confirmed that Sammy had fallen asleep on the pullout bed, his laptop and sketchbook abandoned at his side. The night was quiet, except for the distant rasp of crickets and the occasional rumble of a passing truck.

Aden closed his eyes, willing his brain to shut off. But it wasn't the stress of work, or the phantom sounds of Coco's relentless shrieking keeping him up this time. From the back, on the beat-up couch, Aliza's muffled giggles pierced the stillness.

"What's so funny?" Aden whispered, turning his head toward her. Considering their current circumstances, he wasn't sure he could find anything funny right now.

"Nothing," replied Aliza, not looking up from her screen. "Just talking to Sẹ̀yí."

"Sẹ̀yí?" Aden sat up, his voice sharper than he meant. "Why the hell do you have Sẹ̀yí's number?"

"She gave it to me." Aliza smirked. "Before she left. Said I should keep in touch."

Aden blinked. Suddenly, his throat felt dry. "And what—what are you guys talking about?"

"Nothing much. Although . . ." Aliza bit her lip, clearly savoring his discomfort, the sicko. "She did say something funny. What was it? Oh yeah: *Sometimes it feels like Aden and his brain are fighting, but Aden is winning.*"

"She did not say that," snapped Aden, although unfortunately it sounded 100 percent like something Sẹ̀yí would say.

"Oh, but she *did*," said Aliza, barely choking back her laughter. "She's hilarious. I like her."

"You're not allowed to like her." *She's mine*, Aden wanted to add, but he bit it back.

"Don't worry," Aliza replied, settling deeper into the couch, "we got bored of talking about you. She's telling me about her best friend, the one who's worked with veterinarians in Botswana. I didn't realize you'd meant Sẹ̀yí when you'd brought it up before."

"Yeah. Her best friend from law school is an environmental lawyer." So Aliza must have told Sẹ̀yí about her interest in being a veterinarian. Did that mean that she was still thinking about it? That there was still hope?

Aden hesitated. "Hey, do you—do you still want to go to vet school?"

Aliza's smirk faded.

She glanced up, then back down at her phone. "I don't know. Maybe. It's just, given the circumstances right now, I don't know how it'd be possible. I have to think about Sammy." Her brow furrowed. "I don't want to leave him all alone."

"Yes, but it's your life, too. And you already got into vet school, right? Sammy's not a baby."

Aliza's eyes narrowed. "Wait, how did you know I got into vet school?"

Oops.

"Sammy told me," he answered sheepishly.

"Sammy . . ." Aliza sighed. "Sammy is only thirteen, Aden. And he's been having a rough time at school. It's just the two of us now. He still needs someone to look out for him. I can't just ditch him like—"

She stopped herself. But the look on her face said it anyway:

Like you did.

Still, though. Self-sacrifice and nobility didn't put food on the table, didn't mean shit if you ruined your entire life for someone. If Aliza threw away vet school like this, for good, the bitterness could eat her alive.

"What about when he's a little older, then?" asked Aden, gentler. "People go back to school all the time. You'll still be young."

Aliza let out a soft laugh, but it wasn't her usual sarcastic one. "Yeah, sure. Like that's so easy."

Aden studied her face in the faint glow of moonlight seeping through the RV windows. The shadows carved deep hollows beneath her eyes—angry, purple bruises that spoke of sleepless nights, evidence of a world that had busied itself by socking her right in the face lately. Her short hair stuck out in every direction, a wild, chaotic nest that could be home to a bird on cocaine. Above her eyebrow, the faint glint of an old, dulled scar caught his eye—a silvery remnant from the time she was eleven and decked a neighborhood boy named Justin for trying to stomp on a frog. Aliza was never one to let injustice slide, the nosy idiot. Even if it meant coming back with scars.

"For you," Aden said, "it could be."

He didn't mean it like a compliment. To him, it was just a fact.

Aliza said nothing, just sat there drifting in the undulations of silence. Aden worried if he'd said something wrong—he wasn't in the mood for another argument, was too tired to fight.

But then she looked up at him again. "Did your boss respond?"

"Huh?" Aden reeled from the sudden change in subject. "Oh, yeah. He said I had to be back by Monday. Otherwise I'll probably get in big trouble. Maybe fired."

"Evil corporate overlords, huh?"

"Yep."

"So we really need to hurry and find Coco, then."

Aden nodded slowly. "Yeah."

"When we do, what if . . ." Aliza hesitated. "What if you stayed?"

"Stayed? You mean in New Hope?" Aden shook his head. "That'd be a lot. I'd have to quit my job. Sell my place in Chicago, move back here. Where would I live?"

When Aliza didn't respond, it dawned on him.

"Oh. You mean . . . with you guys?"

"No, I just—" Aliza crossed her arms. "It was just a thought. A stupid thought. It's just, Sammy clearly likes you. A lot. We could stay in the old house. You, me, Sammy, Coco."

Aden stared at her, his stomach sinking like a stone. "The old house? Aliza, I . . ." He trailed off, searching for words that wouldn't hurt her. But there weren't any.

"I'm really sorry," he said softly. "I can't."

"Can't or won't?" Aliza's voice was quiet, but her eyes held him steady.

"Both." He looked away, running a hand through his hair. "It's not just a house to me. Ever since we moved from San Francisco, *that* house, it's . . . it's everything bad that ever happened to me. Every fight with Mom, every time Dad looked at me like I wasn't good enough. The way they treated me like I only mattered when I was being useful to them. And every time I came home, hoping something had changed, only to realize nothing ever would. It's all still there, Aliza. Even with them gone."

"I know, Aden." Aliza's expression was stiff, voice hardening. "I know better than anyone how messed up our parents were. But the fact is, they *are* gone, and you're going to need to get over everything they did to you someday. You can't let it keep controlling you."

"No, you *don't* know," said Aden sharply. "You think you do, but the truth is, I took the brunt of it for years. Shielded you from it. That's why they left you alone."

"Exactly. They left me alone. *Completely* alone." Aliza's voice broke, but she pressed on, like she'd been waiting to say this for a long time. "And then you left, and I had to keep the family from completely falling apart. Mom and Dad became total husks after you left. Like they'd given up. Even Coco—" She sucked in a breath and set down her phone like it was too heavy to hold. "Do you know Coco can only say one name?"

"What does that—"

"*Yours*, Aden. Your name is the only one she ever says."

Aden froze.

"How do you think she felt when you disappeared? How *I* felt?"

His throat tightened.

He'd been her older brother—the one who was supposed to stay. The one who was supposed to make sure she could always keep her head above water.

And he'd left her to drown.

"I'm sorry, Aliza," he said softly. "Trust me, if there was another option, I'd have taken it."

Aliza's arms dropped to her sides, her exhaustion cutting through the anger.

"I'm not asking you to relive the past," she said. "I'm just asking for you to stay this time. For me. For Sammy."

"And what if I screw it up?" Aden asked, his chest splitting open, the words spilling out before he could stop them. "I don't know how to be the big brother you want me to be. I could barely help myself. I nearly—"

He cut himself off. He didn't want to go there.

"Aden . . ." Aliza's voice softened. "What really happened? What aren't you telling me?"

For a second Aden almost laughed. What was there to tell? He'd spent so long burying it—trying not to think about it—that digging it up now felt impossible.

But the pressure inside him shifted, cracked.

He raised his head slowly, feeling something inside him tighten and fray all at once.

"I almost gave up," he said.

Aliza's eyes widened. "What do you mean?"

"Senior year of college. Midterms. I was in a bad place," he began, his words tumbling out unevenly. "I couldn't sleep—had to get a prescription for it. But everything just kept . . . piling up. The higher my GPA, the lower I felt. None of it mattered. Mom and Dad didn't care. To them, good grades just meant I could be more useful. They didn't call unless they needed something: Coco had a competition, or something at home needed fixing." He swallowed hard. "They didn't ask how I was. They didn't care."

His voice thinned, the next words cutting like glass. "So it all added up. I started thinking about ending it. Falling, dying—how peaceful it would be. And then I just . . . stopped feeling anything at all."

Aliza stared at him, her expression frozen with something between fear and helplessness. "Aden, are you saying you—"

"I even called them, you know? Told them I needed help. And you know what our parents said?" His laugh came out sharp, a scrape against the air. "They told me to stop being dramatic and ungrateful. And then they told me I needed to come home that weekend to help around the house."

Aden felt the heat in his throat rise, tears threatening. He fought them back. "That night, I took a bunch of sleeping pills. If my roommate hadn't found me in time, I wouldn't be here. The school put me on psych watch, but the only reason I graduated was because Mom and Dad swooped in and told everyone it was a mistake. That I didn't *mean it.*"

He clenched his jaw. "And now they're gone, and I never got to tell them how much they hurt me. How much . . ."

He trailed off. Aliza didn't say anything, her pale face streaked with tears. She mirrored him in silence, her trembling breath the only response.

"I don't want to go back," Aden said finally. His throat ached with the weight of the admission. "I don't think I'm ready. I don't know if I'll ever be ready."

Aliza stood there, silent. Then, with trembling fingers, she wiped her cheeks with the heel of her hand. "God, I-I'm so sorry, Aden. I didn't know. Fuck. I remember Mom being really upset after some phone call the two of you had, but I had no idea—"

Aden let out a short, hollow laugh, dragging a hand over his face. "Yeah, well. I didn't exactly make it easy to find out. Not really something you drop into casual conversation."

Her lips twitched into a faint, watery smile, but her gaze stayed steady. "But I should have known. You know? I should have . . ." She shook her head. "I'm *so* sorry."

Aden turned away, staring through the windshield into the dark. "It's fine. I'm fine. Really." The words hung brittle and thin in the air. "I just can't go back to that house. That's all I'm saying."

For a long moment Aliza stayed quiet, her gaze lowering to her hands. Finally, she nodded, almost imperceptibly. "Okay," she whispered. "I get it. I understand."

The words felt heavy, not like understanding but like surrender. Aden pressed his lips together, pretending not to notice, and looked out at the stars.

"I just wish you'd called me. Even once."

"I know. I'm sorry."

"Mom and Dad . . . they really spiraled after you left," Aliza added softly. "They didn't know how to do anything without you. Dad kept forgetting to pay the bills, kept arguing that it'd been your job to remind him. Mom couldn't even handle the grocery shopping—she kept forgetting things, and I'd have to go back and get them myself. And then they'd get mad at Sammy for not stepping up fast enough, like he was some backup version of you. They tried to make him trim Coco's nails, prune her feathers, take her to competitions. It's another reason I didn't go to vet school. I had to make sure they didn't ruin his life, too."

Aden knew she wasn't telling him this to make him feel guilty, but still. Knowing what they'd gone through after he left didn't leave him feeling all sunshine and flowers.

Aliza exhaled, her voice thick. "But I had no idea *that's* why you'd left. They acted like you'd left for no reason, like you didn't care about us. That one day you'd come crawling back."

"I'm not surprised," he muttered.

"They needed something to blame," she said, her voice quieter now. "And I guess it was easier to focus on you—or Coco—than admit how broken everything already was." She shook her head. "It was always about her, you know? Even when they fought about you, somehow it would turn into a debate about her, I don't know, *feathers* or her next competition. Meanwhile, Sammy and I were just . . . there, picking up the pieces." She looked up at him tiredly. "But it made me feel bad for Coco, too. I don't think she was happy, either. With their obsession with her."

Aden blinked, the words landing somewhere deep, in a place he didn't know was still raw.

They didn't love Coco, either.

He hadn't thought of it that way before. His whole life, she'd been untouchable. The center of their parents' world. He'd resented her for it, for stealing the attention he was starving for.

But now, as Aliza's words settled in, so did reality: It wasn't love. It was pressure. Coco wasn't their favorite child; she was their pet project. Their desperate attempt to control something, anything, as the rest of their lives unraveled.

He pictured Coco in her cage, always pacing, always preening. Not out of vanity, but out of compulsion. Not because she wanted to, but because she had to. Because that was expected of her, wasn't it? To perform. To win. Be perfect.

Maybe she'd been a casualty, too. Maybe that was why, despite everything, he'd slipped her extra mango slices with Aliza when their parents weren't looking. Why he'd gently stop her from stress-plucking her feathers during competition season. Why sometimes he'd sing to her under his breath when the house was quiet.

Maybe, deep down, he'd always known.

Aliza's voice dropped lower, almost to herself. "Sell the house if you need to. Sammy and I—we'll figure it out."

Aden swallowed, his throat dry. "You won't be completely alone," he said awkwardly, his words halting. "I'll help with the . . . you know, the transition. I meant what I said. I won't abandon you."

Aliza's lips curved into a small, sad smile. "But you'll be in Chicago."

"I'll be in Chicago."

"Right . . ." She nodded again, her gaze dropping to the edges of her sleeves. "I guess that's better than the alternative. It means you'll be closer to Sẹ̀yí at least, right?"

"A lot of good that's done me."

"I really like her," said Aliza. "I think she'd be good for you."

"I just don't know if *I'm* good for *her*."

"You could be."

This time, Aden smiled. "Thanks," he said, and he meant it.

"Gross." Aliza stretched out her arms. "I'm going to bed."

"Sure. Good night, 'Liza."

"Good night, loser."

As she put away her phone, curling up beneath the blanket on the couch, Aden gave her one last look in the rearview mirror.

For a moment, in the corner of the mirror, he could have sworn he saw the faint shift of movement from the pullout bed where Sammy was supposed to be sleeping.

Chapter 22

Aden sat outside the RV, watching the morning light spill over the desert horizon. The landscape stretched in every direction; red rock bluffs and saguaro cacti silhouetted against the pale pinks and golds of dawn. It was the kind of view that made people fall in love with the desert, though Aden mostly found it unsettling. The sheer emptiness of it all. Like the world had been picked clean and left out to dry.

The highway carved a stark line through the dust and scrub, the asphalt still slick and shimmering faintly from the overnight rain. Aden had been awake long enough to watch the stars disappear, the black sky softening into a bruised shade of purple before melting into the first streaks of gold. He told himself he stayed outside because he liked the quiet, but the truth was, he didn't want to go back in. The air inside the RV felt heavy, cluttered with things unsaid.

The coffee didn't help. He nursed the Styrofoam cup like it was a lifeline, even though the vending-machine brew tasted like someone threw depression in a blender and hit "Purée." But it was something to hold, something warm against his hands.

Aliza's words kept coming back to him, uninvited. *You'll be in Chicago.*

Not "if" or "when." Just "will."

The way she'd said it made his chest ache, like she'd already made peace with the inevitability of his absence. Like it wasn't worth fighting over.

He hated that she'd read him so easily. But maybe that's who he'd always been—the one who left. The one who'd go back to Chicago. Back to his dead-end job, to pining over Sẹ̀yí and the childhood he'd lost. As if nothing had changed.

Had anything changed?

Aden stared up at the sky. He wondered whether God was laughing up there.

A sudden gust of wind kicked up, scattering fine sand across the RV's windshield. He flinched, blinking against the grit in the air, and didn't hear the door open until Aliza stepped out, rubbing her arms against the morning chill.

"Couldn't sleep?" she croaked, voice still scratchy from disuse.

He shook his head, taking a long sip from the Styrofoam cup. "You?"

"Barely," she admitted, leaning against the RV. Her gaze lingered on the horizon, scanning the empty road. "Sammy's still out cold, though. He must be exhausted."

Aden smiled faintly. "He's still a growing kid. Sleep is his job."

"I know. But it's weird. Normally, he's up before me."

"Maybe he woke up in the middle of the night," Aden said. He hesitated, then added, "I thought I heard him moving around."

Aliza frowned, her brows knitting together in a way that immediately put him on edge. "You think . . ." Her voice faltered. "You think he heard us talking?"

Aden didn't answer right away. The thought planted itself in his mind, as unsettling as ants crawling across his skin. "I—maybe?" he said finally, his tone carefully neutral.

She exhaled sharply, already turning toward the door. "I'm checking."

Aliza stepped back into the RV, Aden close behind, bracing himself. It was dark, the curtains still drawn over the windows. There was a long lump still in the pullout bed—convincing enough to look like a person. Like Sammy.

Aliza reached for the blanket, her fingers trembling slightly. She drew it back in one swift motion, and her breath caught.

Sammy was gone, replaced by some strategically placed pillows.

Aliza swore under her breath. "Sammy!"

Aden darted around the RV, half hoping Sammy would pop out from some corner, grinning sheepishly, saying it was all a joke. But Sammy's laptop wasn't on the little makeshift desk where he'd spent hours drawing, and his backpack, which had practically fused to his side over the course of this trip, was gone.

"Shit," said Aden, his pulse stuttering. Worst-case scenarios barged into his brain. "Where could he have gone?"

Aliza scrambled for her phone, her movements sharp, frantic. "I'll call him."

Aden's foot hit something hard under the table. He stilled, his stomach tightening, then crouched down to look.

There it was: the familiar black cover, worn at the edges from constant handling. Sammy's sketchbook.

He picked it up gingerly and turned it over in his hands. It felt heavier than he expected—though that was probably just the weight of dread settling in his chest.

"Sammy?" Aliza's voice cracked as she pressed the phone to her ear. Then, more insistently: "Where are you?"

Aden stood, sketchbook in hand. "Put him on speaker."

A moment later Sammy's soft, determined voice filled the RV. "I'm fine," he said. "I'm on a train. Someone said they saw Coco in California. I'm going to get her."

Aden's stomach took a nosedive. "Sammy, I thought we agreed that doing something like this is a stupid idea," he said, massaging his brow, hard—as if he could milk the frustration out of his skull. "Does *no one* in this family have any sense of responsibility?"

Aliza opened her mouth to protest at the thinly veiled insult, but thought better of it.

"I know." Sammy's voice on the other line was resolute. "But I can do this. I just . . . I want to help for once."

Aden's grip tightened around the sketchbook, and Aliza glanced at him, more worried than he'd ever seen her. It was impossible to imagine exactly what the kid was thinking—Sammy was always so damn quiet, so reserved with his feelings, only to drop some incredible insight out of nowhere, something that left them both scrambling to catch up. Maybe that was why Sammy was always observing—

It clicked. Aden turned to Aliza.

"He overheard us last night."

Aliza's face paled as she remembered: The way they'd talked about Sammy—about shielding him from their parents, about how she'd had to sacrifice vet school to protect him.

The guilt they'd handed him without meaning to, wrapped in a neat little bow.

"Shit," Aliza muttered. She spoke up louder this time. "Sammy, what train are you on? What's your next stop? Stay put—we'll come get you."

"I told you, I've got this. Please, just let me do this."

"Sammy, you don't have to help. You don't have to do *anything*," said Aden, frustrated. "You're thirteen, for God's sake. The only thing you need to do is be a kid."

"I know. But I want to." Sammy paused; there was a muffled voice on the other end—the sound of a conductor, maybe. "I gotta go. I'll text you later. Sorry."

"Sammy, wait—" Aliza began, but Sammy hung up.

The RV seemed to tilt under Aden's feet. It wasn't, of course. It was just his brain short-circuiting.

"What now?" Aliza asked, fists clenching.

"You don't happen to have him on Find My Friends or anything, do you? Something that would make life easier for once?"

"Even if we did," she said, "he'd turn it off."

"Right. Of course. Nothing's ever easy with this family." Aden raked his fingers through his hair. Was he still shedding? He didn't want to think about it. He made a mental note: When Sammy was older, he'd make him chip in for a hair transplant in Türkiye. It was only fair.

"We'll just have to head to California, too," he said grimly. "*Where* in California is a whole other question."

Aliza nodded, but she looked unconvinced. "So that's it, then—Coco's still headed west?"

"Apparently." Aden pulled out his phone, swiping through a half dozen tabs. Wasn't *heading west* a euphemism for dying?

No. Another thing not to think about.

He found a map of Amtrak routes and squinted at it. "Closest station is Salt Lake Central—chances are, Sammy probably left from there. We can check schedules, track him that way."

"But what if he gets another tip that Coco's headed somewhere else? Sammy might get off the train to chase after her, and then it'd be impossible to tell where he is." Aliza frowned. "I think we're going to need help. Maybe from the Lowells? Or Sẹ̀yí?"

"You really think the Lowells can track Sammy any better than us?"

"I mean, they have birder friends. They know bird tracking. Same skill set, kind of."

"I don't think it works like that."

Aliza shrugged. "So, Sẹ̀yí, then? Maybe she can take a flight. Catch up with Sammy before we can."

Aden hesitated. His first instinct was to tell her it was a terrible idea, and his second was to admit that yes, Sẹ̀yí would be helpful, as always, and would come up with some clever way to find Sammy—or, at the very least, do whatever she could to try. Which would mean relying on her yet again.

Neither option made him feel particularly good.

"You need to learn when to ask for help," said Aliza, not unkindly.

"I'm sorry, did you get a PhD in psychology when I wasn't looking?"

"I'm serious. Call her."

"I can't just call her for another favor! I don't want to be some douche that takes advantage."

"If you don't call her, *I* will," Aliza said. "Our baby brother is *missing*, Aden! What if he gets lost? What if someone tries to kidnap him, like a, like a—"

"A serial killer?" Aliza threw him a glare, and Aden sighed. "Okay, okay. I'll do it."

He quickly shot Sẹ̀yí a sheepish text—Are you free to talk for a second?—and she called back within minutes.

Aden blinked, briefly distracted by the lush sweetness of her voice on the other line, before refocusing. He summarized the situation as quickly and succinctly as possible, and Sẹ̀yí, bless her, was as calm as always—a rock in a storm.

"Assuming he took a train west from Salt Lake Central," Sẹ̀yí said, "it looks like the last stop is in . . . San Francisco. I could take a flight there, try to intercept him at the station if he makes it there?"

San Francisco. The words hung in the air for a beat too long, like the ring of a tolling bell. Aden's chest tightened, a sharp, reflexive squeeze. Was that really where Sammy was headed, where someone had last spotted Coco? But that was absurd.

Then again, that was the last place his parents had been. It was where they died. Could that mean Coco—

"Aden?"

He shook off the thought, swallowing hard. He was being ridiculous.

"Hey, sorry," Aden said finally, his voice a little hoarse. "That would be amazing, if it's not too much trouble."

On the other line, Aden heard a voice in the distance—Sẹ̀yí's dad. *Who are you talking to, omo mi?*

"No one, Baba," Sẹ̀yí answered before lowering her voice. "Something like this is never too much trouble, Aden. I just hope Sammy's safe. I'll text you once I book my flight, but I'll head out there as soon as I can."

"Thanks, Sẹ̀yí," he said softly, and hung up.

He stared at the phone for a moment, a hundred formless thoughts ricocheting across his brain in the world's worst game of *Pong*.

"So, San Francisco," he muttered.

But no—how was that even possible? Birds weren't that smart, were they? Was Coco really heading back there?

"Aden, come look at this," said Aliza suddenly, her voice pulling him back to the present.

Aden sighed and walked over, trying to shake off the heaviness of the conversation with Sẹ̀yí. He looked down at the sketchbook as she flipped through the pages. The sketches were familiar—places they'd been: the tiny Bird Enthusiasts of Appalachia building, a charming, green-roofed hut; and the hideous hulk of the RV from the outside, parked on a dusty roadside by a gas station. There were those sketches Sammy had posted on Reddit, too—like the one of Coco on the tree in Michaux State Forest. Graceful, even in a drawing.

Aden slowly flipped through the pages, taking them all in.

Then he reached the last one.

It was a drawing of him from behind, his hands on the RV's steering wheel, loose and relaxed. Aliza was beside him in the passenger seat, her head tilted back, laughing.

It wasn't perfect—the angles were a little off, and Aliza's hair looked like it belonged to someone in a cheesy shampoo commercial. Not to mention the back of his head was slightly too big—or, at least, he was pretty sure it was. But none of that mattered.

Sammy had captured Aliza's laughter. Her true laugh. The one that made her nose wrinkle just a little, like she was surprised by her own joy. It wasn't something Aden saw often. And it wasn't something he'd appreciated in the moment—not while the RV groaned under the weight of their journey, not while the miles stretched endlessly behind and in front of them.

But here it was, frozen on the page. A perfect, tiny snapshot.

Aden stared at it, his throat tight.

Aliza shifted beside him, wearing a proud smile. "He's really good, huh."

Aden nodded, then asked in a whisper, "Why did he draw this?"

"Sneaky little kid." Her face softened. "I wonder if—if he wanted to remember. Us, together."

Aden swallowed hard, his gaze fixed on the drawing.

Mom and Dad had rarely taken any photos of them growing up—he certainly had never seen one of him and Aliza together. Seeing one now, though . . .

It felt surreal. Painful, almost. Like rediscovering something you hadn't even known you'd lost. It was a version of themselves he hadn't known they'd ever been.

And yet, here it was, sketched out like proof that it existed, if only for a moment.

"Sammy's so quiet all the time," Aliza added softly. "But he . . . sees things. Things we miss."

"Yeah. I'm starting to get that."

The silence lingered between them, but it wasn't heavy. It felt like the pause between one chapter and the next.

A breath before the leap.

Aliza carefully closed the sketchbook, smoothing her hand over the cover before setting it aside. "We're going to find him," she said, her voice steadier now. "And Coco, even if it means giving her over to the Lowells. We have to."

Aden thought of Sammy's quiet focus, the way his little brother had clung to his sketches like they were maps leading somewhere only he could see. He thought of Coco's impossible flight west, the sheer distance they'd all traveled—literally, figuratively, despite everything stacked against them.

And then, unbidden, Marcy's words floated back to him, soft but insistent: *The moment you give up the search, it's over—so the important thing is, no matter what, you keep going, too.*

He'd rolled his eyes when she'd said it, brushing it off as fluffy, fortune cookie crap—the kind of nonsense platitude that would be at home on a poster of a sunset over water, hanging in some beige office waiting room. Or worse, it was the kind of saccharine consolation offered to someone about to make the kind of mistake they couldn't walk back from, a sticky, cloying Werther's caramel meant to tempt someone back from the edge: *Please, dear, life* is *actually worth living—see? Here's a candy.*

But maybe, sometimes, that was all anyone could offer: a caramel, a platitude, a placeholder for the hope they didn't quite know how else to give. Something small and inelegant, maybe even absurd—but something, nonetheless.

And maybe Marcy was right—maybe moving forward was all you could do. Put one foot in front of the other, even if you weren't sure where it was leading. Just keep going, stubbornly, stupidly, until the thread you were following took shape, until the road made sense.

"Yeah," Aden replied finally, resolute, his eyes meeting Aliza's.

"We will."

The Return (Home)

City screams in many colors. So many faces, small-small, rushing and big-smell, big screech, no trees, no sky, no home. Coco tired.

No Big Faces. Should be here. Coco click beak—soft, like whisper. Where? Where? But Coco remembers. Big Faces laughing, food in hands. A-den, too, and small ones. Warm, so warm. Not warm now, though. Coco shivers. Hungry. Wrong air, taste like metal.

Wind whispers strange, cold song: Alone, alone, alone.

Coco does not answer. Coco does not understand.

Chapter 23

Driving into San Francisco felt like crawling, purposefully, into the maws of a great, silver-toothed beast.

Emphasis on the *crawling*.

The traffic was horrendous, borderline criminal. It was the kind of congestion that made you reconsider every life choice that had led you to that particular freeway. If this was what people on the West Coast dealt with on the daily, Aden was practically grateful for Chicago. And that was saying something, considering Chicago's traffic could make grown adults cry.

From the back seat, Aden heard a loud sigh.

"Are we there yet?" said Aliza, only half serious, but with enough edge to hint that she was teetering toward a full-on meltdown.

Aden gestured at the windshield, at the endless sea of brake lights winking at them. "What do you think?"

She groaned in response and slumped back against the seat. Her phone buzzed again—just one of many interruptions in what had become a steady stream of texts, emails, and calls from strangers claiming to have seen Coco.

The article about their wild cross-country drive had gone live that morning. Apparently, Lorraine had pulled some strings and fast-tracked it, despite what she'd originally said. While, in theory, the attention was supposed to help, so far it had only unleashed a tidal wave of spam and dubious claims—ranging anywhere from *Is this your bird?* with an attached photo of a pink shirt caught on a powerline to PESKY BELLY FAT? BURN IT OFF WITH OPTI-SLIM.

Every time a new notification popped up, Aden could feel Aliza's patience fray a little more. And with Sammy having gone radio silent since their last phone call nearly twelve hours ago, her stress levels had officially reached DEFCON 1.

"Social media was a mistake," Aliza muttered, tossing her phone onto the seat beside her.

"To be fair, you're the one who said that article would help us find Coco."

"Yeah, well, but that was before Sammy ran off on his own, too."

Aden snorted. "Come on, it's practically a family trait."

"Ugh."

His eyes flicked to his phone resting on the passenger seat. The screen lit up, and for half a second he thought it might be Sammy. His heart jerked in that split second of hope—a cruel little jolt—only for the notification to be about a mundane work email.

Friday. He should've been in the office right now, preparing for a client pitch or sitting through another soul-sapping meeting. Instead, he was stuck in crawling traffic outside San Francisco, chasing a brother he should've never let out of his sight.

And Ṣẹ̀yí—Ṣẹ̀yí had dropped everything. Boarded a plane. Soon she'd be scouring the city for Sammy. She texted when she'd landed at San Francisco Airport. Cut her vacation short just for this.

He owed her, more than he could ever say.

The thought sat heavy in his chest, pressing against the parts of himself he'd tried to ignore. It wasn't exactly just gratitude—it was too big for that, too unwieldy.

It felt more like guilt, gnawing at him in silence.

Ṣẹ̀yí had her own life now. Her own family. Maybe she'd started dating someone new—someone more dependable than he'd ever been.

And yet, here she was. Helping him. Helping his family. The way, he supposed, real family would.

But that was Sẹ̀yí: the kind of person who remembered birthdays and left handwritten notes on his fridge. The kind of person who cried when he'd filled her bath with rose petals and lavender-scented bubbles to surprise her after her exams. As if he'd given her the world.

She'd always deserved better. He'd known it then, and he knew it now.

But maybe, when everything finally settled down—

No. Not "maybe."

By some miracle, she had come back into his life. Dropped everything, despite everything. And it made no sense. He'd given her every reason to walk away, especially after the way he'd pushed her out.

He could still remember that night. Her face had twisted, like she was trying to swallow glass. She'd lingered at the door while he sat on the couch, boring holes into the floor with dead eyes. Waited for him to stop her.

He never did.

What a shithead.

Aden took a shaky breath and ran a hand down his face.

But if Sẹ̀yí still believed in him—after all the pushing, the silence, all the ways he'd made himself impossible to love—then maybe he could try believing in himself, too. Enough to stop running. To be someone worth showing up for.

For her. For Sammy. For Aliza.

Hell, even for himself.

"Sammy!"

They spotted him standing beside Sẹ̀yí outside Emeryville Station, a seventeen-minute drive from San Francisco. He looked so small with his backpack slung over his shoulders, his face pale under the harsh station lights.

Aliza didn't hesitate. She ran to him, wrapping him in a hug so tight that he stumbled a little. "God, don't ever scare us like that again!" she said, voice trembling. "Are you okay? Why didn't you answer any of our calls?"

"I forgot my phone charger in the RV," he mumbled into her shoulder.

"Ugh, *Sammy.*" She loosened her grip just enough for him to breathe, but her hands stayed firmly on his shoulders, as if letting go would mean risking losing him again. "You took off ten years of my life!"

Aden stood a few feet back, hands shoved into his pockets. He was trying to process the flood of relief and anger swirling inside him—anger that Sammy had done something so reckless, but mostly anger at himself for not seeing it coming. He glanced at Sẹ̀yí, who stood calmly by Sammy's side. She caught his eye and gave him a small, knowing smile.

"I caught him trying to get on a bus to the city," she said. "He's a sneaky one."

"Thank you," Aden said. "For—for everything."

"Hey, I didn't do it for you," said Sẹ̀yí lightly. "I did it for Sammy."

Aliza looked over at them, her brow furrowed, but there was a flicker of something else in her expression—was that a smirk? Aden quickly reached out and mussed Sammy's hair, eager to change the subject.

"What about Coco?" he asked. "Any update from the person who spotted her?"

Sammy nodded weakly, his face falling. "They tried to catch her, but she flew off again. She really doesn't look good, Aden."

Of course she didn't. The bird had traveled across the entire country to get here. It was a miracle she was even still alive. And yet, hearing it from Sammy hit differently—because if Sammy was seeing it, if Sammy was willing to admit it, it had to have been bad.

Coco.

"All we can do is wait for more sightings," Aden said gently, even though the words felt hollow.

Sammy didn't respond. He just looked down, kicking a loose pebble on the ground. Aden reached out and squeezed his shoulder—an awkward gesture, but it was all he could manage.

Sẹ̀yí cleared her throat. "Do you need anything else from me? I have a flight tomorrow morning."

"Oh." Aden fidgeted with his collar. "Do you, uh—do you want to grab some food or something? With us?"

Aliza perked up immediately. "Yes, please. I need caffeine, and I'm not leaving Sammy alone for a *second*."

"Maybe a few seconds, because I need to pee," Sammy said.

Sẹ̀yí chuckled. "Sure."

As they headed toward the car, Sammy walked in the middle, flanked protectively by his siblings. Aden watched the way Aliza kept a hand on Sammy's backpack, like she thought he might bolt again. How Sẹ̀yí walked beside them, perfectly in step, her trench coat billowing gracefully behind her.

For a moment, Aden let himself wonder what they'd do if Coco didn't make it. If this whole journey ended with nothing to show for it except exhaustion and frayed nerves. If they just let her go and went back home without her.

But then Sammy looked up at him—really looked at him, with something between trust and guilt—and Aden pushed the thought away.

The café was a patchwork of mismatched furniture and chipped tile floors, like it had been put together with whatever scraps the city had left to spare. Aden stared at the flickering neon sign outside the window—**OPEN 24/7**—its hum barely audible over the low din of voices and clinking mugs. Across the room, a barista wiped the counter with slow, practiced indifference, her earbuds firmly in place.

Aden cupped his hands around his coffee mug, feeling its fading warmth seep into his palms. Across from him, Aliza twirled her straw in a circle, watching the ice melt into her soda, while Sẹ̀yí sipped from her mug of green tea. Reunited with his sketchbook again, Sammy was drawing, the sound of pencil on paper just audible enough to remind them all he was there.

"She must be so terrified," Sammy said, his voice soft, like he wasn't sure he should be speaking at all.

Aden glanced up. "Coco?"

Sammy nodded.

Aliza sighed. "Of course she would be. Everything she ever knew had been turned upside down. She probably hadn't been able to truly rest, and she's been out there for so long . . ." She trailed off, staring at the condensation on her glass.

"Yeah, but she's tough," Aden said. "She survived living with our parents."

Aliza snorted, a small, reluctant sound that almost resembled a laugh. "True."

The conversation lapsed again, settling into the kind of silence that wasn't entirely uncomfortable but wasn't exactly easy, either.

Sammy set his pencil down, his brow furrowed. "When I was on the train," he said, "I kept thinking about that time she almost flew out the window. Remember?"

Aliza blinked. "Wait, how come—God, that was ages ago. I barely remember. Sammy, you must have been, like, three or four."

Aden glanced at Sẹ̀yí. "Jesus. I must have just been about to graduate college."

"Maybe. I don't remember all the details. But you were cleaning her cage, I think, and Mom left the window open. Coco went right to the ledge. And you were freaking out because you hadn't clipped her wings in a while." Sammy smiled faintly. "Mom was *so* mad."

Aliza rolled her eyes. "Like it was Aden's fault," she muttered.

"But Coco didn't leave," Sammy continued, almost like he hadn't heard her. "You were so surprised. You thought she'd just fly away. But then she turned around. Like she was saying, 'Fine, I'll stay.'"

Aden frowned, his hands wrapping around his mug. "I don't remember that."

"But it happened," Sammy said. His voice softened, his pencil tracing aimless circles on the paper. "She trusted you. Even when you thought she wouldn't."

"Ugh," Aden muttered, just as Aliza said, "Aww."

Sammy ignored them, his gaze dropping to his sketch. He traced the lines of Coco's feathers, his voice quieter now. "That's why I thought maybe I could do it, you know? Find her by myself. Like, if I called her, maybe she'd listen to me, too."

Aliza's face fell, her brows knitting together. "Sammy—"

"I wanted to help for once, okay?" Sammy said quickly, cutting her off. "Like, do something instead of just . . . messing stuff up all the time."

Aden stared at him for a second, trying to find the right thing to say. "You don't mess stuff up."

Sammy shrugged, his shoulders hunched. "You're just saying that because I'm your little brother."

Aliza opened her mouth, but Aden awkwardly raised a hand, stopping her. "No, seriously—this isn't, like, just me being your older brother. I mean, yeah, I *am* your older brother, but I'm not saying it *because* of that. I'm saying it because it's *true*, okay? You don't need to prove shit to anyone. Least of all us."

Sammy looked unconvinced, his pencil pausing mid-sketch.

Aden shifted in his seat, running a hand through his hair. "Look, I know being so young sucks because you always feel like everyone's making decisions without you. But if you feel guilty because of the choices Aliza has made . . ." He shook his head. "I mean, look at her. Do you think she regrets her decisions for even a second? Even the really, really, really bad ones?"

"Aden!"

Sammy hesitated, finally looking up from his sketch pad. His voice was barely audible. "But I—I feel like I held you back," he said, his eyes darting to Aliza's.

Aliza's expression softened, and she reached for his hand across the table. "Never. You've *never* once held me back. And if I had to make the choice again, I'd still make the same one. Some things are more important than vet school." She took a quiet breath. "Some things are more important than anything."

"I know what it feels like, to think you're a burden," Aden added. "It probably doesn't help that we're a lot older than you. But that's just your brain lying to you. Got it? Next time, tell it off."

Sammy gave a small nod, his eyes drifting back to his sketch pad.

Sẹ̀yí, who had been quietly sipping her tea, glanced at Sammy's drawing, her mouth tugged into a small smile. "You're really good at drawing birds," she said, nodding toward the sketch.

Sammy blinked, startled, and muttered shyly, "Thanks."

"She's important to you," Sẹ̀yí continued, her voice thoughtful now. "To all of you. That's clear. It makes me wonder . . ." She paused, setting her mug down with a soft clink.

"What?" Aden asked, his brow furrowing.

"Coco," she said. "The way you've all described her. She doesn't seem like she'd just . . . fly off randomly. If she had the chance before, but she didn't, then maybe something changed."

Aliza blinked. "What are you saying?"

"I don't know. What if this whole thing isn't just about fear or instinct? What if it's not random?" Sẹ̀yí said, her tone thoughtful now. "You said your parents . . . died here, right?"

Aliza and Sammy nodded silently, their expressions cautious.

"So maybe Coco came here out of a sense of longing," Sẹ̀yí said. "Maybe she's searching for them—for closure."

For a moment no one said anything. To be fair, that was mostly because Aliza and Sammy were deep in thought, reflecting on Sẹ̀yí's words, while Aden was distracted by the way Sẹ̀yí's hands—her long, elegant fingers—wrapped around her mug.

Aden realized he was staring and shifted uncomfortably in his chair. "Yeah, but she's a bird," he said finally, breaking the quiet.

"True." Sẹ̀yí smiled faintly at him, and his stomach did a little flip.

"But birds migrate, Aden," Aliza suddenly spoke up. "They follow migration paths to spots passed down through generations. And even animals feel things like loss. You'd be surprised by what they remember."

Sammy tapped his sketchbook with his pencil. "So you think she's . . . looking for Mom and Dad? Is she trying to find the hotel where she last saw them?"

"I don't know," Sẹ̀yí said gently. "This is all just speculation. I'm not an animal behavioralist or biologist. But maybe she's just looking for the feeling of them. Of better times. Of home."

Home.

There was something about the word that made Aden's brain snag on it, the sound of it reverberating in his chest.

"Either way," whispered Sammy, "we need to find her soon. The picture that person sent me on Reddit—it was scary. She looked really sick. I almost didn't recognize her."

Aden felt his stomach twist. Coco was already in bad shape the last time he'd seen her—he didn't want to imagine how she looked now.

Suddenly, Aliza reached into her bag. "That reminds me," she said, her voice softening as she pulled out the photo Aden had given her weeks ago. The edges were slightly worn now, as though she'd looked at it often.

She smoothed it flat against the table and pushed it toward Sammy. "I meant to show you this earlier. Look at Coco," she added, a faint smile tugging at her lips. "She was only, what, seven or eight here?"

Sammy traced a finger along the edge. "Oh, whoa. You were so small." He glanced at Aliza. "Where was this?"

"In New Hope," said Aliza, but then faltered. "At least, I think."

Aden looked at the photo. "No. That wasn't in New Hope." His paused. "This was in San Francisco."

Aliza frowned.

"But—that doesn't make any sense. I thought we'd moved to New Hope as soon as I was born," she said. "That's what Mom told me."

Aden let out a laugh. "Of course she did. But you were around three. I—I *remember*."

Memories unfurled easily now: their little blue house with the overgrown rosebushes, Coco's first flight in the backyard. Laughter. Tire swings in a nearby park. Birthday cake.

A time before their parents quit their jobs, hoping that this would give their life the shake-up they craved. But when that didn't work, they did what scared people always did when they had no other options: clung to a shiny distraction. In their case, a bird named Coco Chanel.

Aden doubted they'd named her with any kind of symbolism in mind. But sometimes he wondered if, on some level, they'd chosen the name for what it promised: Coco Chanel, the designer who could take an ordinary woman, an ordinary life, and make it beautiful.

Maybe that's what their Coco was meant to be. A symbol of the life they wanted, not the one they had.

But the point was, they'd been good once. Normal. In San Francisco, before the fear took hold. Before it warped them.

Just as it had warped him.

But he wouldn't let it anymore.

Aden stood suddenly, the chair scraping against the floor.

"I know where she's going," he announced. "We're going to need help to get her, though."

Chapter 24

It all began almost twenty-three years ago, when Aden, Aliza, and his parents moved from San Francisco—from a little blue house with pink roses—to New Hope, Pennsylvania. And not long after that, his mom, a systems analyst, and his dad, a programmer, decided to leave their cushy tech jobs to instead dive full-time into the care and training of Coco, their Major Mitchell's cockatoo.

A blue house with pink roses. The first home Coco had ever truly known. Which meant that all they had to do now was find it.

Easier said than done in a big city like San Francisco.

So the next day, the four of them—Aden, Aliza, Sèyí, and Sammy—awoke bright and early, prepared to spend the next twenty-four hours in a blur of dead ends and wrong turns.

But first, Aden made a call.

It was an awkward, stilted conversation—with Reema khala as blunt as ever—but when he explained the situation, her tone softened.

"I can't give you an exact address," she'd said, "but if I recall—I believe your old house was near the Mission somewhere. When you all first moved there, your mom told me how she liked the houses—small, but charming. Storybook, almost." He could almost hear her faint smile on the other line. "But yes, I do remember the roses. Pink. Like Coco, your mom said."

His mom had said that? The memory stirred—her voice, unusually soft, pointing out those roses on a walk home. He hadn't thought much of it at the time—he'd been practically a toddler—but it was one of those rare, fleeting moments when she'd seemed almost . . . sweet.

"Thanks, Reema khala. That helps."

It wasn't much, of course. But it was more than they'd had before.

Now, armed with Reema khala's tip, Aliza squinted at her phone, using Google Maps to cross-reference areas around the Mission District with the vague fragments Aden could remember. Sammy had his sketchbook open on his lap, scribbling furiously.

"And are you sure the roses were pink?" Aliza asked, not for the first time, her voice tinged with exhaustion.

"Yes," Aden replied, staring out the window. "Pink roses *everywhere*, like an infestation."

"Roses don't *infest*, Aden. Unless they're a multiflora rose."

"They do in my memories," Aden said dryly, but the edge in his tone softened when Sammy nudged him.

He'd sketched a rough outline of the house: two small windows flanking a bright-red door, roses climbing the trellis. A white picket fence. Something out of an American dream, the kind immigrants conjured up while filling out hundreds of immigration forms until they were met with the concrete, highway-filled reality.

"Maybe we could show this picture to people," Sammy suggested shyly.

Aden hesitated. The idea of knocking on strangers' doors with a drawing of their childhood home felt ridiculous, but it was better than the aimless circling they'd been doing all morning.

"This is great, Sammy," he said.

Sketch in hand, they began enlisting the help of strangers. A barista with a silver nose ring at a tiny corner café took one look at Sammy's sketch and said, "Oh, that's *definitely* the Mission. Could be somewhere near Potrero. Lots of cute little houses like that there."

As they stepped out of the RV in the Mission, an older woman walking her dog pointed them toward an overgrown lot where a blue house might have stood once, though no roses bloomed there now.

"The city's changed so much," she said, shaking her head. "But good luck to you. It sounds like a special place."

Somehow the small moments of kindness—people leaning out of windows to direct them, a man at the hardware store pulling out old city maps for them to examine—kept them going. Sẹ̀yí had changed her flight after Aden, nervous but trying, asked her to stay—with only a small, pointed cough from Aliza to nudge him along.

Even Aliza's normally sharp wit softened into something hopeful as they canvassed together. "This is the weirdest freaking scavenger hunt in the universe," she said as they drove through yet another neighborhood. "And instead of treasure, we win a traumatized bird."

Aden raised a brow, amused. "Yeah, and who wants that?"

"I do, actually. Very much."

"Sicko."

Aliza elbowed him while Sẹ̀yí laughed.

Eventually, they turned in to a neighborhood, and Aden was hit with a strange sense of déjà vu. He slowed the RV to a crawl.

"Aden?" asked Sẹ̀yí, noticing the look in his eyes.

"This feels . . . familiar," he said quietly, almost to himself. He pulled over abruptly and stepped out in a trance, barely aware of Aliza and Sammy calling after him.

He wandered deeper into the neighborhood—and knew, instinctively, to turn left into a cul-de-sac. Here, the brightly painted bungalows stood close together, divided by white picket fences. The closer he got, the more a strange, magnetic pull seemed to guide him. It wasn't just the house, or his eagerness and desperation to find it. It was something older. Something instinctual.

The air smelled faintly of salt and damp earth, and something in the slant of the afternoon light struck a chord so deep he couldn't explain it.

He walked slowly, his eyes scanning the rows of houses, until he saw it.

Half hidden behind an overgrown fence was a small, weathered blue house. A different shade of blue than he'd remembered, but perhaps they'd given it a new coat of paint. The rosebushes, too, were huge, wild, spilling through white trellis and fence like they'd been growing unchecked for decades.

"That's it," he said, his voice thick.

Aliza was at his side, breathing hard. "Are you sure?"

Aden nodded.

The house radiated a strange familiarity, like a hazy dream slipping just out of reach. His first day of school—he could almost see himself leaving through that same front door as the bus pulled up. Mom waiting in the doorway, Coco perched on her shoulder. *Bye, Aden! Bye, A-den!* Sitting on the couch while Mom and Dad explained that he and Coco would have a new baby sister soon.

He remembered the night they brought Aliza home from the hospital. He'd been left behind with someone—Reema khala, maybe. Aliza had been so tiny, swaddled in blankets. There'd been a bright-red stain between her brows. Dad had called it a stork bite, and Aden had laughed. Years later, when Ṣẹ̀yí showed him a photo of her best friend, Olive's, newborn, he'd pointed out the stork bite, too. Ṣẹ̀yí had given him a curious look, the kind that always made him feel like he'd said more than he'd meant to.

Such normal memories. They'd been a normal family once. In this house.

Ṣẹ̀yí and Sammy came up behind them. "Should we knock?" asked Ṣẹ̀yí. "Ask if anyone's seen her?"

"Y-yeah." Aden suddenly felt anxious, to the point the spicy burn of the breakfast tacos threatened to crawl up his throat.

But he stepped up to the door and took a deep breath. His knocking echoed through the quiet street. There was a long pause.

"Maybe no one's home," Aliza said, rocking back on her heels.

Just as Aden was about to agree, the door creaked open.

A man appeared, mid-thirties, with sandy-colored hair that stuck out at odd angles, glasses perched slightly askew, and a warm, if slightly frazzled, expression. He looked like the kind of man named Peter or

Todd—someone who probably danced awkwardly at weddings but always made sure you had a slice of cake. At least, Aden hoped.

The man blinked at them, clearly surprised to find a small group standing on his porch. Before Aden could figure out how to explain, Aliza barreled ahead.

"Have you seen a really big pink bird?" she asked, holding her hands apart to demonstrate Coco's size. "Cockatoo, about this big. She's loud. Goes by the name Coco."

The man frowned, confused. "A . . . cockatoo?"

Aden sighed and stepped in. "Hi, sorry. We used to live here when we were kids," he explained, his voice measured. "Our bird flew away a little while ago. We think she might have come back here."

Recognition flickered in the man's eyes, and his expression softened. "Wow. That's . . . I mean, that's kind of amazing. But I haven't seen anything like that. I'm really sorry."

"Well, is there any way you can keep an eye out? I'll give you my number," said Aliza, already fishing for her phone from her pocket. "It would mean a lot to us."

The man smiled weakly. "I'll do what I can, but we're leaving on vacation in a couple days, so that might be difficult. I'll let the neighbors know, though. Is that all right?"

"That would be great," said Aden. "Anything you could do."

"Of course. Good luck. I hope you find her."

Aden was about to thank the man and turn back to the RV when a little voice cut through the conversation.

"Daddy!"

A girl—maybe six or seven—came bounding into view. She wore a striped shirt, her brown hair in two messy pigtails and a pair of binoculars slung around her neck. She reminded Aden of Aliza when she was around that age.

"There's a *huge* bird in the apricot tree!" she said.

Aden and Aliza exchanged a glance.

"Wait. Can we please come—" Aliza started, her voice barely contained.

The man hesitated, his protective instinct visible. But then he sighed.

"All right, yeah. Come on. Please take your shoes off, though—we've got a no-shoe policy here."

They obliged and followed him and the girl, Nora, through the house. It was small but cozy, filled with mismatched furniture and the scent of coffee lingering in the air. A half-finished puzzle sprawled across the dining table, and Aden noticed a crayon drawing taped to the fridge: a lopsided bird labeled *Passenger Pigeon* in bright letters.

As they stepped into the backyard, Aden felt something tighten in his chest. The yard was compact but lush, bursting with flowering and fruit trees, their branches heavy with apricots and plums. And roses—so many roses.

"This is my bird-watching station!" Nora announced proudly, pointing to a small plastic chair beside a birdbath. A pair of tattered field guides lay open on the ground, and a makeshift feeder dangled from the apricot tree.

"She's been hyperfixated on birds ever since she had a school project," the man explained, gesturing to the binoculars around Nora's neck. "Good timing, though, huh?" He smiled, but Aden barely heard him.

His eyes locked on a flash of pink in the branches above.

"Coco?" Aliza called out for her tentatively.

When they got no response, Aden squinted and moved closer.

But there she was, an unmistakable pop of pink against the dark wood of the apricot branches:

Coco.

Except Sammy was right: She looked worse for wear. The bird shuffled on her branch, feathers sticking out at odd angles, her whole frame drooping like she was barely clinging to life.

"She's beautiful," Nora whispered, clutching her binoculars.

Aliza nodded and whispered, "She is."

"I'll get a ladder," the man offered, already turning toward the house.

"Wait!" Aden called after him, his voice sharper than he intended.

The man half froze, confusion etched on his face.

Aliza looked at him, worried. "What's wrong?"

Aden hesitated, glancing between Coco and the man. "The ladder could scare her."

"Shit. You're right." Aliza's jaw tensed. "We can't let that happen. If we don't catch her now—we can't *afford* to have her fly off again."

"She looks really tired, though," Sammy murmured, his quiet voice cutting through the tension.

Aden nodded, swallowing. Coco didn't look like she had another flight in her. Her wings drooped, her talons flexing against the branch as though even standing up there was becoming too much.

But she wasn't coming down, either. Too scared. Too disoriented.

"What do we do?" Aliza asked, her voice cracking, her desperation bleeding through. "God, if only we had that stupid QuickCatch Net. Should I run back and get some of the fancy birdseed? You think that would entice her enough?"

"Would she even notice it from up there?" asked Sammy.

"Maybe talking to her would work," Sẹ̀yí offered gently, her gaze flicking between them and the bird. "Calmly. Let her know she's safe."

"It's a start." Aliza took a tentative step forward, her hands trembling at her sides. "Coco," she called softly, her voice lilting awkwardly, like she was trying to be coaxing and confident at the same time. "Coco-baby, come down. We're here. We'll take you home."

"Coco, it's okay," Sammy added, his soft voice like a warm breeze. "You're safe now."

Even Nora pitched in, her tiny voice barely above a whisper. "Come on, pretty birdy."

Coco did not move. Instead, she stared off into the distance, her focus elsewhere.

"She's not listening," Aliza muttered, her shoulders sagging. She looked at Aden, her expression crumbling into something like defeat. "It's like she doesn't even recognize us anymore."

For a moment the three of them stood frozen, the silence broken only by the rustle of leaves and the soft hum of bees around the roses. Then Aliza's head snapped up, her eyes wide with an idea. "Wait. What about Mom?"

"What?" Aden asked flatly.

"Her voice," Aliza said, breathless. "Mom's voice. Coco always heard her, right? Even if she didn't like it, maybe on some level, she'd still remember. Isn't that why Coco's here? Because she's looking for something familiar?"

Aden opened his mouth to argue—Coco barely listened to anyone, let alone obeyed—but stopped himself. The look on Aliza's face was desperate, pleading.

"I'm afraid that ship has sailed as of ten days ago," he said instead, gently.

"No, but we have her voicemails!" Aliza said, ignoring him as she scrolled furiously through her phone. "Hang on. I saved some of them." Her fingers trembled so badly she nearly dropped the device.

Aden watched her, silent. He hadn't saved any of their mother's messages. Not one. He'd deleted them all years ago—the passive-aggressive reminders, the accusatory tirades. Eventually, he'd blocked both his parents' numbers.

"Got it," Aliza said finally. She held up her phone and hit play.

Their mother's voice crackled through the speaker, clipped and distant.

"Aliza, it's me. I don't know where you've run off to, but Coco needs more cuttlebones before we go to San Francisco. Get two packs this time, please."

The voicemail ended abruptly. The silence afterward was deafening.

"Ah, yes, good ol' Mom," said Aden.

Sẹ̀yí gave him a sympathetic look.

Coco, meanwhile, did not budge.

"Aden," Aliza whispered, her voice breaking. She looked at him, helpless. "It's not working."

For a moment, Aden said nothing. He glanced at Coco, at Aliza, at Sammy, who was watching his older siblings with wide, uncertain eyes. The weight of it all pressed down on him—the years apart, the words unsaid, the absurdity of how far they'd come to end up here, under an apricot tree, begging a bird to come home.

He looked back at Coco.

And then, before he could think—before the voice in his head could remind him of the futility of it all—he stepped forward, pulse hammering in his ears.

"Coco," he said softly.

The bird's head tilted just slightly. Her eyes were dark and glassy, unreadable.

"Hey, pretty bird," he tried again, gentler this time. "It's okay. Aden's here. I promise, I've got you."

Aliza went still, her mouth parted like she didn't dare exhale. Sammy didn't move as Sẹ̀yí rested a hand over her heart.

Aden took another step, just enough to feel the cool shadow of the tree against his skin.

"You've been through a lot, huh?" he said. His voice didn't shake, but the rest of him did. "I get it. I do. The world's a mess. People let you down. It's easier to just say 'Screw it' and fly away, huh?"

He swallowed hard.

"But you don't have to run anymore. You're safe now."

For a beat, nothing.

Then—soft, tentative—a breath of sound from above. A squawk, more air than voice. Coco's talons shifted on the branch.

"Aden," Aliza whispered.

He could feel his own throat tighten. "That's it. I know. I know, pretty girl," he murmured, a faint laugh catching in his chest. "Life sucks and then you die, right? But guess what? You didn't. We didn't.

And I'm—" His voice dropped. "And I'm sorry. I said some pretty horrible things to you before? But you're just trying to live. Same as me. Same as anyone."

The wind rustled through the leaves above them. Coco didn't look away.

"So come on," Aden said. "Let's go home. Please?"

A pause. A silence so long it felt unbearable.

Then movement: a small, hesitant flutter of wings. Coco let out another sound, this one stronger.

She hesitated, then launched herself forward, gliding shakily toward his outstretched arm.

Her landing wasn't graceful—she almost lost her balance, legs wobbly—

But she landed. She stayed.

Aden could barely breathe.

"She came down," Sammy said, awestruck.

Ṣèyí squeezed Aden's shoulder; he hadn't realized it until that moment, but he was shaking.

Aliza approached carefully and reached out to pet beneath Coco's crest. As if to prove to herself she was real.

Coco leaned in to her hand, just slightly.

"You did it," Aliza said at last, her voice trembling—like she didn't know whether to cry or laugh.

She looked at Aden for a long moment, something unspoken passing between them. Then, without a word, she pulled him into a hug.

Aden stood stiff at first. But he didn't push her away.

Sammy joined a beat later, his small hands clutching at Aden's back.

The knot in Aden's chest uncoiled—a first breath after being underwater.

For the first time in years—maybe ever—he let himself lean in, too: Aliza's steady arm across his back, Sammy's awkward, warm grip at his side, Coco nestled safely between them.

Like buoys weathering a storm.

Like—he thought, amused—a flock.

When Aden looked up, the man and Nora were still there, standing near the apricot tree with its sprawling branches. Nora clutched her binoculars tightly, her wide grin revealing two missing front teeth.

"Thank you," Aliza said, nodding toward them.

The man returned the gesture, though his gaze lingered on Coco with something like relief. "Take good care of her."

They crossed the front yard, the grass soft and springy beneath their feet. Coco nestled into Aliza's arms, her beak twitching faintly like she was dreaming.

At the edge of the lawn, Aden paused. The house stood quiet behind them, the rosebushes casting long shadows in the fading light. Nora and her father were still watching from the front porch.

He hadn't even learned the man's name. And still, he'd helped.

How . . . *bizarre*.

Aden climbed into the driver's seat, the leather sticky with the day's heat. Sẹ̀yí slid into the passenger side while Aliza settled into the back, adjusting Coco until she was perched securely on her lap. Sammy took his usual spot at the table, already flipping open his sketchbook.

Aden stared at the steering wheel. He exhaled through his nose and turned the key. The RV rattled to life, the engine grumbling like always.

"All right," he said, steady now. "Let's get the hell back home."

"Can you drop me off at the airport first?" asked Sẹ̀yí.

"Oh. Right. Of course. I mean—not that you're not welcome to come home with us. Obviously. If you want."

Sẹ̀yí smiled. "That would be fun, Aden, but unfortunately, I have work. Maybe . . . some other time?"

"Yes!" Aden said too quickly. "Yes. That would be great. Rain check. It's a date." He cleared his throat. "Okay, so airport first, then we go home. Then . . . I call you."

Aliza groaned. "Ugh, *finally*."

"Shut up," Aden mumbled. "And make sure the windows are closed, because I swear to God, if Coco flies off again, I'm letting her die."

"Not funny, Aden!"

Epilogue

"They sent a picture of Coco!"

"Damn, that was fast." Aden leaned over Sammy's shoulder to get a better view of his phone screen. "Where?"

Early-morning sunlight flooded through the kitchen window above the sink; it was a Tuesday, a school day.

Sammy opened the attachment on his email, and there she was: a bright-pink Coco, her feathers catching the light in a way that made her glow—the way a person did after a lengthy vacation to Jamaica. She was sitting on a branch-like perch, her cheeks puffed in that familiar, slightly smug but very pleased way. It had been only a month, and already she was looking much better.

Aden let out a breath, his ribs shuddering in relief. She was okay.

In the end, the three of them had decided to give Coco to a bird sanctuary in Del Mar, California, before they drove back to New Hope. They'd signed off on some paperwork—Aliza had asked the sanctuary owners a hundred questions about her care, about the facilities—and that was that. Coco was free.

They'd stayed up the entire night, debating what to do with her. But they had all agreed eventually that Coco was a lot of work. More important, for years, their parents had dragged her around to perform, to compete, to be in absolutely perfect condition at all times. She had never had the time to just be a *bird*. To socialize with her kind.

This would be their gift to her: a life where she wasn't a family pet, but a cockatoo in her own right.

She deserved to be free.

The Lowells had been disappointed, of course. But even they relented, eventually. After all, it was what the siblings had decided would be best for her, and who could argue with that?

Now the three of them were back in New Hope. Aden had sent an email to Richard, his boss, informing him that he would not be returning to work. Instead, he would be moving back home to be with his brother and sister as they picked up the pieces post their parents' funeral. And here Aden would stay—at least until Sammy graduated.

So no, for now, Aden would not sell the house. Not until the three of them were ready.

As for Aden's future plans, well—he always thought he'd be a good boss, if only to himself. Starting his own one-man law firm seemed like a good fit: He could do general practice, be a Swiss Army knife of lawyers. Even if it was easier said than done. He still had to get malpractice insurance, set up a support network, find a decent CPA, win over clients. He had some savings he'd squirreled away the past few years, but he'd still need a little more if he wanted his own office. The whole idea was daunting, if he was being honest. The idea of building something on his own.

Well, at least not *entirely* on his own.

For the past month, Aden had put in the work to repair his relationship with Ṣèyí—not with grand gestures or words, but with quiet, steady effort. He showed up when he said he would. Called her every night, just to talk. Brainstormed his plans for the future with her.

He didn't push her to trust him. He gave her time to see that he was serious.

And slowly—cautiously—she'd started meeting him halfway. Awkward calls turned into conversations that stretched long enough for her guard to slip. The texts stopped feeling like tests. Eventually, she stopped sounding like she was bracing for him to let her down.

Even now, Aden knew there were things they hadn't fully worked through—things they'd have to keep untangling as they went. But they were trying. And for once, Aden wasn't waiting for everything to fall apart.

Baby steps—that was what Sẹ̀yí had reminded him. It all started with baby steps. And if their trip across the country had proved anything, it was that he could be resourceful when it truly counted.

Baby steps. First the law firm, then—the moment he could—a ring for Sẹ̀yí.

One step at a time.

"Is that Coco?" came Aliza's voice as she hopped down the stairs into the kitchen. She was in her black vet-tech scrubs—running a few minutes late, Aden noted—for her next shift at Blackwood Veterinary.

She'd thrown a hoodie on over her scrubs. One of his old ones.

"Is that mine?"

"Nope," Aliza said breezily, tousling Sammy's hair without missing a beat.

She leaned over his shoulder to look at the picture of Coco on Sammy's phone. "Oh, she looks *fabulous*. Tell the people at the sanctuary we want to FaceTime her. With all the donations you keep sending them, it's the least they could do."

"Amen to that," said Aden before sipping his coffee. "Sammy, eat your damn toast. I need to drop you off before school gets too crowded."

Sammy took a bite, deliberately slow. "Yesh, Moam," he mumbled through a mouthful.

"Aww, Mommy Aden! We should get you an apron for your next birthday," said Aliza, grinning. "We'll get it embroidered and everything."

"Sẹ̀yí, unfortunately, would love that." Maybe Aden would get her a matching apron, too. A gag gift. But he could place the ring in her pocket and—

"Ooh, good point," Aliza interrupted. "In that case, maybe we should get you one that says *Wifey for Lifey*." She cackled.

Aden's eyes narrowed. "Aren't you late?"

Aliza checked her phone. "Shit. You're right." She grabbed her tote bag and water bottle, slinging the bag over her shoulder. "Okay, I'm off. Aden, don't get too bored!"

"Wait." Aden stood and crossed to the counter, where he'd neatly stacked the mail into a small pile. He picked up the envelope and turned it over in his hands.

He'd thought about this for weeks—how to phrase it, how to make it not sound like pity. It had seemed easier in his head, but now his nerves itched under his skin. What if she hated it? What if she thought he was meddling?

Baby steps.

He approached her, trying to hide his nervousness, and handed her the envelope. "Take this."

Aliza raised a brow. "What's this?"

"A Christmas gift."

"How sacrilegious," she said, opening the envelope. "Especially since it's still only Septem—" Her voice trailed off as she pulled out a slip of paper.

Her eyes darted to his. "Aden, why are you giving me a check for five hundred dollars?"

Aden shifted uncomfortably. "Read the description."

Aliza's eyes trailed back to the check as she read: "For . . . vet school applications."

"I don't know if that's enough," he said quietly, "but I guess it's a start."

She stared at it for a long moment. Then at him. "Oh my God, Aden. No, this is—this is definitely enough," she said, letting out a weak laugh. "But wha—*why?* This is a lot of money, how did—did you rob a bank or something?"

"I might not be rich, but I am a lawyer, remember?" Aden shrugged. "And before you say anything, this isn't from Mom and Dad's money. That's all still tied up in probate." His voice faltered; he hadn't yet told her about how he'd been planning to pass on his cut and give the inheritance to her and Sammy. That, maybe, he'd reveal as a birthday gift.

"The point is, this is from me," he went on. "I just thought you should . . . reapply. Give vet school another shot. But it's up to you. So if you want to use it to buy overpriced lattes, or invest in, say, a sketchy new tech start-up instead, be my guest. It's your money now. I just . . . want to make sure nothing is holding you back anymore."

Aliza said nothing, staring at the check as though it might evaporate in her hands. The paper trembled slightly.

She swallowed hard, and for a moment Aden thought her eyes reddened. But she blinked quickly, sniffing once.

"Okay," she said finally, her voice steadying. "But, you know, you could have just done a direct deposit instead of a check. What a waste of paper."

"It's the *symbolism*, okay!" Aden barked. "Jesus, just—get out of here, you brat." He gave her a gentle shove toward the door.

Aliza laughed, tucking the check into her bag. "Thanks, Aden. I mean it."

"Yeah, yeah," he said gruffly, waving her off with a flick of his hand.

"Bye, Sammy!" Aliza called over her shoulder.

"Buh, Uhlizha!" Sammy's voice rang out from the kitchen, muffled by what Aden assumed was another mouthful of toast.

At the doorway, Aliza turned back, her tote slung over one shoulder. She hesitated for just a second, then grinned. "Bye, Aden."

Aden's expression softened almost imperceptibly. Then he smiled.

"See you later."

Acknowledgments

When Flaco, the Eurasian eagle owl, escaped from the Brooklyn Zoo, I thought—rather cynically, the kind of cynicism one uses to blanket a bone-deep sadness—*Well. Goodbye, poor bird.*

I decided it would be a matter of days before the news reported his death. They'd shove his obituary somewhere on page five, in a tiny column slotted between all the important world news, and that would be that.

Because that is the way the world works, right? It is a cold, unfeeling place for a bird. It is a cold, unfeeling place for a human. Creatures fall through the cracks all the time. People look away. Life moves on.

What I saw instead was news of hundreds of birders flooding Central Park, where Flaco had made his new home, to track his movements and help in his recapture. Determined to do what they could to save him. Willing to spend their days, their energy, their hope, on a single bird.

Flaco didn't make it. Real stories often suffer from a lack of neat-and-tidy endings. But the point, I felt, was that people had tried—really, *really* tried—when they had nothing to gain.

Birders, I realized, are the best of us.

And so I want to start by thanking birders, who first planted the seed of this story in my mind—for how they inspire human stewardship of the most vulnerable among us. A small reminder that kindness still matters.

I also must thank Hannah Bowman, my agent and friend, for not laughing at me when I asked if this book idea was absolutely bonkers. Thank you, Hannah, for always taking me seriously (even when I probably shouldn't be) and for inspiring me to be a better human.

Thank you to my wonderful editor extraordinaire, Laura van der Veer, for ushering this book to life and for being such a delight to work with; and to Tashan Mehta, for her insight and care into making this book stronger. And to my team at Amazon / Lake Union Publishing, including Tree Abraham (art director and absolute genius), Rachael Clark (marketing manager and very likely the reason why you're holding this book in your hands!), and of course, Karah Nichols (production manager and the most patient wrangler of manuscripts): Thank you for being the heroes that make the cogs of publishing *sing*.

Thank you to the brilliant Ploy Siripant for her beautiful, vibrant cover design, and Logan Matthews for their design support. The cover makes me smile every time I see it.

Thank you to Ramishah, Thya, Humnah, Maya, Ayushi, Nihaarika, Jawayriya, Azanta, Lili, Rem, and all the readers who have, for years now, sent me supportive messages. You're the wind beneath my wings, truly.

Thank you to my sisters, Farheen, Hiba, and Sana. We may not share blood, but we share something far deeper, far more important: being the eldest siblings in our respective families and being utterly traumatized by it.

Thank you to Cara, who puts up with my whining every time I write and comforts me simply by existing. Love you.

Thank you, as always, to Stephen: for feeding me, for dealing with Deadline Me, and for being the best partner in crime.

Thank you to my brother, Shaz, for teaching me that, for better or worse, no one will ever understand each other better than siblings.

Thank you to Kisa, the best cat and family pet I could ask for. Thank you for watching over me for the past sixteen years.

And finally, thank you to the sweet old man whom I saw sitting outside on South Street with a cockatoo perched on his shoulder. I'd been debating whether to write this book—had almost decided against it—but then I saw you, and the way your eyes twinkled while petting your beloved friend.

I thought, well, if that's not a sign from the universe, I don't know what is.

About the Author

Photo © 2023 Linette and Kyle Kielinski

Farah Naz Rishi (she/they) is the author of *I Hope You Get This Message* and *It All Comes Back to You.* A Pakistani American writer and voice actor, she received her BA in English from Bryn Mawr College, her JD from Lewis & Clark Law School, and her love of weaving stories from the Odyssey Writing Workshop. When Farah is not writing, she's probably hanging out with video game characters. For more information, visit www.farahnazrishi.com.